THE CRISP POLEWARD SKY

A ZEKE TRAYNOR MYSTERY

JEFF SIEBOLD

Book cover design and interior formatting by Tugboat Design

ISBN: 978-0-9979570-9-9

Acknowledgements

The author wishes to acknowledge Elizabeth Bruno, his editor, for her sharp eye and constructive comments. And the author also wishes to acknowledge Deborah Bradseth of Tugboat Design for her excellent creative work.

ALSO BY JEFF SIEBOLD

Zeke Traynor Mysteries
Lilac and Old Gold
Bluegrass and Crimson
Ardmore Green

Dedicated to Karin. Always an adventure with you!

CHAPTER 1

"This one is already getting dicey," said Clive Greene. "You may want to step in early."

On the other end of the call, Zeke Traynor was enjoying a lobster roll and a frosted mug of Beach Blonde, a craft beer local to Cape Cod. He swallowed and said, "It's escalated, then?"

"I'd say so, yes," said Clive in his proper British accent, clipping his words aristocratically. Zeke wondered whether there had been an Earl in Clive's lineage at some point.

"Hate to leave the Cape," said Zeke, mostly to himself. "I just got situated here."

Zeke occupied rental cottages, mostly along the East Coast of the United States, moving further south in the winter months, and braving the northern locations during the summer. He had recently moved from Marie Island on the west coast of Florida to an ocean front cottage in Hyannis Port. The cottage, which was actually the guesthouse of a seasonal oceanfront estate, suited him perfectly.

There was no reply from Clive.

"So you want me in Phoenix? That will take us away from our Cambridge thing," said Zeke.

"True, but I need your help out there," said Clive.

"It gets hot in Phoenix," said Zeke.

"Good boy, it gets hot pretty much wherever you are," Clive exclaimed.

Zeke smiled. "When and where?"

"Phoenix Sky Harbor airport. We've got you booked for a 1:24 arrival tomorrow afternoon. Sally will get you the details. Kimmy will pick you up there."

Sally was Clive's girl Friday and the best researcher at The Agency, Clive's consulting business. Staffed with former intelligence and FBI agents, The Agency contracted with various government entities for high-risk assignments. Clive was former MI-6 and was well known as a recruiting wizard.

Kimmy, an ex-Mossad agent, worked with Clive and Zeke.

"All right," said Zeke. "I'll be there. What's the current status?"

"It looks like Mr. Diaz and his crew are about to make a move," Clive said. "Possibly out of the country. Our client would prefer to keep him on U.S. soil."

"And your client is…?"

"The Deputy Director of DHS, Clark Hall. He requested our assistance with Mr. Diaz and his operation," said Clive.

"Are we ready to take the operation down?" asked Zeke.

"Well, yes, unofficially." Clive smiled grimly.

"So no assist from the local authorities?" asked Zeke. It wasn't the first time.

"Hmm." Clive made a noise that could have been an affirmation, or not.

"Human trafficker, not much sympathy for Mr. Diaz," said Zeke.

"That's in our favor," said Clive. "I've spoken with the Phoenix ICE team. They'll clear the way for you. Run interference with the local law. But they can't be involved." ICE was the U.S. Immigration and Customs Enforcement arm of the Department of Homeland Security.

The Phoenix office of ICE had recently suffered some bad press when they attempted a raid on a warehouse, said to hold human traffic victims and boxes full of uncut heroin. Unfortunately, their confidential informant was unreliable—dyslexic or high or both—and gave them the wrong address. The result was an early morning raid on a cake factory. Bakers start early, and a pastry chef and six hardworking employees were arrested in the fiasco that came to be called the "Betty Crocker Raid" and "Cake-gate" by the media. While the address mistake was being sorted out, the heroin and the victims were quietly moved to an unknown location by their owners. On the heels of that fiasco, ICE was keeping a low profile in Phoenix.

"No local police and no ICE involvement. Any other assist?" asked Zeke.

"Well, I've sent Kimmy out there already. She lunched at the Rose and Crown in Phoenix, by the way. They have an excellent Pork Pie," Clive said, distracted. It was well known that Clive favored British fare.

"You sound jealous," said Zeke with a smile. "Kimmy will

have the weapons, I expect."

"Quite so," said Clive, now back in the conversation. "As well as restraints, if you need them. I'll have Sally send you the latest status. We'd all like the problem to go away."

"I'll see what I can do," said Zeke.

"Good, and then we'll get on with the Cambridge affair," said Clive, somewhat dramatically.

* * *

Zeke finished his Beach Blonde, wiped his mouth with his napkin and left the restaurant. A short drive in his vintage BMW returned him to the rental cottage where he opened a carry-on bag and went about the business of packing for the Phoenix excursion. He wondered for a moment whether he'd have enough time for a stop in Atlanta on his way back from Phoenix.

His cell phone rang.

"Hello, beautiful," he answered, noting the incoming caller ID.

"Hello yourself," said Tracy Johnson.

"I guess you could sense me thinking about you," said Zeke. "I was working out a plan to stop by and see you."

"Again? Already?" said Tracy with a smile. Tracy was in her late twenties and worked as a Secret Service agent in Midtown Atlanta.

"Well, I'm on my way to Phoenix, and a layover in Atlanta actually sounds pretty good," he continued. "Unfortunately, the job won't wait, so I'm thinking of stopping by on my way back. I could fly Delta." Delta's southernmost hub is located in Atlanta's Hartsfield-Jackson airport. *Southernmost,* thought Zeke. *It edges out Los Angeles by a third of a degree latitude, maybe eighteen miles.*

"Sure, keep a girl waiting," said Tracy, feigning hurt feelings.

"Don't want to do that," he said under his breath.

Zeke was average height, five foot ten inches, a couple inches taller than Tracy, and muscular in a well-toned way. His balance and efficient movements exuded competence and coordination. Zeke's blond hair, worn slightly long, set off his slate-blue eyes.

"You could stay longer on the return trip, I suppose," said Tracy, out loud but sort of to herself.

"I could," said Zeke.

"I suppose I could make time for you," she said.

"If nothing better comes along," he teased.

"Well, sure, that," said Tracy with a smile. "That goes without saying."

* * *

Zeke spotted Kimmy waiting with a small crowd in the lobby just outside the TSA area of Sky Harbor Airport. The airport was bright with sunlight flooding in through the large windows. Kimmy was wearing a flowing, ankle length beige skirt and a bright red shell that matched her sandals and toenails. Her thick black hair was held back with a hairband that looked like a princess's silver crown.

"You look right at home here," said Zeke as they headed for the exit.

"Well, more so in Sedona, actually," said Kimmy, referring to the eclectic town about a hundred miles north of Phoenix. "That's more my style. Ethereal and spiritual. You can feel the energy."

Zeke nodded in neutral agreement. "OK, so what's going down here?" he asked, sidestepping a discussion about Red Rock Country.

They were walking toward the exit and the parking garage.

"Benito Diaz has set himself up as a human trafficker, kidnapping young people—mostly female—and selling them. It's been going on for years. Many of his victims are illegals, up from Mexico or Central America. They have something to hide, so they can't call the authorities even if they trusted them...which they don't," Kimmy added.

"Do they keep them here," asked Zeke, meaning within the United States, "or ship them out?"

"Both, we think," said Kimmy. "Some of each."

"Connections with the Eastern Europeans?" In recent years, Eastern Europe had become a hotbed for prostitution and Internet porn. Along with identity theft and computer malware.

"Probable. The world's becoming a smaller place," said Kimmy matter-of-factly. "You make your money where you can."

Kimmy bounced on the balls of her feet as she walked beside Zeke, moving her hands and constantly changing her expression. Her whole being was like a bundle of kinetic energy.

Lots and lots of joules there, thought Zeke with a smile. *She's electric.*

"So this guy Diaz, he's set up here in Phoenix. Lives in Scottsdale, but he does his business in Phoenix, east to El Paso, and west to Tijuana. Some up in Vegas, too."

"Sounds like a pretty big operation," said Zeke.

"He's got hundreds of people working for him," said Kimmy. "Well, 'working for him' is a loose term. Most are on a contract basis. Bring Diaz a good deal, and he'll pay you well. He's built a reputation on that alone. And he's in the market for runaways, illegals, even kids on vacation."

Outside, now, Kimmy stepped ahead of Zeke and led the way to their parked car.

"Can I assume that he's into drugs and prostitution as well? They usually go hand in hand," said Zeke.

Kimmy stopped at a white Cadillac SUV with gold piping along the sides. She clicked a key fob and the four doors unlocked simultaneously.

"Yep, he sure is," said Kimmy.

Zeke opened the back door, passenger side, and set his carry-on bag on the seat. The interior felt hot. By the time he was seated in the passenger seat, Kimmy had the engine started, the air conditioner blowing, and the GPS initiated.

"Here you go." She handed Zeke a handgun, a Walther PPK.

"Thanks. Where to?"

"Thought you'd want to be officially briefed on the situation," said Kimmy. "So, our first stop is at Immigration and Customs Enforcement."

* * *

Kimmy turned the SUV into a large parking lot before the car had had a chance to cool down inside. They were only about a mile from the airport. The ICE building looked as if it may have been a one-story retail mall at some point but had been converted to government offices.

"Find a shady spot," suggested Zeke.

Kimmy circled the large lot twice before she pulled into a spot being vacated by a dark blue sedan. It was under a small tree, quite a distance from the building.

Zeke stepped out into the parking lot and walked to the back of the car, near the trunk. Kimmy met him there and he heard the four doors snap locked as she pushed the key fob.

"Who're we seeing?" asked Zeke.

"We're meeting with Jorge Ramirez. He's Agent in Charge of the DHS's Immigration and Customs Enforcement here in Arizona. ICE."

They started toward the main entrance of the building, across the hot asphalt. Zeke could feel the heat through the soles of his shoes.

Without warning, two black SUV's squealed in from around the building, blocking their path to the entrance. Six doors flew open simultaneously and six Hispanic-looking men jumped out of the vehicles. Two were holding M-16 rifles, now pointed at Zeke and Kimmy. The others held what looked like semiautomatic handguns.

Zeke reacted immediately, diving low between two cars and scampering away from the shooters before they could get fully oriented. He pulled his weapon from its holster, glanced back, and saw that Kimmy had vanished.

Six bogies, thought Zeke, *and I've got seven rounds in the magazine. Nothing to waste.*

The six men, all dressed in untucked, long sleeve flannel shirts and khaki pants fanned out in a large semicircle and began moving toward Zeke and Kimmy's last position. They moved slowly, carefully, their large work boots noisy on the paved lot.

Suddenly, Zeke heard two shots, and the two men with the assault rifles fell to the ground. The others instinctively turned to their right, pointing their guns and looking for the source of the unexpected sounds.

Zeke moved quickly between the cars, flanking the men to their left, dropping farther back into the parking lot. When the men turned toward him, he'd moved past their peripheral vision, and was almost behind them.

The four remaining men looked confused, now. They stepped forward, the drivers following behind, creeping along slowly in their SUV's. Then the men ran quickly, closing in on Zeke's last position. But there was no one there.

Zeke sat on the hot ground, directly behind the man farthest from the building, shielded by the large tire of a small Hummer.

His PPK was in his right hand, held loosely at his side. The gun made him feel a little like James Bond, who always carried a PPK in the movies. *At least he did until 1997,* Zeke thought.

He spotted Kimmy, ducked down and hiding behind a decorative stone wall closer to the entrance to the building. Civilians had disappeared from view, either running back into the building, or hiding behind cars across the parking area. The killers looked suddenly disoriented.

Two drivers, four killers left, thought Zeke. *Hardly fair.*

Zeke stood and shot the man closest to him in the back, then pivoted quickly and shot the next in line as he was turning toward the sound. The other two men sprayed bullets in his general direction while diving for cover.

Then Zeke shot each of the SUV's from the rear, the bullets entering through the back windows and exiting through the windshields. The window safety glass shattered but stayed in place.

Spider webs. So much for visibility, Zeke thought.

Simultaneously the two remaining men turned and ran back toward the SUV's, their guns in hand. The drivers backed the vehicles into crescent-shaped turns, sawed forward, then back, and were ready to accelerate away from the action.

At that moment, a dozen agents came crashing out of the building dressed in SWAT gear, each with a large, yellow ICE stenciled across his chest and back. Carrying shields and short riot shotguns, they immediately surrounded the two vehicles. Two agents shot the tires on each SUV, disabling the vehicles. Then they tossed teargas into the broken windows.

Zeke heard one of the drivers yell, "Mierda," and as he moved closer the driver's door flew open and a short, squat driver jumped to the ground and started running, away from the agents and directly toward Zeke.

Zeke stepped into his path.

He's got a low center of gravity, and he probably outweighs me by sixty pounds, Zeke thought instinctively, sizing up his opponent.

Running at Zeke full speed, the man put his hands out to push Zeke's chest and shove him out of the way. But Zeke wasn't there when he arrived. Stepping to the man's right, Zeke avoided the violent, two-handed push and slapped the man's arms down. He hooked the man's nose with his left hand fingers and with his right elbow hooked the man's neck, effectively stopping his head as his body continued to run forward. In a moment, the driver was flat on his back on the ground, his nose bleeding badly and the wind knocked from his lungs.

Two ICE agents moved forward to retrieve him from the parking area. The other driver and two gunmen had been subdued by the agents. The SUV's sat empty in the parking lot, shot up and looking like relics from an abandoned junkyard.

* * *

"Gang bangers," said Agent in Charge Jorge Ramirez, after the action was over. Kimmy and Zeke were sitting in Ramirez' office, an hour and a half after the ICE agents had arrested the four remaining Hispanic men. "They're from L.A," he added.

"Long way from home," said Zeke.

"They were probably sent here on a special assignment," said the agent. "Wouldn't surprise me if they were hand-picked by Diaz."

"They came here for us," said Kimmy, seriously. "They knew what we were doing."

"Do you think they followed you?" asked Ramirez.

"Doubtful," said Zeke. "We drove about a mile from the airport parking lot to your offices. I'm not sure how they'd be able to find and follow us. And they were actually around the corner of the building when we parked and started walking in.

"Well, you can see how difficult this whole thing is," said Ramirez. "Diaz has too much money to work with. And he spreads it around, which guarantees him some righteous intel."

"You have a leak?" asked Zeke.

"Anything's possible, I suppose," said Ramirez. "What do you think? Remember when El Chapo escaped from prison in Mexico? In a mile long tunnel? Everyone in that prison was on his payroll. Had to be."

Zeke nodded.

Ramirez thought for a minute. "But, no, I don't think we have a leak in this office."

"So what's your plan?" Zeke asked Ramirez.

"Well, we need to move quickly on this," said Ramirez. "Our latest information is that Diaz is in town, in Phoenix, for a transaction."

"As in buying boys and girls?" asked Zeke.

"Yep. We think it's a group from Honduras and El Salvador this time. They're lured here with promises of a good job, maybe as a cook or a nanny, with a big paycheck. But once they arrive it all changes."

"How so?" asked Kimmy.

"Lots of ways," said Ramirez. "There's usually a language barrier, and the traffickers take their identification papers and their money away, if they have any. So they're told that they're illegals in this country. Then they're held somewhere, maybe a warehouse or a rental house, until their captors accumulate enough people for a bulk sale to someone like Diaz. Meantime, the victims of the sex trafficking are raped and locked up, degraded, and mostly given drugs to control them..."

"So the victims aren't all brought in for sex trafficking..." started Kimmy.

Ramirez apparently disliked being interrupted by a woman. He said, over her, "Other than sex trafficking, there's a big interest in human trafficking for labor." He directed his comment to Zeke and ignored Kimmy, who just smiled.

"Domestic work, agriculture, food service, landscaping... even street begging. They bring people in, control them, and threaten them with deportation and injury to their families if they don't cooperate. It's a pretty ugly business," said Ramirez.

"You said the attackers were 'gang bangers,' said Zeke. "Where are they from?"

"They're not talking yet," said Ramirez. He shook his head. "But Diaz would know where to find them. It looks like they're all members of MS-13." He paused for effect.

"Mara Salvatrucha," said Zeke. "The Mara's. From California and El Salvador. You can confirm it by their tattoos."

"Correct, we're working on that," said Ramirez, sounding slightly deflated. "They're all over. Drug smuggling, arms trafficking, carjacking, assault... They wouldn't hesitate to accept a contract from Diaz to kill you."

"So what's your plan for Diaz?" asked Zeke.

"We've been surveilling the traffickers," said Ramirez. "They've been accumulating victims in a house in west Phoenix. We've got a team watching it."

Surveilling? thought Zeke. *Who says 'surveilling'?*

"Apparently, they know you're coming soon," said Zeke. "They didn't waste any time trying to sabotage your operation."

Ramirez looked slightly offended. "We won't let that happen," he said. "We're going to move tonight."

"We're here to assist," said Zeke. "Your Director requested that we..."

"We've got this," Ramirez interrupted, with a sudden flash of anger in his eyes. "Sorry to make you come all the way out here." He looked around the room. Then he said, "Look, I've gotta make a call."

* * *

"The MS-13?" asked Kimmy. "I've never run into them."

"In from Southern California, with a growing presence in Arizona and in the northeast," said Zeke. "They've made a move into Spain recently, but they're not very prevalent in

Europe, Israel or other parts of the Middle East."

"You said they're from El Salvador?" asked Kimmy.

They were sitting in the Cartel Coffee Lab, a small coffee shop near Ramirez's offices. Zeke had an iced coffee and Kimmy was sipping herbal tea. The Bohemian atmosphere of the place complimented Kimmy's persona. *She fits right in*, Zeke thought.

"The gang was started in L.A. by refugees from El Salvador and Honduras. Mara means "gang" from the word 'marabunta,' which is some type of fierce ant. The Salvatrucha guerrillas fought in the Salvadorian Civil War all through the 1980s. That name stayed with them: 'Mara Salvatrucha'. MS-13."

"Why 13?" asked Kimmy.

"From the 13th letter of the alphabet, 'M,' for Mara, 'gang.' Most all their tattoos are symbolic, and somehow result in symbolic 13's," said Zeke. "They're very proud of the symbolism."

"These are bad boys?" asked Kimmy.

"Their motto is 'Rape, control, kill,'" said Zeke, "and they do. So, yes."

Kimmy's expression turned grim.

"How do you read Ramirez?" asked Zeke.

"Macho," said Kimmy. "For him, it's about pride and respect. And he has to be right, be in charge."

"Which can get in the way of reality," said Zeke.

"Do you think he sees the leak?" she asked. She took a sip.

"Probably not. Maybe in a general sense," said Zeke. "But he wouldn't want to admit it to himself, despite what he says."

"So we work around him?" she asked.

"We do our jobs, and we make sure he doesn't get in the way."

"And tonight?" asked Kimmy.

"You heard the man. Tonight we observe the raid."

CHAPTER 2

Zeke reviewed the file. The house was a one-story structure with a neat dirt yard and a shingled roof. Most of the houses on the street looked similar, even identical. *Built by the same developer,* he thought.

There was a carport and a brick accent wall, and a large cactus in the middle of the front yard. Strings of Christmas lights were still hanging from the fascia board. There was no activity evident.

Zeke studied the pictures of the house, taken from the front and side, as well as the aerial close-up provided by Ramirez's team. He could easily approximate the layout of the house, and his estimates were confirmed by a builder's blueprint.

"It's small," said Jose Fernandez, Ramirez's second in command. Fernandez was a Unit Commander in DHS's Immigration and Customs Enforcement agency. His team had been preparing for the takedown.

"How many are inside?" asked Zeke.

"We think there are as many as fifteen people crammed

in there," said Fernandez. "We've been watching for a while. Only two people ever go in and out of the house, but from what they bring with them, food and such, and the frequency of their visits to resupply, we think there's a crowd in there."

"When do we do it?" asked Zeke.

"We moved the schedule up after the attack on you. We go tonight," said Fernandez. "But you're not part of it. You observe only."

Zeke looked at Fernandez. "Ramirez's orders," he said, and shook his head.

"Have you been with this agency long?" Zeke asked Fernandez.

"Since before we worked for DHS," said the Commander. "So, yeah."

Zeke nodded to himself. "Diaz won't be at the house, though."

"No, we're not lucky enough for that. He'll make the payoff remotely, and the illegals will be transported to his people and put to work. Diaz won't dirty his hands," said Fernandez.

"We won't be able to convict him then," said Zeke.

"No, unless we can flip one of the handlers or one of the transporters."

"The ones that are hands-on with the victims?" asked Zeke.

"Right. But it hasn't happened yet."

* * *

Six heavily armed ICE agents exited the black SWAT truck in a single-file run, stocks on their shoulders, rifles up and pointed along their line of sight. The truck was parked in the driveway of a suburban ranch home, and they edged along the side of the house and into the back yard. The owner's black poodle was barking frantically from inside the house.

"Target is directly behind, over the hedge," said the Team Leader into his com device. "On my count."

The team of ICE agents assembled on the near side of the hedge, crouching to leave no profile. When they were in position, the Team Leader called, "Stand by."

At 4:23 AM, on Jose Fernandez's signal, which was a double click on his open radio microphone, a buzz-buzz sound, all hell broke loose. The six armored ICE agents, who were wearing steel helmets and face paint and carrying Heckler & Koch MP5 submachine guns, stormed the three entrance doors of the small bungalow in Glendale. Two of the agents breached the front door, which led directly into the living area and was closest to the bedrooms. Two agents entered through the kitchen door, located under the carport. The remaining two agents entered the house through the rear sliding glass door, which also gave access to the kitchen. They met at a small round table that was littered with dirty dishes and empty plastic cups.

The entry was anything but quiet, and anything but orderly. The front door burst open and the ICE agents crashed into the small living space yelling commands and screaming, pointing their floodlights and their weapons everywhere.

Tense, the team leader waited, listening for gunfire, shouts or radio communications.

"I have five souls in the rear bedroom," said a voice over the radio. "Had to knock a padlock off the door."

A moment passed.

"Check that, six souls, female," said another voice. Then, away from the radio he said, "Restrain them."

"Clear," called another voice. "Living room and kitchen are clear."

"Hall bathroom is clear," another contributed.

"Six souls in the master bedroom," said another voice. "All female, all Hispanic."

The Team Leader heard frightened voices speaking rapid Spanish, pleading for mercy. "Please don't send us back," he heard a woman's voice calling out, over and over again.

"Anyone else in there?" he asked. "Are we clear? Are we secure?"

"I have five more souls locked in a spare bedroom," said another voice.

The house was only 1,600 square feet in size and had a total of five rooms and two bathrooms. It took less than four minutes for the team to secure the premises and begin the process of restraining the frightened women.

"Aye, Skipper," said one of the agents over the radio. "No bogeys, seventeen souls. We're clear."

Within thirty seconds, everyone present was subdued, restrained with zip ties and lying face down in rows on the floor. A more thorough search confirmed that there were seventeen people in the house, mostly teenagers and young adults, and all female.

* * *

Across the street, Zeke and Kimmy had observed the action from a car parked in a neighboring driveway.

"That'll disrupt the transaction," said Zeke, "but Diaz and his contacts won't be touched. They're too smart to be caught with the victims."

"Doesn't seem right," said Kimmy. "Any chance one of the handlers will flip on him?"

"Flipping on Diaz would likely be a death sentence," said Zeke. "But if they stay quiet and do their jail time, they stay alive, and their families are cared for financially."

"So how do we get to the guys at the top? The Director of DHS hired us for Benito Diaz, not these low level guys, right?"

"Yep. Let's start with what we have. Benito Diaz won't be happy about this raid. And I'm thinking it may keep him in town longer than he'd planned."

* * *

"The local guys wanted the takedown themselves," said Zeke. "Wouldn't let Kimmy and me help out."

Zeke and Kimmy were sitting in Zeke's room, sipping hotel coffee from paper cups. Zeke was talking with Clive on a secure cell phone, his speakerphone activated.

"They wouldn't? That's odd. The Deputy Director contacted me personally. He implied that the southwest offices of ICE were cowboys. A bit out of control," said Clive.

"That's an accurate description," said Kimmy. "The Special Agent in Charge here is making up the rules as he goes."

"Hmm," said Clive. "Well, no harm, I guess. How about the assassins who met you at the ICE offices? Anything there?"

"Four are in custody," said Zeke.

"Four of eight?" asked Clive.

"Well, yes," said Zeke with a small smile toward Kimmy. "They were outnumbered."

"Quite so," said Clive.

"How did they know about you, do you think? About your arrival?" Clive asked.

"The timing was almost perfect, so they must have been waiting for my arrival at the airport, then saw me deplane and meet up with Kimmy."

"Had Kimmy been to the DHS offices prior to your visit?" asked Clive.

"I had not," Kimmy said. She'd hopped up and circled the bed and was standing at the window. "I talked with Ramirez on the phone, but just to let him know that we were planning to visit."

"So you think there's a leak in the organization?" Clive asked.

"Almost certainly," said Zeke. "Benito Diaz runs a well oiled machine. He undoubtedly has law enforcement on his payroll. Federal as well as local, I'd guess."

"So you're planning to interrogate them? The assassins?" said Clive.

"Yes, after they're arraigned tomorrow morning." said Zeke.

"By that time, I'll be on a plane back to D.C.," said Kimmy. "I'm returning tomorrow."

"Quite so," said Clive. "Good."

"I'll let you know how it goes," said Zeke.

"We'll be very interested in the outcome, old boy," said Clive.

* * *

"It's a real uphill battle," said Jorge Ramirez. "These guys aren't going to say anything against Benito Diaz."

Zeke nodded. They were waiting in a small, concrete block room with a single window and a metal door. The window was a mirror on the inside, and the door had a small glass area, about five feet off the ground and center, to allow the guards to determine who was on the other side before they opened it.

Ramirez and Zeke stood at the heavy aluminum table that was centered in the room, but positioned toward the back wall. A single aluminum chair was bolted to the floor behind the table. The chair was empty. Two more portable chairs sat empty across the table and a video camera on a tripod was positioned beside the far end of the table.

"You think we'll get anything from the Mara's?" Zeke asked, watching Ramirez.

"No, I don't," said the Agent. "We've been through all this. They won't give Diaz up. They won't give anyone up." He was blinking rapidly.

Zeke nodded and looked away.

"These guys are all liars anyway," said Ramirez. "They don't know what the truth is. You know they're lying because their mouths are moving, you know?"

Zeke said, "Sure."

"Look, we've interviewed these guys already, and we're going to interview them again, anyway. And I can tell you from experience, they won't say anything. They're scared to death of Diaz," said Ramirez. "They know he'll flay them with a dull fish knife."

"He's a bad dude," said Zeke, mostly to himself.

"He is. And as bad as the Mara's are, they've got two reasons not to give him up," Jorge Ramirez continued.

"How do you figure?" asked Zeke.

"First, they know all about the repercussions, the fallout from Diaz's fury. It'll touch them, their families, their brothers in the gang...everyone. A total scorched earth approach."

"What's the second reason? Asked Zeke.

"Financial. They know that talking would be the end of their financial arrangement with Benito Diaz. And honestly, he makes them a lot of money."

Zeke said, "Makes sense."

"I'm not sure what you think you'll be able to get out of this. We've done everything there is to do. They just won't talk. It's a waste of time." He stared at Zeke intently.

"Yeah, I think you're right," said Zeke. "We can cancel all of this. You've convinced me there's nothing here."

Ramirez paused for a moment. Then he visibly relaxed and

a small smile crossed his face. "OK, sorry to waste your time," he said, and he moved to the door and rang the bell that called the guard.

Zeke said, "I'd like to interview one of the women from the raid last night, though. One of the victims."

"Sure," said Ramirez easily. Then to the guard as he exited the room, "We're closing this down. Cancel the interviews with the Mara's. Bring us one of the vic's from the raid instead."

The guard nodded.

* * *

"She doesn't speak English," said Agent Ramirez. "Should I get a translator for you?"

Zeke was sitting across the aluminum table from him, waiting for one of the victims to be brought into the small room for questioning. The video camera was still on a tripod next to the table, and there was a manila folder in front of Ramirez on the table with a DHS/ICE stamp on the front of it.

"No worries," said Zeke, absently.

"You speak Spanish?" asked the agent. "Street Spanish from El Salvador?"

Zeke smiled. "Sure," he said.

"Oh," said Ramirez. "Vea."

"Yep, for real. Vea. I speak fluent Arabic, too."

"Huh," said Ramirez, and he looked away, suddenly disinterested.

A few minutes later there was a knock on the door and

a uniformed female ICE agent escorted a girl into the room. The girl was thin and angular and had short, black hair. Her features gave the impression that there was some Indian blood in her lineage.

She sat, and Ramirez said, "Hola, Rosita," in a condescending tone.

The female agent looked around for a chair, then, seeing none, went and stood near the door.

Rosita cowered, looking at the tabletop.

Zeke said, more gently, "Hola, Rosita."

Rosita looked at Zeke and nodded and repeated the greeting. Then she looked at the table again. When she spoke, Zeke noticed two upper teeth were missing on the right side of the girl's mouth.

In Spanish, Ramirez explained to Rosita that they wanted to interview her about her situation since she entered the United States.

The girl nodded at the tabletop but said nothing.

"You're from El Salvador," said Ramirez. "Where did you live there?"

"San Salvador," she said.

"You were in school there? Where did you go?" Ramirez continued.

The girl looked up. "Externado San Jose," she said.

San Jose Day School, thought Zeke. *A Catholic school.*

"How old are you, Rosita?" asked Ramirez, looking through his file.

"Sixteen," the girl said.

"And you came to the United States for what?" he continued.

Rosita looked around the room, and then at Zeke. She said, "I was threatened many times in San Salvador. Men from La Mara followed me home from school almost every day. I was…"

Here she faltered for a moment and looked at Ramirez.

"Yes?" asked Zeke gently. She looked at him.

"I was beaten and raped twice."

"So you escaped to the United States, is that it?" asked Ramirez.

Rosita nodded.

"Did you come to Phoenix?" Zeke asked.

The girl shook her head. "No, I was offered a job in Los Angeles. As a housekeeper for a rich family."

"Who offered you the job?" asked Zeke.

"An uncle. My mother's brother."

"And how did you get to Los Angeles?" asked Zeke.

"Uncle Hector, he arranged it," she said. "He paid a man to bring me into this country."

"After you'd been beaten and raped," said Ramirez. "Twice."

"Si, yes," she continued. She looked ashamed.

She's telling the truth, thought Zeke.

"You know that it's illegal to enter the United States without permission," Ramirez continued.

Rosita looked down at the table. Her face turned red.

Zeke's eidetic memory and his skill at spotting lies were well developed during his time with MICECP, the Military Intelligence Civilian Excepted Career Program. He had served that organization as a contractor to the U.S. Army for years, prior to going to work for The Agency. Now, those skills were automatic.

Rosita did not answer.

"What happened when you got to the United States?" asked Zeke. "Did you get to Los Angeles?"

The girl shook her head. "No, I was brought over the Mexican border in a truck with others from El Salvador," she said. She didn't look up from the table.

"And...?" asked Zeke.

"And I was taken to a house and locked in a room with some of the others. The man took my passport and my money and he told me that I'd go to jail if I didn't obey him."

"Do you know where this was, Rosita?" asked Zeke.

She shook her head.

"And then?" he asked.

"And then, after a few days, we were put in a van and brought here."

"To Phoenix," said Ramirez.

The girl's face looked blank.

"That's where you are. Phoenix, Arizona. United States," he said.

"How long have you been here, Rosita? In the house we found you in?" Zeke asked.

"Many days. Maybe ten," she said.

"Did you recognize any of the men who were holding you?" asked Ramirez. He sounded impatient.

"No. But their tattoos...they were Mara Salvatrucha. And they were proud of it," she said.

"Waiting to sell you to Diaz," said Zeke. "You and the others."

"I don't know," said Rosita.

"Did they make you work while you were here?" asked Zeke.

A flush began to creep up the girl's face. She nodded slightly. "They took me out in the evenings."

"Did they make you have sex?" Zeke asked. "For money?"

She nodded again, her eyes on the tabletop.

"The Sisters, the nuns, they said that I should remain pure until I marry," said Rosita, "but I'm no longer pure. I will go to hell, now."

"But you were forced, weren't you?" Zeke asked. "It was against your will."

"Yes. But I should have been stronger. I was afraid."

"The money you earned, did they take it from you, Rosita?"

The girl nodded again. "Every day," she said.

CHAPTER 3

"Benito Diaz is in Scottsdale," said Clive from the other end of the phone line. "We have intel that he's staying in his home there."

Zeke nodded. "Ramirez's raid blew up in his face," he said. "Diaz knew he was coming."

"I suppose he'll take another run at it," said Clive. "Diaz, I mean."

"It's what he does," said Zeke. "I doubt that he's concerned about disposing of a couple of Federal agents. Or their consultants. That's just a part of doing business."

"So what do you see Diaz doing next?"

"I'm sure he'll stay out of sight until ICE loses focus, and then he'll go for the exchange again," said Zeke. "The MS-13's will replenish the supply. There's a lot of money in human trafficking. There were seventeen victims ready for this last exchange."

"They're watching Diaz, but he probably won't get near the action next time," said Clive.

"I agree," said Zeke.

"He'll probably send his guys to get the victims and drop them at one of his warehouses in Pahrump or Amargosa Valley," said Clive. "Sally researched it and said Diaz owns a couple of brothels there."

Zeke knew that Clive was referring to brothels in rural Nevada, some of the many run by Benito Diaz. It was trickier in Nevada, because prostitution is legal in most of the state. And although it is highly regulated, all of the prostitution takes place away from the larger cities in small towns, perfect settings for subtle and effective bribes.

"And he can inventory them there," said Zeke.

"Won't he still need to meet with the MS-13 leaders? Pay them?" asked Clive.

"Mostly the meeting is about mutual respect," said Zeke. "Acknowledgement of the status of the MS-13 gang leaders. After the botched raid, they'll probably forego the meet in favor of the enterprise."

"The enterprise?" asked Clive.

"Sure, this is one small part of Diaz's world. And for the MS-13's, underneath it all the money is more important than the status. They roll this along, making this exchange on a regular basis, I'm sure," said Zeke.

"So Diaz stays out of it, sends some guys to pick up the victims in, what, a panel van? And takes them to upstate Nevada."

"Most probably. Yes, a couple of panel vans or maybe a U-Haul truck, maybe an eighteen wheeler, something like that," said Zeke.

"Then how will ICE get to Diaz?" Clive asked.

"Good question," said Zeke. "Maybe we can help them with that."

* * *

"Jose Fernandez," said the voice on the phone.

"Commander, it's Zeke Traynor."

"Sure, Zeke, what's up?"

"You said you've been with ICE for a while," said Zeke. "Do you have any contacts in Nevada? State police-level?"

"I do, as a matter of fact. We've run several joint operations with them. They're only three and a half hours away…Vegas, that is."

"What type of operations?" asked Zeke.

"Well, last time it was a couple of illegals hiding out at the Hualapai reservation up north. They robbed a grocery store in Peach Springs, shot a cashier, then ran across the state line to Laughlin, Nevada. Just over the border. We tracked them there."

"Cell phones?" asked Zeke.

"Part of it. They got jobs as janitors at a casino on the river. Thing was, they were gambling with a lot of cash when they got off work, and the security guys became suspicious."

"So you went after them?" asked Zeke.

"Yep. We talked with the Nevada State Police and they said, 'Come on over.'" Course, we're Federal, and they're in our territory, more or less, so it was just a polite invitation," said

Fernandez. "So we went. Took them down in a rented hotel room."

"Could you do it again?" asked Zeke. "Get the invitation, I mean."

"I think so."

"Let me tell you what we've got," said Zeke.

* * *

The girl sat huddled in the dark, her arms wrapped around her knees despite the oppressive heat. She had stopped sweating an hour ago, her body mostly empty of the fluids it needed. A small electric lantern that someone had set on the floor in the corner was providing feeble light, but that light was being blocked by all the sweltering bodies, uncomfortably crammed together and seldom moving.

What did I do, the girl thought to herself. This is so much worse than it was at home.

Her head was down and her eyes closed as she endured the long ride. They had been brought ashore in a metal container at the Port of San Diego two days ago, then told to wait quietly for transport. Any noise would bring the Federales, and then they would all be sent back to San Salvador, or perhaps put in jail.

Thank god this container is ventilated. Those buckets in the corners really stink! she thought. Now that the water they'd held was gone, they were being used as improvised toilets.

The container had been quickly loaded from the ship to a

tractor-trailer, and a short time later, it was attached to a big rig truck and towed from the port. There were thirty people in the container, and no one had eaten for hours.

At the beginning, it seemed so long ago, men holding machine guns, their faces covered with bandanas, had herded the refugees into the small space, warning them repeatedly to be silent. They were assured that the bags of food and the buckets of water would be sufficient for their trip. This had proven to be false.

Her name was Isela. Her mother had told her that it meant 'care giving, but dangerous'. She later found out that it also meant 'rare beauty'. But now she sat, huddled and sick to her stomach, weak and feeling anything but beautiful. And she missed her sister, who started this journey with her but had been separated from her at the very beginning.

"Hola," said a voice.

Isela looked up to see a shadowy face in the weak light. He was young, she saw, perhaps her own age, fifteen. He looked unsure, uncertain.

He said, "Hola. I am Miguel." Then he looked away.

"Hola, Miguel. I'm Isela." Her name sounded foreign as it fell from her lips in this strange place.

"We must almost be there," said Miguel. "We must," he repeated.

"Where?" she asked.

"At the ranch. For the work they told us. I will be a vaquero, a cowboy. That's what I was promised." He looked away.

"What are you looking at, baboso?" said an older boy. He

was sitting a few feet from Isela and was in his twenties. "Do you want trouble?"

Miguel looked away, safely at the floor. "No, no…"

Isela looked at Miguel. "I was told we are going to a restaurant. To work in a restaurant," she said.

Miguel said nothing. He looked up at her for a moment, disappointment in his brown eyes. Then back down at the plywood floor of the container.

"Perhaps you misunderstood," said Isela, trying in a way to comfort the boy. "Or I may have…"

* * *

The truck drove on, and it seemed to Isela that it was getting hotter and hotter inside the container. She was propped with her back against one of the side walls, breathing the hot air slowly and preserving her strength. It was miserable and stinking inside the box, and she could see the sweat stains on the clothes of those around her.

Miguel had moved away, intimidated by the older boy, and Isela was numb, simply existing to get through this journey.

Without warning, the truck slowed and made a fast right turn, and bodies inside the container were thrown to the left. Several who were standing ended up along the interior plywood wall of the trailer, stepping on others who had already been sitting there.

Isela was jostled and avoided being stepped on by moving slightly and making space for a large man's boot that hit the floor with some force.

"Lo siento," he mumbled.

Isela was silent. She didn't have enough energy to talk.

The two back doors to the trailer were thrown open and everyone in the container moved toward the back, toward the light. Isela saw three men standing on the ground, just outside of the open doors. They were small men wearing plain white sleeveless t-shirts and jeans and leather boots. Isela saw that they had tattoos on their faces and that one was holding a large gun, like the hunting rifle her father used to shoot, but bigger and more complex looking. The other two wore pistols tucked into their belts.

"Get down," said the first man in Spanish. He was closest to the container. "Get down and stand over there." He pointed with his rifle toward a small corral area just to the side of the truck. It was a dusty place, fenced-in with split logs. It was empty.

One by one the people in the trailer stepped down out of the truck and shuffled toward the corral. As they made their way across the dirt road, they each passed a woman who was standing near the gate to the corral and watching carefully. She was of average height and slim, wearing jeans and silver studded cowboy boots. Her hair was raven black, pulled into a ponytail and held in place by a hairband that matched her long-sleeve, maroon shirt. She looked to be in her forties, and Isela thought that she might be the most beautiful woman she'd ever seen.

"You," said the woman to one of the immigrants. "You come over here." She spoke Spanish in a melodic voice, soft and without accent. But her presence commanded attention.

She was talking to a young girl, younger than Isela by a couple years, and clearly frightened. The girl stopped and looked around, uncertain. Then she stepped toward the woman, slowly.

"Don't worry, darling," said the woman. "You're safe, now. Stand over here, please." She gestured for the girl to stand near her, but just outside of the corral.

"What's your name, dear?" the woman asked the girl.

"It is Rosa," the girl said.

"Rosa. I am Ximena. How old are you, Rosa?"

The girl looked away. Then she said, "Fourteen. I will be fourteen this month."

"Good. Wait here, please." The woman went back to inspecting the refugees as they passed her on their way to the corral. Isela stepped down from the truck in turn, and followed a short, heavy man toward the corral. He had gray-black hair and brown skin and the loose skin of his thick neck hung over his sweat stained collar. He smelled of body odor and garlic and stale urine.

"You, girl, come here," said Ximena. Her soft voice was almost hypnotic, demanding attention in its subtlety. Isela looked up and saw her brown eyes, sharp and piercing, and she stepped out of the line toward the woman.

"Your name, please?" asked the woman.

"Isela," she said and looked at the ground to avoid the intense stare of the woman.

"Stand over here," she said.

And somehow Isela knew that her life had just changed forever.

＊ ＊ ＊

She took a plastic bag from a cardboard box sitting next to her. "You'll want to shower and then change into this," said Ximena, almost kindly. Most of the refugees were standing inside the corral, uncertain of what to do next. Several were sitting on their heels as they waited.

Isela nodded and took the small bag of clothes from the woman. She stood still until the woman pointed to the back of a whitewashed building and said, "You can change in there."

Isela walked to the building, tired and hungry and dirty, even filthy. She followed several other girls from the container into the back door of the building. Just inside, there was an open room where the chosen girls were changing into their new clothes.

"This is pretty," said one girl holding up a short green dress. She quickly pulled it on over her head and smoothed down the front with her open palms. "And it fits pretty well."

Isela looked around. What she saw were several girls from the container, maybe twelve to twenty years old and chatting excitedly with each other about the new clothing. From the looks of it, the outfits ranged from schoolgirl uniforms to one-piece shifts and mini-skirts with tight tank tops. There wasn't much left to the imagination.

"Why are we to wear these clothes?" she asked the girl in the green dress.

"I don't know," the girl said. "But this is so much better than the shorts I've been living in for the past few days. Those were really dirty."

"Where did you put them?" she asked.

"In that bucket," said the girl, pointing toward a large barrel filled with suds and smelling of chlorine. "And the showers are over there." She pointed.

Isela opened the bag she was holding and took out a pair of short jean shorts. She slipped off her pants, soddened and dirty, tossed them in the barrel and walked into the shower area. When she was done, she toweled herself off and pulled on the new shorts and the accompanying sleeveless top.

Just then, Ximena opened the back door and entered the room. She looked around the room at the girls and said in Spanish, "When you're finished dressing, go through this door to the front of the building."

Several girls moved toward the door and the first girl there—the one with the green dress—pushed it open and walked through. Isela waited her turn, then stepped into the front room of the building, following the girl in front of her.

"This is where you'll be working," said Ximena, gesturing around a wide living room that was tastefully decorated with sofas clustered into conversation areas. There was a white grand piano in one corner of the room and two open doors that led to hallways off the walls near it. The floor was hardwood covered with area rugs defining the conversation areas. There was no one in the room except a tall black man wearing a white shirt and tuxedo trousers. He ignored the intrusion.

"Working?" asked one of the girls in front of Isela.

"Yes, of course," said Ximena impatiently. "You must pay us back for bringing you here to the United States. Do you have money?"

No one said anything. They looked down.

"No? So you will entertain our customers to earn money. Men come here to gamble and to be entertained by young women," she continued. "They will treat you well, and you will make them happy."

* * *

The tall black man with the white shirt and tuxedo trousers was named 'William.' Isela couldn't remember ever hearing him say a word. He stood near the front door of the brothel, which was named "Susie's Ranch," and he watched everything that went on in the big room. He had shaved his head and wore a frown as his permanent expression.

Once, one of the girls stormed out of the building after being groped by a drunken customer. William had gone after her, and moments later they returned, William's large hand holding her twisted fingers, leading her by the arm back to the Ranch. She was crying from the pain and humiliation, but after that, she had been compliant.

One of the customers told Isela that they were in Pahrump, Nevada. There was nothing around for miles except flat desert land and scrub, with formidable mountains in the far distance. The temperature rose above 100 degrees every day, and there was nowhere for the girls to run.

"It's time to work," said Ximena as she entered the girl's room, looking around. "You cleaned up your room—good. Now, it's time for your medicine."

The girl came closer and the woman poured some white powder from a small vial she was holding. Without much thought, she leaned over and used a small straw to inhale the cocaine. It seemed to make things more bearable.

Once she had figured out what was expected of her, Isela settled into a routine. She slept until after noon each day, then rose and showered and ate. Around three each afternoon, she dressed in what Ximena called her Barbie Doll outfit, and made her way to the main living room, where she 'entertained' the men who came to visit. She'd learned how to use the credit card machines.

When the man she was with was ready, Isela took him down one of the halls to a private bedroom, where they finished their date. Then, usually, they would join the others again in the big room. She kept at this until all of the visitors were gone, and then she showered and went to bed.

Isela didn't know how long she'd been at the ranch. She'd become numb and managed the routine by rote. Their expectations of her were small and predictable and unwavering, and she seemed to exist only in the moment. After a time, her memories of El Salvador became indistinct, and she carried out her duties at the ranch numbly, without much feeling or thought.

* * *

"This is Mr. Carl, Isela," said Ximena, leading a large blond man to the sofa she was sitting on. "Mr. Carl thinks you are beautiful like a wild horse."

It was Ximena's way of breaking the ice for their shy customers, and Isela translated it to mean, "He likes it rough, so charge him more." It didn't matter, as all the money went to the Ranch anyway.

Although she had told no one, today was Isela's birthday, and she'd spent much of the morning awake and thinking about her family. When her mother had heard of the opportunity to go to the United States from her brother-in-law, Isela's uncle, she was excited. It was a chance for her to get Isela and her sister out of the city with its gangs and crime and war and strife, and to "go north and work for some rich Americanos," her mother had said with a smile in her voice. This is what she had dreamed of for the girls!

But along the way they had been separated. Isela was put on the container and shipped directly to Nevada, while her sister had been separated from her before she'd arrived in Mexico, and God knows where she was now. She had cried silently, missing her sister, Rosita.

* * *

It was the first time Isela had seen him. Many of her customers came to see her regularly, but this man hadn't been to Susie's Ranch before, at least since Isela had arrived. She would have remembered. He looked almost exactly like her older brother, Ricardo.

He had come into the big room around dinner time when the customers began to show up in earnest, and he'd looked around, teased with a couple of the girls, and then left the building, which was in itself odd.

Thirty minutes later, Immigration and Customs Enforcement agents, accompanied by the Nevada State Police, had arrived at the front door. With no hesitation the SWAT team took control of the building, dragging one guest out of a bedroom in his shirt only, and another in even less. No shots were fired.

"Sit on the floor, there," shouted an agent holding a frightening looking rifle. "Let's go, right there," he pointed. "Sentarse Alli."

The girls sat cross-legged on the floor while the agents tied their wrists with large, black zip ties.

* * *

"That actually went extremely well," said Agent Ramirez. He was in his Phoenix office with Zeke. They were discussing the prior day's action in Pahrump.

"So apparently the Mara's ship the incoming refugees directly to the brothels. Must have been to avoid the warehousing in Phoenix or wherever," said Ramirez, repeating Zeke's analysis as if he had figured this out himself.

Zeke nodded and smiled.

"We've got ten illegals, and several of them under-aged girls," he continued. "And we closed down the Ranch. That should slow Benito Diaz down some."

"Good work," said Zeke, simply.

"And I think we've effectively closed down his pipeline," added the ICE agent.

"I'm sure you have." In fact, Zeke was pretty certain that Benito Diaz's pipeline was much more extensive than Ramirez perceived.

"Were you able to arrest any MS-13 members?" asked Zeke.

"No, no one was there. The girls said they were dropped off and then the men who took them to Nevada, their 'handlers,' left."

"Think we may want to find them?" asked Zeke.

"Well, they came in on a container, a TEU, you know? An intermodal container that was rigged to keep them alive. One of the girls said they started out in Mexico and a couple days later they were let out of the box in Nevada."

Zeke nodded.

"And the pretty girls were put to work in the brothel," said Ramirez.

"How about the others?" asked Zeke. "And the men?"

"They were put to work as laborers, we think, or domestics, or on a farm, something like that. Maybe a pot farm. They stay oppressed because they're illegals and they have no money or papers. And they don't want to be shipped back."

Zeke nodded.

"Often they're abused by the people they work for, since they have no recourse. They're at the bottom of the food chain," said Ramirez.

"Sure," said Zeke. "So will you go after the MS-13's who brought them to Nevada?" he asked again.

"Well, they're either in northern Mexico, or somewhere in Southern California. L.A. is where the gang started, at least in the states. So we've got some jurisdictional issues," said Ramirez. "We had enough trouble getting permission to pull off the raid in Puhrump, Nevada. It would be almost impossible to do something like that in L.A. Besides, we don't have the manpower for that."

Zeke made a mental note to chat with Clark Hall about it. Then he stood and excused himself.

"Sorry, I've got a few things to do before I head back east," said Zeke. "Congratulations on the Nevada action."

CHAPTER 4

It was a clear day with a clear sky and good visibility. "If I were a pilot, I'd call this near perfect weather. This was a great idea," said Bruce Narber. "I've never been to the Grand Canyon before."

They were on the south rim, strolling the paved sidewalk that adjoins and parallels the canyon itself. To their right was a parking area, one of many. To their left was the very colorful 6,000-foot deep hole in the earth.

"I know," said Jerry Sebastian. "This is spectacular."

Crowds of tourists walked with them and toward them, couples dressed in desert boots and floppy sun hats, large families with parents struggling to keep them all together, groups of teens and independent retirees. Bruce navigated around a girl looking down at her iPhone screen and stepped to the edge of the sidewalk, looking north.

"Wow," he said. "You don't get the perspective from the pictures. Not even the aerials."

"I thought it would be worth the trip," said Jerry. They had driven up from Phoenix that afternoon, a three and a half hour drive, and then followed the line of cars into the park. "You need to see it at night."

"I'll bet," said Bruce, still gazing at the scenery. "I'll just bet."

Bruce Nabor was 32 and fit, and he worked as an air traffic controller at Phoenix Sky Harbor airport. He told Jerry that he'd recently transferred from Albuquerque to this airport hub, which was a step up, and that he was settling in nicely. He'd met Jerry Sebastian at an after-work party at a bar in Tempe. Jerry didn't work at the airport; he said he was in software.

"Hey, let's grab something for dinner and come back after dark," said Bruce. There were waves of people moving past them in some sort of chaotic sequence. "I could use a beer."

A short time later the two men were seated at a table in the Arizona Room restaurant in the Bright Angel Lodge, one of the better restaurants in the park. They ordered draft beer and thick steaks, and the sun was just setting as they finished their meal.

"Delicious," said Jerry. "Plus, what a great view!"

"I'm afraid it would be like fine art," said Bruce. "After you see it for a while, you kind of get used to it. It becomes invisible. To you, anyway."

"Let's walk back to the rim and check out the nighttime views," said Jerry.

"Sure. But we can see it from here," said Bruce.

* * *

Jerry Sebastian pulled the SUV into a parking space close to the edge of the rim. At this time of night, the park was comfortably empty, populated only by overnight campers and the random walker. It was dark, and the few people on the sidewalk were carrying flashlights.

"What time is it?" asked Bruce.

"Look at those stars, man!" said Jerry, pointing enthusiastically. He looked at his watch. "It's eleven thirty."

"It was smart to book that room. I don't much feel like driving back to Phoenix right now."

"Me either," said Jerry. He walked to the edge of the canyon and leaned forward, looking while holding onto a small sapling for stability. "Whoa, that's a long way down," he said.

Bruce stepped up next to him and grabbed the sapling and looked down. "Sure is," he said. He leaned a bit and looked into the dark.

What they saw was a small area that paralleled the sidewalk, sloping downward, mostly covered with medium sized rocks and brush, and an occasional small tree. Just beyond that, the ground fell away quickly in a steep grade, and then it became the wall of the canyon.

"Vertigo," said Bruce, looking down.

Jerry said, "Yeah," and pressed his taser against Bruce's hand, the one holding onto the tree. The shock first contracted his muscles, tightening his grip, and then he lost control before collapsing onto the rim and rolling forward off the edge and into the darkness. He made no sound as he fell.

* * *

"There's a wake of buzzards circling the canyon floor," said Alice Donnelly, the Chief Ranger in charge of the South Rim National Park. "My people just reported it to me. Can we get a UAS down there to check it out?"

It was Sunday late morning, and the hot Arizona sun had been beating down on the canyon's south rim since it rose, seven hours ago. The buzzards wasted no time following the strong odor of death to the canyon floor.

"Can do, Chief Ranger," said the voice on the other end of the line.

UAS was an acronym for Unmanned Aerial System, a fleet of drones owned by the park and used for search and rescue missions.

"What coordinates are we looking at?" asked the head of the UAS Team.

Donnelly told him, and he agreed to check the area and let her know what they found. She hung up the phone.

"They're sending the drones in," Donnelly said to the Rangers standing next to her. "Might want to get a rescue team ready. They're bound to find something down there."

Typically, the team would find mid-sized animals— coyotes, mountain lions, even Big Horn sheep—that had died. These were the most prevalent reason for the buzzards. Mostly the deaths were the result of contact with predators. But occasionally, they found a human being. Then the rangers had to plan for the rescue considering location, time of day and safety concerns for the rescue team.

"God, I hope it's a coyote," said the Chief Ranger to herself.

* * *

They were watching the live streaming video from the drone on computer screens in the operation room. Two of the park's four UAS devices were circling the area at the base of the south rim, working their way toward the buzzards, which were clustered in a pack, standing on the ground and apparently busy with an unidentified carcass. The birds were large and awkward looking and they screamed and shouldered each other aside for access to the body.

"There's something," said the Chief Ranger.

The drone slowed and the ground grew closer on the monitor. Some of the buzzards looked up at it as it approached, threatening it with screams, but not giving up their positions.

"That's a body," said the drone operator, watching the screen.

"Definitely a human body. Looks like we have a man down."

Chief Ranger Donnelly watched the screen to confirm the assessment, and then she turned away. "Let's get a rescue team down there. We'll need to hurry, but we can get the body out before dark."

* * *

"It's taken care of," said Luis Cruz.

He was speaking into a prepaid cell phone that fifteen minutes before had been on display on a rack in the Walmart just off Interstate 40 in Flagstaff, Arizona. Right now, Luis was driving seventy-five miles an hour south toward Phoenix.

"Si," said Raul Diaz on the other end of the line. "What name did you use this time?"

Luis paused for a moment. Then he said, "Jerry Sebastian. I was Jerry Sebastian."

"Was there any problem?"

"No," said Luis. "No problem."

"OK. I'll tell him you called. Check back tomorrow afternoon," the man said in guttural Spanish.

Luis Cruz held down the button in the SUV's center console until his window was all the way down, then he tossed the cell phone toward the scrub on the side of the road. It shattered when it hit the pavement and the pieces flew in every direction.

He raised the window and turned on the radio.

* * *

Ever since he was a boy growing up in south central LA, Luis Cruz had been different. He had never felt much empathy for the other kids, or adults either for that matter. Much of his life had been spent on the shadowy edges of honesty, dealing in half-truths and clever lies.

When he was fourteen, he found himself on the wrong side of a robbery. A petty theft, actually, when he and a friend tried to exit a local grocery store with several pounds of bacon stuffed down the front of their pants. The grocer had witnessed the theft on a security camera and sent his twin twenty-year-old boys to retrieve the meat. In their enthusiasm, they had kicked the boy unconscious. Luis woke to find himself in the hospital, with both arms broken and contusions all over his body. Any remaining empathy he'd felt toward his fellow man dissipated during his five-month recovery.

Luis Cruz looked like a CPA, or an engineer, or maybe a software programmer. Software development was a big thing in Phoenix, with ASU located in Tempe on the fringes of the city. Luis comfortably fit himself into that role. He was thirty-five, although he could have passed for younger, and was meticulous about his appearance and clothing. He wore geekish short-sleeved shirts and black-rimmed glasses, and worked hard to look harmless. His black hair was the only clue to his Latino heritage. His mother had been an Angelo woman with fair skin.

Luis made the call the following evening, using a new Walmart cellphone. He'd selected a flip phone, because it was cheap and he was going to use it only once. He dialed the number from memory.

"Hello? Who is this?" asked the voice in Castilian Spanish, very proper with correct enunciation.

"It is I, Luis," he replied.

"Yes," said the voice. "You've completed your assignment, I see."

On television, thought Luis. "Yes."

"We have another project for you."

"Very well," Luis said with no discernible accent.

"Come and see me," said the voice.

Luis knew that this man liked face to face contact. He prided himself on being able to read a man's soul by looking into his eyes. Luis knew this belief had served the man well in his professional life.

"Very well," said Luis. "Tomorrow." He closed the flip phone and removed the sim card. Later he would drop the phone into a hotel toilet, wrapped in a small hand towel. He knew that it would easily fit through the four-inch pipe and be washed with the rest of the sewage to the nearest water treatment plant.

Luis lived on the fringes of society, alone and alert. He was constantly reading and studying anything that might give him an edge. Unlike in the movies, to be effective an assassin had to be patient and willing to devote as much time as necessary to the project at hand. Sometimes it required months to get close to his target, to develop a relationship and build trust. But Luis was good at it. He reflected the empathy he saw in other people, and although soulless, he practiced the appropriate reactions to various situations constantly, developing intricate scenarios in his mind and then putting himself in the place of each of the participants. He studied movies and television for clues to human responses. He would meet people and befriend them as practice. When they bored him too much he moved on.

Inside, Luis felt very little. He knew he was different and clever, and he was driven not by emotion or desire, but by his secret need to be superior. He often laughed to himself about the people who had trusted him, and how easily he had gained their friendship. Human beings were a needy lot.

In the end, though, he was a loner. He worked alone and preferred his own company. For his work, his preparation was impeccable, and his reputation grew quietly. Eventually he'd been sought out by some of the richest men in the world. Like his current employer, the man he had just spoken with.

Luis returned his rental car to the airport, entered the terminal, and took an Uber ride to downtown Phoenix. He checked into a Marriott hotel and began to make plans to meet with Benito Diaz.

* * *

In the hotel, Luis thought back over the recent past. Almost four months ago, Benito Diaz's brother Raul had contacted him with the assignment. Luis had been considering a brief retirement, a respite, but the phone call had reminded him that he was attached tightly to the Diaz brothers. He didn't like the feeling.

"So, Luis, you need to come out here," Raul had said tactlessly. He was Benito's younger brother, and he assumed Benito's power as if it were his birthright.

Luis clenched his jaw and said nothing.

"Do you hear me, Luis?" he asked.

Luis sighed. "I do hear you, Raul," he said.

"So you can come here now," said Raul. It wasn't a question.

"Of course," he said.

* * *

"Come in," said Raul, who was sitting alone at a dining room table and cutting a papaya with a steak knife. He glanced up, and then went back to his task.

Luis waited, standing just inside the door.

"So I want you to kill someone for me," said Raul.

Luis said nothing.

The room was decorated with Mexican knickknacks, painted bowls and glazed flower pots. There was a yellow and red bowl of fruit on the table, heaped full of papayas and avocados. The ceiling had large wooden beams affixed to it, running laterally. The single window looked out onto a large area covered in stone and bordered in shrubs and small fruit trees.

"Do you hear me, amigo?" Raul asked, not looking up. "I was in prison, you know. It's not just my brother you must respect."

"Yes, I heard," said Luis. *It would be so easy to gut this pig,* he thought. *One day I will.*

Luis stepped into the room and walked to the table. The house was a beige low-rise that sprawled across an oversized lot. It was one of many in this upscale development.

"Who is it?" Luis asked.

Raul looked up for a moment. "Bruce Narber. He testified in L.A.," said Raul. "Carlos was sent to jail because of him. He is an *informador.*"

Luis nodded. He remembered the headlines. The trial had

resulted in two leaders of the Mara Salvatrucha being sent to jail for kidnapping and drug trafficking. The government's key witness had been an airport employee, an air traffic controller on a break, who had seen drugs and illegals being loaded onto an airplane late at night.

"And now he is in witness protection. He thinks he's safe there."

Luis nodded, thinking, *Here comes the rant.*

"But he cannot hide from us. We are everywhere! We have eyes and ears everywhere! This man is already dead!"

By my hand, thought Luis. Then he interrupted, "How do you want me to do it?"

"An accident," said Raul. "We don't need to send a message with this one. The right people will know what has happened."

"Certainly," said Luis. "I'll see to it. I'll request my usual retainer."

"Of course," said Raul. "Fifty percent. It will be deposited into your account in small increments over the next two weeks as usual." Then he looked up. "You are paid too much for this work."

Luis said nothing and stared down at the man. His black eyes were empty and ominous. He was as still as a snake.

Raul looked up and saw something in Luis' face that suddenly made him feel uncomfortable, nervous. He began to look around the room, to fidget with his knife. And then he was suddenly preoccupied with his papaya, taking a slice, looking at it, putting it in his mouth. After a moment he said, "OK?" He didn't look up again.

Luis stood still for a moment longer, then turned and left the house.

* * *

"Were you followed here?" asked Benito Diaz. It was a sincere question asked without emotion.

"No. No one knows I'm in Phoenix," said Luis Cruz. "I arrived last night, after we spoke."

"Very well." Diaz's use of Castilian Spanish had the affect of extracting a proper response from those around him. It also lent a sense of formality to his meetings.

Diaz asked, "How did the last project conclude?"

"There was no problem," said Luis. He looked directly at Diaz as he spoke.

Diaz nodded slightly. "He had to be taken care of. He'd seen too much at the airport, and he testified about it." He paused and looked at Luis. "This next is a more difficult project."

Luis nodded, patient.

The two men were sitting on the back deck of the Scottsdale home where he had last met with Raul Diaz. They were sitting at a small table that held two plastic water bottles. Camelback Mountain was visible in the distance. The yard was entirely enclosed by a five-foot high concrete block and stucco privacy wall painted desert brown. A series of patio misters surrounded the porch and sprayed constantly, the water evaporating before it reached the ground. It was over 100 degrees outside and very dry.

JEFF SIEBOLD

"It involves law enforcement," Diaz continued.

"Alright," said Luis. "I was told that your men have control of the local authorities. That you have men in place."

"You were told that?" asked Diaz. "By whom?"

"It doesn't matter," said Luis.

Diaz waited, watching quietly.

"By your brother Raul," said Luis.

Diaz nodded. "Yes," he said to himself. "Well, this is a special situation."

It was Luis's turn to listen.

Diaz thought for a moment. "We anticipate interference from a contractor. A man who has been hired to help the Federales find us and close us down. His name is Zeke Traynor. He was involved in the recent raid on our Phoenix warehouse." Diaz smiled to himself. "And it seems that they are determined to cause trouble between us and our suppliers."

MS-13, thought Luis. He was very still, patient.

"And so we would like to send him away," Diaz continued. "Dispatch him."

"As you wish," said Luis. He waited.

"Some men made an attempt to do so last week," said Diaz.

"Yes?" Luis was interested. *And why am I here?*

"But they were not effective. They failed," Diaz continued.

The Mara's, thought Luis. "The victim is aware, then? Of the attempt?"

"Yes."

"So they would be expecting another?" asked Luis.

"Most probably. But you will be successful."

58

Luis thought for a moment and then nodded slowly. He simply said, "Yes."

* * *

"The body had been there for most of the day," said the voice on the phone.

Chief Ranger Donnelly nodded as she said, "Yes."

"It's likely he fell last night and was on the bottom for fourteen or fifteen hours."

Donnelly was talking with the office of the medical examiner for Coconino County.

Poor bastard, she thought. "Anything out of the ordinary? Cause of death?"

"It was a hell of a fall," he continued, ignoring her questions. Harold Shiner had been Chief Medical Examiner in the county for almost forty years, and he used every opportunity he could to draw out his own importance. He wasn't a man to be hurried along. "Looks like he hit every rock on the way down. Till he got to the edge, of course. Then it would pretty much be a free fall."

"Died of the contusions, then?" asked Donnelly.

"Hard to tell, exactly. Broken ribs that pierced some vital organs, a concussion, broken legs and multiple contusions. He was a mess before the birds got to him."

"Hmm," said the Chief Ranger.

"Have you figured out who he is?" asked Shiner. "Anybody come up missing in the park?"

"Not yet. There's been a lot of traffic since yesterday. Could you identify him from the body?"

"Not much chance of that. The birds did a number on his face while you were trying to get to him," Shiner said. He made it sound as if it were Donnelly's fault.

She paused. "We'll keep looking," she said.

CHAPTER 5

"I suppose we'll need to pay some attention to the Cambridge thing soon," said Clive. "The colleges." He had called Zeke in Phoenix from The Agency's Washington, D.C. office.

"All right," said Zeke.

"Ramirez seems intent on self-destruction," Clive continued. "Let's leave him alone until I chat with his superiors."

"OK," said Zeke.

"Meantime, we need to take a close look at this student loan fraud. It appears that there are literally millions of dollars being stolen through institutions of higher learning in the Boston area alone."

"That sounds like a well-oiled machine," Zeke commented.

"Indeed. It been going on for quite some time, you know. I'm sure it didn't happen overnight."

"Who's our client for this?" Zeke asked.

"Actually, it's the Executive Branch. The U.S. Department of Education."

Zeke paused for a moment. "How did they get your name?"

"They didn't say. Very mysterious and all that. But I'm fairly certain that it came from the FBI."

"What's our next move?" asked Zeke.

"Well, I've arranged a meeting on Tuesday with the Assistant Deputy Director and we'll get a feel for the problem from him. Fellow named Cy Stiles. Assistant Deputy Director Stiles to us, I suppose," he said with a smile in his voice.

"What time Tuesday?" asked Zeke.

"Mid-afternoon. It'll give you enough time to fly into D.C. on Monday. From Atlanta, I mean," Clive said, tongue-in-cheek. "And we'll bring you up to speed Monday afternoon."

Zeke shook his head and smiled. "I guess it's time for another layover. I'll be in your offices Monday noonish."

"Looking forward to it," said Clive.

* * *

"Told you I'd be back soon," Zeke whispered softly in Tracy Johnson's ear.

She shuddered lightly, pulled away and smiled. "So glad you're here," she said.

"The last time I was met in an airport by a beautiful woman, eight assassins came after us," said Zeke with a smile. "We should be careful on our way back to your place."

Her place was a Midtown Atlanta condominium, close to the Secret Service office where she worked. Tracy and Zeke had met while protecting a counterfeiter-turned-informant who had escaped from a Mexican Cartel. They'd been maintaining the long-distance relationship for a couple of years.

"I packed spare riot guns under the seats," Tracy assured him. "And a couple of hand grenades. We should be OK."

Zeke gave her a kiss on the nose before letting go of her upper arms. "Oh, good," he said.

Tracy was wearing distressed jeans with low boots and a heavy, colorful cable sweater in various shades of blue and white.

"You're not wearing anything under that sweater, are you?" Zeke whispered.

Tracy gave him a quick smile and took his hand as they walked through the airport concourse. They then took the train to baggage claim and ground transportation. Her Mazda Miata was parked on the third floor of one of the concrete parking garages, marked 'South Terminal Parking.'

"New wheels, nice," said Zeke, admiring the MX-5.

"Thanks, it's fun to drive," she said.

"Take me home, then." He tossed his carryon into the back seat.

"Yes, sir," she said. "That was my plan all along."

* * *

"I'll need to fly to D.C. tomorrow morning," said Zeke. "I have a meeting with Clive."

Tracy had lost the sweater and jeans, and was lying on the couch with Zeke modestly covered by a light blanket they shared. "Hmm," she said.

"That sounded happy," said Zeke. "What did you like?"

"Hmm," she said again. Then, "All of it. Every. Single. Moment."

"Good. Me, too."

She snuggled closer, absorbing his body heat. He smelled her clean, fruity scent.

"What are you wearing?" he asked.

"Well, nothing. You know that." she purred.

"No, your cologne, what brand is it?"

"It's El Nihilo," said Tracy.

"Out of nothing," Zeke said to himself.

"What?" she asked lazily.

"El Nihilo. Latin. It means 'Out of Nothing.' Like, 'God created it out of nothing.'"

"Really?"

"Yes," said Zeke.

"Odd. Because the name of the scent is 'Devil Tender,'" she said.

"That's clever. I won't forget it," said Zeke as he smelled her neck. And then he kissed her again.

* * *

"It sounds like your Phoenix trip was pretty dangerous," said Tracy Johnson. "Those Mara guys are bad news."

"They are," said Zeke.

They were seated at an outside table at The Lawrence, a popular restaurant well known for its cocktails. It was an easy walk from Tracy's midtown condo.

Tracy was working on something that contained Lavender Mint Tea Vodka, and Zeke had a house Old Fashioned, made with small batch Bourbon.

"And there were eight of them, just waiting to kill you?" Tracy asked.

"Well, I assume they were there to kill us. They were pretty fierce. And they didn't hesitate."

"Do you think you're safe now?" she asked.

"I do. I think they were there to stop the ICE raid. I'm pretty sure Benito Diaz hired them to break up ICE's efforts and cause some confusion. But I'm not sure how they knew that Kimmy and I were on our way to help."

"Sounds like they may have an inside guy," she thought out loud.

"It does," said Zeke, and took another sip. "How're things at the Secret Service?"

"Not bad. But we don't have anybody shooting at us in the streets right now," she said.

"It was a parking lot," he said with a smile.

Tracy pulled a face, feigning exasperation. She sipped her drink.

"Are you hungry?" she asked.

"No, not really," said Zeke. "You?"

"Not yet."

"Let's stop at a market on our way back to your condo, and I'll make us a dinner later, when we get hungry."

"OK," said Tracy. "But what will we do in the meantime?"

"I vote for soft music, a low fire in the fireplace and a glass of wine while we get to know each other again."

"That sounds romantic," she said.

"I hope so," said Zeke.

"What else do you have planned?"

"Well, I was thinking about the quickest way to get you out of those clothes…" he said.

"These clothes?" Tracy looked down at her knee-length dress and smiled. "Well, since you asked so nicely."

* * *

"Every time we're together it's like magic," said Tracy.

They were sitting on the couch in her condo, sipping wine and listening to "Of Monsters and Men" on the sound system. The small fire was warming the air-conditioned room.

"It is," said Zeke.

"Why is that?" she asked.

Partially the dopamine, he thought. But instead he said, "It's almost electrical. When I'm away, I can't wait to get back here to you."

"Now I'm a magnet?" asked Tracy with a grin.

"You certainly are," said Zeke.

"What's next?" she asked.

"The clothing, I suspect," he smiled.

"No silly, I mean what's next for us?"

"You're in a hurry?" asked Zeke, tongue in cheek. "Are you going somewhere specific?"

Tracy looked at him for a moment with a blank face. Then she smiled a spectacular smile.

"The only place I'm going is Cape Cod," she said. "I think I'd like it this time of year."

"You will," said Zeke. "And so will I."

* * *

"Tell me, old boy, just what's up with the ICE agency in Phoenix?" asked Clive. Zeke and Clive were meeting in Clive's Washington, D.C. office, across from the FBI building on Pennsylvania Avenue. It was rush hour, about 6:15 in the evening, and through the large window they saw the streets were filled with an assortment of slow moving vehicles.

"What do we know about Jorge Ramirez?" asked Zeke. "Have we done a credit check on him?"

A 'credit check' by The Agency included a comprehensive and thorough review of a person's school records, criminal records, military service records, and a variety of other information, including an actual credit check.

"Asked Sally to run that down when you called," said Clive. "We have the results here. There are some irregularities. Quite a bit of money moving through his bank accounts. So, what tipped you off?"

"Counterintelligence training," said Zeke. "Ramirez was lying and trying to get me to abandon the investigation."

"How did you know?" asked Clive.

"Lots of small things," said Zeke. "The way he looked at me

when he lied." His blink rate changed. He touched his face. A couple other things. But I confirmed it when I agreed that he was probably right, that there was nothing else for me to find out."

"What happened then?" asked Clive.

"He smiled. Just for a quick moment. A smile of relief that I'd bought into his lie and agreed to his suggestions," said Zeke.

"But you obviously haven't," said Clive.

"Once we determine what we're up against, I'll be heading back to Phoenix to interview the assassins."

* * *

"Glad you could make room in your schedule for us, Assistant Deputy Director," Clive said. He and Zeke were sitting around a low coffee table in the man's office. Coffee, tea and oatmeal cookies were set out on the table before them.

"My pleasure, Mr. Greene," said Cy Stiles. He was a short man with long, gray hair that was brushed back away from his face and apparently kept there with a substantial amount of hair spray. His face was tanned and his shoes were well polished.

"As you know, we're here about the student loan issues," Clive continued. "We need your perspective."

A young woman, presumably one of the ADD's aids or interns, shrunk back away from the table and attempted to disappear into the sofa cushion. Stiles eyes flashed red for a moment, then he regained control.

Sensitive subject, thought Zeke.

"Yes, of course," said Styles. "First, nothing we discuss can leave this room. I have your word on that?"

Both Zeke and Clive nodded.

"This could damage the President!" said Styles. "We have to keep it under wraps." He sighed a deep sigh. "But we do need your help."

"Yes?" asked Clive.

"Well, apparently it's been going on for years. Maybe for three or four administrations. Billions at stake, here," said Styles. He spoke in short, clipped sentences, many of which had an exclamation point at the end.

Pretty dramatic, thought Zeke.

"This is my aid, Sarah Helms. She's been looking into it for us. She brought it to me, actually. Tell them, Sarah."

Zeke noticed that she was a tall, thin woman in her thirties with brown hair and watery green eyes. She wore a woman's business suit over a white shirt with a bow at the neck. She wore no wedding ring, but had a small, gold Cartier watch on her left wrist. Sarah adjusted herself and sat forward on the couch.

"Well, we were looking at defaults, actually," she said. "A small team of the Director's staff. Student loan defaults. And we started examining them in detail." Her voice was deeper than expected, almost masculine.

"How many are there, typically? In default," asked Zeke.

"Millions of loans a year. More during a recession."

Zeke nodded. "How much money are we talking about?"

"In default? About $137 billion last year. That was up 14% from the year before."

Zeke whistled softly. "How many are involved? In the entire program, I mean."

"I know, we get used the size of it," said Styles. "There are about 42 million people involved. They owe a total of 1.3 trillion dollars in Federal student debt."

"So we noticed that there was a pattern of students receiving loans, then dropping out almost immediately," said the aid. "A higher than expected percentage. Much higher than the typical college dropout rate," she added. Her clipped speech mirrored the ADD's vocal patterns. She kept her body very still as she talked.

Zeke nodded. "What about repeat offenders?"

"Yes, some applied more than once. Received funding then dropped out. Sequential years," she said.

"You can do that?" asked Clive.

"It's a government program. It's a matter of understanding the rules and using them to your advantage," said Stiles.

"We figured money was being stolen," Sarah continued. "But the proceeds of the loans go directly to the schools. Not to the individual students."

"So to make it work, someone in the schools would have to be involved," said Zeke.

"It seems so," said Sarah. "We thought it would be some of them. So we started looking for schools that meet the pattern."

"High, early dropout rate and high delinquency in student loans? Then repeat the next year?" asked Zeke.

"Yes, the anomalies," said Sarah, nodding.

"And you found...?" said Clive.

"We found a number of them."

"You'll need to excuse me, gentlemen," said Stiles, looking at his watch. "Another meeting."

"Certainly," said Clive.

"Stay here. Get what you need from Sarah. Remember, confidential!"

He stood, shook hands all around and left the office.

"Do we have any idea who's behind it?" asked Clive, once Stiles had gone. "It sounds like it's a fairly organized effort."

"We don't," said Sarah. "But yes. You'd need the student identities. The right employees at the colleges. Access to the funds."

"I assume you have a list that we can start with," said Clive.

"We do. Most likely candidates on the student side. Most likely colleges. We used a number of criteria," said Sarah.

"Like a low threshold for admissions?" guessed Zeke.

"Yes," she said. "Schools that are easy to get into. Hungry for students and the accompanying tuitions."

"Sounds right. Who has access to the schools' finances?" asked Zeke.

"It differs from one institution to the next. But most colleges have a similar organizational structure," said Sarah.

"It's usually the responsibility of the Vice President of Finance and Administration, I'd guess," said Zeke.

"Yes. I'll get the lists for you," she said.

"Good," said Clive. "And we'll want an introduction to the schools from this office, some sort of pretext to give us access to the right people and records."

"Sure. The ADD has a lot of influence. We'll work you both into our normal oversight team. Maybe as government auditors," Sarah said, thinking aloud.

"Good, yes," said Clive. "We'll get this going as soon as that's ready."

CHAPTER 6

The inside of the truck cab was painted red. Red like one of those older trucks, maybe a farm truck from the 1930s, a faded, matte red that favored a pinkish hue. It was the original paint, in a truck that had seen too many summers and was seemingly waiting to be put out to pasture.

Susan pulled open the truck door and it closed behind her with a groan. Dressed in jeans and a tie-dyed shirt, she repositioned herself on the overstuffed seat, getting comfortable. She set her small backpack between her legs on the floor. The driver said, "Where ya heading?"

"Going to Des Moines," she said easily. "But I'll ride with you as far as you're going."

"I'm turning north at Iowa City," the man said, "but I can take you that far."

They were about ninety miles west of Chicago, where the man had stopped on the shoulder of the interstate ramp to pick up the hitchhiker. In 2005 in the Midwest, hitchhikers were not an unusual sight.

"Thank you," she said. "Every ride helps." She smiled warmly at the man.

They rode in silence for a while.

"I'm Henry," the man said. "I have a farm near Cedar Rapids." He said it as if to impress Susan.

"Hello, Henry," she said. "I'm Susan. Heading home from college for the week."

Henry nodded at the woman, who he estimated to be in her mid-twenties.

"University of Chicago?" he asked.

"No, University of St. Francis. In Joilet."

"Which is why you're on Interstate 80," said Henry. Henry Rothier was a farmhand. But he was also a petty thief and had been arrested four times for stealing, and twice for drunk and disorderly behavior. Now, he was working on his sister's Iowa farm, making a few extra dollars for beer and whiskey. He was thin, in his late thirties, and had a pronounced stoop in his shoulders, even while driving. He wore worn workboots and denim overalls and a yellow t-shirt under it that had started out white a few days ago. His hair was uncombed, as if he'd slept on it recently. He smelled of farm.

"Which is why I'm here," she agreed with a smile. "Do you mind if I roll the window down?"

"No, that's fine," said Henry, agreeably.

She cranked the window down manually and took a deep breath of the outside air. "It always smells so nice out here," she said. "Like fresh hay."

Just before they reached Moline traffic slowed to a crawl.

A large truck with a lighted arrow on the back was stopped in one lane, directing traffic to merge right. Four State Police cars were blocking the shoulder and the lanes and the officers were looking into each car.

"What's this?" asked Susan.

"A roadblock," said Henry. "Not sure why. They must be looking for someone."

Henry pulled his truck up to the roadblock and rolled down his window. "What's up?"

The officer looked into the truck at Henry and at Susan, then waved them through without answering.

"You don't see that very often," said Henry.

The truck bumped along on the Interstate, rattling and groaning with unexplained noises. Eventually they passed Moline and took the Bypass around Davenport, across the Mississippi River into Iowa.

"I never get tired of seeing the river," said Susan.

At the Iowa I-80 truck stop, Henry exited the Interstate and pulled up to a gas pump.

"Do you need to go inside?" he asked, delicately.

"No, I'm good," said the girl.

"OK, well, I'm going in," said Henry. He turned and smiled a silly smile at her.

She nodded.

He opened the driver's side door, which apparently hadn't been oiled for a half century. It groaned loudly as he stepped down to the pavement. Then he started to walk toward the building. Susan looked through the back window. The rear of the truck was open and covered with loose hay. There were several rolls of barbed wire and a dozen or more fenceposts loaded on top of the hay.

Susan considered her options. She could stay in the truck, fairly invisible, all the way to Iowa City, and then catch another ride, probably south to Hannibal or St. Louis. Or, she could continue west to Des Moines, and then south to Kansas City, her original plan.

* * *

"OK, I just need to pump some gas, now," said Henry, squinting a bit.

Susan smiled at him and nodded her understanding.

Henry fiddled with the gas cap and the fuel pump, and when he had it right, he jumped back up in the cab.

"They had the news on in there," said Henry. "They were saying something about a husband and wife being killed, over in North Utica, pretty close to where we just came from."

He had a low country accent that smoothed out the consonants as he spoke.

Susan made her eyes large for a moment, looked at Henry and said, "Oh. I guess I'd better be careful, hitchhiking and all."

"It can be dangerous, that's for sure," Henry contributed.

"Can we turn on the radio? It's probably on the news," said Susan.

"Radio doesn't work," said Henry. "Hasn't for years."

They sat for a while longer.

"Did you spill some paint?" she asked.

"Huh?"

"In the back, on the hay, there are some red splashes," she said, casually.

"Oh, that's barn paint. we spilled some," said Henry. Then he looked around and said, "Tank's about full."

He jumped out of the truck and finished up with the gas pump, replacing the cap and looking around carefully before he climbed back into the truck. "I guess everybody's inside, still watching the news," he said as he started the red truck and shifted into low gear.

They rode the Interstate in silence for a while. As they drove, Susan sensed Henry becoming increasingly nervous, fidgety, anxious, like a schoolboy getting ready to ask a girl to dance. It made her feel nervous, too. The cool steel of the switchblade low and horizontal across the skin of her stomach under her panties, was reassuring.

Susan looked out her window and watched the farms slide by. It was getting dark out.

A half hour later, Henry finally spoke.

"I guess I'm going to have to let you off up here somewhere," he said.

"OK, sure," said Susan. "How about right at the intersection of 380?" She was referring to the north south Interstate that Henry would be taking home to Cedar Rapids.

"Well, I can drop you, but there aren't any gas stations or restaurants there. Nobody really stops there," said Henry. Then he said, "There's nothing south of there, either, except that quarry. I could take you with me one exit north. There's a couple of gas stations and stores there."

"Well, I'm heading west, so it might be better to stay on this road," she said.

"I guess you can, but it's pretty dark, now. You sure you'll be OK?" asked Henry. "Especially with those killings and all…"

Susan smiled to herself in the dark. "I'll be OK. I'm sure," she said.

* * *

"I work in the auto center up at the Walmart," he said. "Mostly do tires and stuff."

Susan had just settled herself in the passenger seat of a black mustang with tinted windows, gold piping and loud pipes. The driver, a pale, pudgy twenty-something with longish hair and a fuzzy beard, had stopped abruptly on the shoulder of Interstate 80, then backed up, spinning his tires, to pick up the lone female hitchhiker. She was heading west.

"Which Walmart?" she asked, to be polite.

"Over in Coralville," he said, sticking his right thumb over his right shoulder. "I'm going home now."

Susan took this to mean that the store was behind them.

He waited a beat, then said, "You like my wheels?"

"Very nice," she said. He pumped the accelerator so she could feel the power as the car responded, jumping forward.

"Know why it's black with gold trim?" he continued.

"Why?"

"Iowa Hawkeyes colors, that's why!" he laughed to himself. "Best wrestlers in the country!" Then, "How far you going?"

"I've got a ways to go, to Des Moines," said Susan. "I'll ride with you as far west as you can take me."

"I'm about thirty miles from home. I live in Victor with my ma," he said, jovially. Then, "What's your name?"

"I'm Susan."

"How come you're hitchhiking?" he asked.

"Just trying to get somewhere," said Susan.

"Well, yeah," he said. "My name's Albert, by the way."

He smiled at her quickly and she noticed his dead tooth.

"Hello, Albert. I appreciate the ride."

"Sure. It gets lonely driving up and down the interstate every day," he added.

"I can imagine," said Susan.

"Hey, did you hear about the killings?" Albert asked. "In North Utica?"

"I did. Is there any more information? Did they catch the killer yet?" she asked innocently.

"Don't know. The guys saw it on TV in our waiting room. The waiting room for the auto service. Said a family was killed, dad and mom. They had two young girls, " Albert said. "The cops said it was a home invasion."

"They were killed in their home?" asked Susan.

"They said so on the TV. Said it must have been before school let out, but after lunch. A neighbor girl found the bodies around three thirty when she stopped by to visit, I guess. Stopped by before she got her kids off the school bus."

"Why after lunch?"

"TV said the mom called a neighbor at lunch time, and they talked about the Burgoo Festival."

"The what?" asked Susan.

"It's a big deal around here," said Albert. "Lots of arts and crafts and food and stuff. Most everybody gets a booth and sells stuff. Ma sells pies."

"And it's called a Burgoo Festival?" she asked, curious. "Isn't that some sort of a sexual term?"

"No, not this Burgoo. Burgoo is like a thick stew. It's usually one of the more popular dishes at the festival."

Susan waited a beat. Then she said, "Did they say who the victims were? Of the killings?"

Albert seemed anxious to share what he knew, warming up to the task of providing data.

"Said they'd lived there, in North Utica, for a year and a half or so. Said their last name was Simpson," Albert said. "That sort of thing doesn't happen much around here."

"I imagine not," said Susan.

Albert thought for a minute. Then he said, "Did you read, *In Cold Blood*, that book by Truman Capote? Those murders took place in Kansas. That's not too far from here."

Susan nodded, realizing that Albert wasn't waiting for a response.

He plowed ahead. "Same thing, right? A family was killed. Small town, farm area. Hey, maybe it was a copycat…"

Nope, Susan thought. She said, "Wasn't that a long time ago?"

Albert thought. "Well, it was. But someone could have read the book and thought about it…"

"Maybe you should be a detective," Susan added.

Albert nodded enthusiastically. "I already applied to be a prison guard at the penitentiary down in Ft. Madison. They didn't need me, but they've still got my application. And I passed the drug test."

"Admirable," said Susan warmly.

"They'll call me when they need me, Ma says. At least I'm on their radar."

They drove on for a little while.

"Did the police say whether they have any suspects?" she asked.

Albert shook his head. "Not that I heard about. But that was a couple hours ago. I'll check when I get home. Ma always has the news on."

A while longer, Albert said, "This is my exit. I'll need to drop you here. Is the truck stop OK?"

"Sure," said Susan. "That's perfect."

"You've only got another 75 miles to go to Des Moines," he added.

"I appreciate the ride," she said.

* * *

The truck stop was average in condition, but with overflowing trashcans near the pump islands and a fast food restaurant attached to the building. There were a few cars refueling under the main canopy, and five eighteen-wheelers parked around the side of the building, a couple with their engines running.

Susan ate something that tasted like it may have had soft chicken parts in it, drank a diet coke, and used the restroom. Then she wandered into the retail area of the building.

A tall man with a bushy beard and bright green eyes was standing in line, getting ready to check out. She got in line behind him and asked, "By any chance, are you heading west?"

He turned and looked at her for a minute. "You're not a hooker, are you?" he asked. "'Cuz I don't want any of that kind of trouble."

Susan smiled what she hoped was a disarming smile.

"No," she said, "I saw you from the restaurant window. You came in on the westbound off-ramp, so I figured you're headed west."

The man nodded, as if satisfied. "I guess I could use some company. How far are you going?"

"Des Moines," she said. "Just an hour or so. I could really use the help."

He was wearing a flannel shirt, dirty jeans and a baseball cap that read, 'Kubota' above the bill. His face was pock-marked in places, but his eyes were almost cat-like. He said, "Sure," and turned back toward the counter.

* * *

"I'm a preacher," the man said, once they were seated in the cab of his old Kenworth. "People call me 'Father Fred.'"

"I'm Susan," she said simply, looking at him directly. "Where's home?"

"Oh, I'm a long way from home," he said. "I work out of Memphis, but I'm heading to Denver on this run. Had to pick up this trailer in Naperville, didn't want to dead head. You know, ride with an empty load."

Susan nodded and said, "I'm a student at Joliet. Heading home for a week."

Father Fred eased the truck out from under a canopy and maneuvered it across the parking area. At the highway, he turned right on the on-ramp for Interstate 80 west. In minutes, they were on their way toward Des Moines.

"The reason I asked about hookers," started Fred, "is that they drive up and down the freeway and try to get drivers to stop at the truck stop for sex." He said it matter-of-factly.

Susan nodded.

"They pull up next to you in your truck and honk their horn and wave out the window. Some of them call out nasty things to you."

Susan nodded again.

"Sometimes there's two or three of them in a car, and they want you to follow them off the freeway. And usually it's to a truck stop, sometimes a rest area."

Susan said, "Well, that's not me."

Fred asked, "What are you studying?"

"Nursing," said Susan. "Only one more year to go."

"What's in the bag?" asked Father Fred, looking at the back-pack on the floor between Susan's shapely legs. It was light gray and orange, and an empty plastic water bottle was attached by a black carabiner. His piercing green eyes stared at her just a beat too long.

Susan said, "Just some clothes and books. And my laptop. Gotta study." Then she thought, *That was an odd question.*

Fred nodded and said, "You can throw it in the back, if it'd be more comfortable."

Susan looked over her shoulder and saw the sleeper section of the truck cab. It held an unmade bed behind an open curtain and a small pile of clothes, probably dirty from the way they'd been heaped in the corner. There was room on the floor for her bag.

"It's OK, thanks," she said, calmly. "I'm only going a little ways."

"Suit yourself," said Father Fred. "Do you go to church?"

"Um, well, I did when I lived at home," she lied. "But not so much, now. But my school is a Franciscan school."

Father Fred nodded, watching the road. "You should go to church," he said.

"That's what my Mom says," Susan said. Then she added, "I know I should."

* * *

Twenty minutes later, Father Fred said, "I'll drop you up here."

They had taken Interstate 235 around the city, a slightly longer route but one that Susan mentioned would take her closer to home. Father Fred eased the truck off the Interstate and a short distance north to the Walmart entrance.

"I'll drop you here. Then I can turn around in the parking lot and get back on."

"Thank you," Susan replied.

"Well, I'm glad you're not one of those truck stop hookers," said Father Fred as he stopped the truck. "But you need to go to church. We all do."

* * *

She spent the night at a nearby Days Inn, paying $59 cash for the room and, more importantly, the shower. Hitchhiking was a tiring business, with the uncertainty of the rides and their erratic timing. But it was a virtually untraceable method of travel, random and without any paper trail. She slept soundly and was up early, back to the on-ramp heading for Interstate 35 south, her knife in place and her backpack slung over one shoulder.

This early in the morning, the traffic included long-haul drivers mixed with commuters. The commuters wouldn't do her much good, but once she cleared Des Moines, she should be able to hop a ride that was a straight shot to Kansas City.

About fifteen minutes later, a State Police car pulled over on the ramp and asked her where she was going.

She said, "Breakfast," and he gave her a ride to a Cracker Barrel, about four miles away. But it was generally in the right direction and it got her to Interstate 35 south. He dropped her off, and she thanked him and went inside and ordered two eggs over easy with toast and sausage and a cup of coffee.

"Here you go, honey," said the matronly waitress, refilling Susan's coffee cup.

"Thanks," said Susan. Then she thought, *The last leg of my journey.*

* * *

The vehicle that finally gave her a ride that morning wasn't at all what she'd expected. After thirty minutes standing outside of the Cracker Barrel on the on-ramp south, Susan decided to use another tactic. She walked back to the restaurant's parking lot and stood close to a long, brown and tan RV. She'd been watching from the ramp for a while and had seen it exit from the southbound ramp. She figured the occupants would be done with breakfast soon and ready to roll.

Seven minutes later, a man and a woman walked out of the restaurant and toward the RV. They were retirement age, she thought, and overweight. The woman walked carefully, as if she might stumble and fall at any moment.

"Hi!" said Susan politely. "Are you by any chance heading south?" She aimed the question at the man, and complimented it with a worried expression.

Susan saw the woman hesitate, becoming visibly defensive, outside of her comfort zone.

She said, quickly, frantically, "I'm trying to get to Kansas City. My Mom was in an accident and she's in the hospital and I've got to get to her." Then she added, "My car broke down, so I've had to ask for rides. Some really nice people have been helping me."

"What happened with your Mom?" asked the woman, more compassionate, now.

"She was in a car accident," said Susan. "They took her to St. Luke's Hospital. They said she's hurt pretty badly."

The man looked at his wife. "We should help her," he said. "We're going that way." That Susan was young and attractive wasn't lost on him.

"Sorry to hear about your mom's accident," said the woman. "Yes, we'll take you. We're planning to be in Kansas City this afternoon, just after lunchtime. Our second son and his family live there."

"Oh, thank you so much," said Susan. "I'm so grateful. I didn't know what I was going to do. No one's stopped for me..."

"That's alright, dear. We'll get you there," said the man, unlocking and stepping up into the RV. He came back out with a step and set it down on the ground and helped his wife into the bus. Then he helped Susan up and pointed to a built-in couch. "That's probably the most comfortable spot to sit," he said. "My name is Eric Stratton, and this is my wife, Sophie. We're retired."

"I'm Susan," said the girl. "Susan Del Gato. Thank you again, so much. I'm frantic about my mother..."

Sophie said, "Poor dear. I can't imagine."

Eric closed the side door and slid behind the wheel of the RV. He started the engine and fiddled with the controls for a moment, then he looked back and said, "Hang on, Susan, this bus is moving."

* * *

The ride was fairly boring, passing farm towns with names like Bevington and Osceola and Decatur City before crossing into Missouri and breezing by Eagleville and Cameron and Kearney, until they finally reached the Missouri side of Kansas City. The trip took three hours, and the Stattons dropped Susan at the main entrance to St. Luke's Hospital. They offered her some money, which she refused, and asked if she wanted them to stay with her while she checked on her mom, which she also declined, but gracefully.

Susan turned and waived goodbye toward the RV, ducked into the hospital entrance, and followed the red stripe on the walls through a maze of corridors and to the Emergency Room, where she exited the building using the ER's oversized sliding glass doors. She walked four short blocks south to a coffee house named Kadin's Coffee. There, Susan ordered a latte and took it to an outside table for privacy.

Once situated, she took out her cell phone and dialed a number from memory.

"Hello?" asked a man's voice.

"I'm here, in K-town," Susan said. "No way to have tracked me here."

"Good," said the man.

"Is your guy here yet?"

"He'll be there tomorrow. He'll pick you up as planned."

"Good. It'll give me time to look around," she said.

* * *

Susan sat on the porch of the house across Metropolitan Avenue from the prison, and watched carefully. She had been sitting on the porch of the old, empty wooden home for about an hour, now. The afternoon sun cast shadows across the small space and made her nearly invisible when she was still.

The house looked like a mill-town house, built for workers in a neighborhood close to their employment. In this case, though, it was one of several houses along Metropolitan Avenue that faced the prison, seven hundred feet away, across a lush grassy open space.

She doubted that anyone from the prison could see her, if anyone was watching. The old structure rose up out of the prairie like a castle. It's solid stone walls extended forty feet up and forty feet underground.

This would be a formidable place to try an escape, thought Susan. But she wasn't there for an escape. This time, it would be something more dramatic.

* * *

At three-thirty on that cloudy afternoon, a gate opened on the east side of the compound and a small man walked out. He looked around, then back at the gate, as if waiting for permission or approval. The gate closed behind him indifferently.

The only vehicle nearby was a yellow cab parked thirty feet away from the gate in a marked parking area. The door to the cab was open and the engine was off, waiting patiently. The man walked over to the cab.

"Are you here for me?" he asked.

The cab driver, a large, rawboned man in his forties, looked up from his newspaper and asked, "Are you Diaz?"

"Yes, Eduardo Diaz," said the man.

"Then I'm here for you," the man said.

Diaz nodded and pulled the cab's back door open. He got into the seat, setting his brown grocery bag next to him. Then he quietly shut the door.

The cab started up and the man said, "Where to?"

"Where do most of the prisoners go when they're released?" asked Diaz.

"There's a restaurant in town, right next to a Traveller's motor court. That's a popular spot," said the man.

"OK, yes, let's go there," said Diaz.

* * *

Susan was certain that she was well off of anyone's radar, after her cross-country trip. No rental car, no trail, everything paid for with cash. Despite her quick lies and plentiful stories, she had actually started this journey in Chicago, three days ago, on April 17, 2005.

Eduardo Diaz was a Federal prisoner and had been held in Leavenworth for his part in an international drug smuggling operation between Mexico and the United States. When the FBI broke up the operation, Eduardo bargained with them for a reduced sentence in return for his testimony against his partners. In the end, he had spent just three years in prison.

His partners were not so lucky. The other leaders were incarcerated for between ten and twenty-five years for their part in the drug smuggling and distribution operation, and were being held in maximum security prisons in other states. Eduardo was quietly processed into Leavenworth and served his time with no fanfare.

Word came to Susan a month ago. "Eduardo Diaz is being released soon. We need you to take action against him for us."

"I can do that," she'd said. "You've called the right person."

When her mother died, Susan Del Gato had decided to become a killer. For years, her father had been an enforcer, a hit man for the Chicago mob, which also meant that he had quite a bit of free time to spend with his daughter. His wife had died of cancer, wasting away for two years before she eventually died, and the loss damaged every member of the Del Gato family, but none as badly as Susan. After her mother died, Susan was overwhelmed with the feeling that she had to pay someone back for it, to get even.

After that, Susan spent her time with her father, learning everything she could about his trade. She approached the profession as a business, studying and practicing. She would work out complex case studies with her father as her coach, and plan the tiniest details of each kill. He involved her in his "projects" and they spent hours together planning his kills.

Her father was an enthusiastic coach, teaching Susan and fueling her efforts with his own energy, energy that he had once hoped would go to help his son follow in his footsteps. But he'd had no son. And he doubted that he'd marry again.

Susan riled against the unfairness of her mother's death. Those who knew her said that she had a chip on her shoulder, something to prove. At first, they were wary of her.

But Susan's reputation grew over time with the help of her father's contacts. By the time he retired from the profession, due to his advancing age and failing eyesight, she was proficient enough to step in and take over the key role.

And now she'd been sent to deal with Eduardo Diaz.

* * *

"I'd like to go to the motor court, please," Susan said to the cab driver. "At Fourth and Poplar."

The Traveller's motel was one of the few located in the Town of Leavenworth, and it wasn't difficult for Susan to determine that room 11 housed her target.

To the desk clerk, she had said, "I'm supposed to meet Eduardo Diaz here."

The clerk looked on his computer screen as a matter of habit and said, "Sure. Do you want me to let him know you're here?"

"Thanks," said Susan. The desk clerk dialed two digits, a number which Susan memorized. Room 11.

There was no answer.

"No one's picking up," he said.

"OK, thanks," she said, "I'll come back later." Then, "I'll bet you're busy on visiting day."

"Oh, gosh, yes," said the young clerk. "Crazy busy."

* * *

In fact, Eduardo Diaz was at that moment across the street from the motel, eating a hamburger with onions and mushrooms heaped on top, and drinking a Coke. The restaurant, a local establishment named for a President, was moderately busy with dinner customers this afternoon.

The server came by to top off his Coke.

"Are you the prisoner they released today?" she asked, seemingly without any judgment for or against him. She was about fifty and overweight. Her fingers were stained yellow from nicotine.

"I am," said Eduardo Diaz. Then he added, "I've served my time."

"Oh, no doubt, honey. I've heard about what goes on in that prison. My nephew was a guard for a while." She shook her head. "Anything else for you?"

"No, I guess not," said Diaz. "Here, let me pay you." He reached into his pocket.

"You can pay at the counter," said the waitress, with a wave toward the cash register. Losing interest, she wandered away.

He finished up his meal, paid with cash, put a tip under his glass to hold it down and left the restaurant, walking back toward the motel.

As he crossed the street he felt a sudden chill in the air. Eduardo wasn't yet used to being a free man, and he found himself looking around to see who was watching him. There was no one in sight.

The room key stuck in his motel door and he had to jiggle the handle to room 11 to make it work. It finally opened and he stepped inside.

CHAPTER 7

The red-eye American Airlines flight from Washington to Logan International Airport took about an hour and a half, and shortly thereafter, Zeke had his rental car aimed at Cambridge. The radio in the Toyota was rocking Aerosmith's "Dream On" as he crossed the Charles River and pulled up in front of the hotel.

"Welcome to the Hotel Marlowe," the girl behind the front desk said as she looked up at Zeke. Then she smiled a big smile. "Do you have a reservation?"

"I do. It's for an early check-in," said Zeke, thinking, *It's the eyes again.* He gave her the details.

"Yes, sir. You'll be staying…three nights?" she asked.

"Possibly longer, but I'll let you know."

"Certainly." She smiled a confident smile and handed him the key.

The room was a corner suite on an upper floor with a view of the Charles River and downtown Boston. Two of its walls were composed of floor to ceiling windows. The decor was traditional, with heavy drapes and lushly upholstered furniture. A king-size bed occupied one section of the large room. Zeke set his suitcase on the bed and dialed a number on his smartphone.

"7423," said a voice on the other end of the line. She'd transposed the last two digits, as always.

"Hello, Tanya," Zeke said. It was a simple word code, using a name that started with the weekday name. Today was Thursday, and the code was enough to confirm his authorization to use this phone line. "I'm in Boston, safe and sound."

"Kimmy's on her way up to meet you. How was your flight?" she asked.

"Uneventful," said Zeke. "I'm staying in the Marlowe."

"Like Phillip Marlowe?" asked Sally in a hard-boiled 'Private Eye' voice.

"Exactly," laughed Zeke. "I see that I'm scheduled to meet with the Finance guy at Raleigh University this morning. What do we know about him?"

"Check your e-mail. I've sent you the details," Sally said. "But the short version is, Dr. Paul Richardson is the VP of Finance for Raleigh U. He's expecting you at ten thirty this morning."

"And I'm an auditor from the Department of Education, Cy Stiles' operation. I'll be interested in looking at the last two years' data on student loans for undergraduates."

"Right," said Sally. "You'll be 'auditing' about a thousand records of student loans. The college has 2,100 students, and two-thirds of them have student loans. When you factor in the number of students that are included in both years, overlapping, you end up at about a thousand files. We actually have copies of them here already and are combing through them as we speak."

"Got it," said Zeke.

"Do we have any leverage on this guy?" asked Zeke.

"Actually, I think we do. He appears to be cheating on his wife. That's from a quick look at his credit card statements, but it's pretty likely. Over the past two months he's booked a hotel room in Cambridge in the middle of a work week. Seven times."

"What hotel?" Zeke asked.

"The Pavilion Hotel, near the University."

"That's good info," said Zeke.

"Seems he goes in for expensive lunches, too," said Sally. "He likes a place called 'Tuscano,' which is Italian and pricey. It looks like he eats there just before he visits the hotel each time."

Zeke smiled. "I'll interview the Vice President and see what shakes out. You're setting up some other interviews while I'm here?"

"I am," said Sally. "So far we've arranged two more."

* * *

"I like Boston," said Kimmy. "As far as big cities go, it has a good feel to it."

At Clive's request, Kimmy had driven up earlier and met Zeke after he'd checked into the Marlowe Hotel.

She and Zeke were now walking down Chatham Street,

alongside Faneuil Hall, between Boston Harbor and the North End. They were on their way to the Boston Police Department's downtown offices on Sudbury Street, about a quarter mile away.

Zeke was quiet.

"It's got good energy, you know?" Kimmy continued. "For so many people living here."

Zeke nodded.

"It's not San Diego, but it has a good vibe," she continued. "So what's the 'Cambridge thing' that Clive was talking about?"

"Clive was contacted by the head of the U.S. Department of Education," said Zeke. "The Secretary asked for his help with some major Student Loan fraud. They got a whiff of it in Washington and they're afraid it'll become an issue before the next elections."

"You mean misappropriation of the loan proceeds?" she asked.

"Partly," said Zeke. "We're trying to get a sense of how deep it goes…and how long it's been going on. Clive got in touch with his contacts at Boston P.D. and they agreed to assist. It's a jurisdictional thing. They're convinced that there's a money scheme going on in Cambridge. In the schools, somehow," said Zeke.

"How many schools are there in Cambridge?" she asked.

"Fourteen colleges and universities, believe it or not. The highest concentration of higher education in the country," said Zeke.

They approached the brick building that housed the main offices of BPD and Zeke pulled the glass door open for Kimmy, then followed her inside.

At the front desk, Zeke asked the receptionist—a uniformed woman with a large Smith & Wesson on her hip—for directions to Deputy Chief O'Malley's office. She pointed at a bench, indicating that they should wait, called someone on a phone behind the counter and went back to work.

A few moments later, a burly young officer appeared and escorted Zeke and Kimmy to the Deputy Chief's offices with no fanfare, no conversation and little interest.

"Glad you came by," said Pat O'Malley, shaking Zeke's hand and nodding at Kimmy. O'Malley's name was displayed on a plaque on his crowded desk, facing the visitor's chairs.

"Clive said high level theft," Zeke said. "What can you tell us about that?"

"Yeah, the operation originated here, you know?" said O'Malley. "Our organized crime guys were looking into something else and sort of stumbled across it. We told the FBI, you know, it's a federal thing, stealing federally-insured money, federal loans, but they haven't taken any decisive action yet."

Zeke smiled. "Can you get at it from the other side?" he asked. "From the schools?"

"That's what we want to do. The FBI said that you'd be coming to help, that you're the man for the job."

"We've set up meetings with several schools, with their finance people. It seems like a good place to start."

"What's your cover?" asked O'Malley.

"Federal auditor," said Zeke. "From the Department of Education."

O'Malley nodded. "OK. Our OC guys said they think the

Boston Mob is in it up to their eyeballs. And I don't doubt it."

"We'll be careful," said Kimmy, sincerely.

O'Malley nodded. "Good. I appreciate you checking in. I'll be sure my friends at the Cambridge PD know about you. Let us know if you need any help."

* * *

"Good morning, Mr. Traynor," said the man. He was noticeably short and immaculately dressed in a navy blazer and gray dress slacks. His solid maroon tie contrasted nicely with the starched white shirt he wore, and his cufflinks and tie clip were a matching sterling silver pattern. He was evenly tanned.

"Hello, Dr. Richardson," said Zeke.

As they shook hands, Zeke noticed that the academic's hair had been recently cut, and that he smelled of bay rum.

Richardson ushered Zeke into his small, neat office and waved at a wingback chair. He sat opposite, across a low coffee table from Zeke.

"I took the liberty of having coffee prepared," said Richardson, and he smiled an unconvincing smile. "French press."

"Great, thanks," said Zeke, and waited.

"So… I understand you're here to audit our student loan records? Is something amiss?" asked Richardson.

"Not that we know of yet," said Zeke. "This is fairly routine, ordered by ADD Stiles."

"Yes, I heard that," said Richardson. Then, in a 'man-to-man' voice he said, "I'm sure there's more to it than that…"

Zeke looked at him and said nothing.

"Isn't there?" asked Richardson, suddenly less sure of himself.

Zeke paused several seconds before he said, "I wouldn't know about that."

"Oh, well yes, certainly. I understand," said Richardson in his 'official' Vice President's voice. "Well, ahh, where do we start, then?"

"Well, first I'll need to interview you, as the person responsible for Finance for the University," said Zeke. "I'm sure you understand. It's all routine." He opened a folder in his lap and looked at some papers. Then he paged through them as if he were looking for something.

"Oh. Well, I'm very busy today. I'm not sure I can spare the time," said Richardson.

"Actually, I could interview your boss, the Dean, if you think that would be better." Zeke looked up at him, a question on his face.

"Oh. Well, no, actually, it should be me, I suppose. Very well. But can we make it quick?"

Zeke ignored the question and said, "Is there a more comfortable space? Somewhere we can spread out, if we need to?"

"Yes," said Richardson, regaining his composure. The requested task was obviously within his comfort zone. "I'll ask someone to arrange that for us."

* * *

They had been talking for just over an hour, and Vice President Richardson was anxious. "Do we have much more to cover, Mr. Traynor?" he asked. "I have a lunch meeting."

"Just a little bit more," said Zeke. He smiled absently at the man.

"Well, all right," said Richardson, as if he were giving permission.

"Let's circle back," said Zeke, looking at the papers in front of him. "Tell me again the reason for the high default rate on student loans here at Raleigh."

"Well, I believe we've covered that…" Richardson started.

"Actually, no," interrupted Zeke. "I asked the question, but you skirted the issue and explained the loan application process to me, instead of answering the question."

"Well, I'm sure I don't know why we would have a high default rate. Are you certain that's accurate?"

"Yes. Does it have to do with the type of students you attract?" asked Zeke.

"What? No, I can't see how it could. We're a very diverse university, but we're also a boutique among the giants here in Cambridge."

"About two-thirds of your students carry student loan debt?" asked Zeke.

"Yes, that's right," said the Vice President.

"And Raleigh seems to have a higher than normal dropout rate," said Zeke, still referring to his notes.

"Not really. I mean, we have students who leave the school, but all institutions like ours do," said Richardson. He shot his cuffs nervously, first the left one, and then the right one.

"Are any efforts made to collect the debt? After a student defaults, I mean."

"No, that's the responsibility of the loan servicer. The University doesn't get involved in that part of it," he said.

"So you lose track of the money flow once a student's tuition is paid? And his room and board?" asked Zeke.

"We don't watch that part," said Richardson, touching his nose. He coughed into his hand.

"All right," said Zeke. "Can you get me these files to start with?" He handed Richardson a list of student names and social security numbers. "And I'll need a room to set up in. This is a sample audit. It won't take more than three days."

Richardson stood up awkwardly, and then walked to the door. "Come with me," he said.

They walked a short distance to a secretarial pool area, which held four desks, presently occupied by three people, each working on their computer.

Richardson walked to the furthest desk. A girl who looked like an undergraduate student looked up as he approached.

"Cheryl, I need you to pull these files for Mr. Traynor to review. He can use the faculty conference room if it's not booked."

"OK," she said and took the paper, apparently not impressed by Richardson's authoritative attitude.

"May I bother you for the Internet password?" asked Zeke.

Richardson said, "Oh, sure. Our network is named 'Netlink' and the password is 'RaleighU', with a capital R and a capital U."

"OK, thanks," said Zeke.

"I have a lunch meeting, and then an appointment off-site this afternoon," said Richardson. "I'll be back tomorrow."

Tuscano's and then the Pavilion Hotel, thought Zeke. *Wonder who the woman is.*

* * *

"He's going through the records, snooping," said Paul Richardson to the man. "He seems to know what he's looking for…"

They were standing on the sidewalk between two of Raleigh University's classroom buildings, the bright sun shaded by the tall maple trees. The man said, "He's an auditor. Of course he's snooping."

The man was tall and almost effeminate in his mannerisms. He wore his gray hair long, pulled back in a small ponytail at the base of his neck. He had a bulbous nose that dominated his face. His glasses had tortoise shell frames and his face was mottled. He wore a nondescript gray suit with bright yellow suspenders. His name was Jobare Worthington and he was the Dean of the Liberal Arts College at Raleigh University.

"I know, but he seems to be zeroing in on the student loan defaults. Almost like he knows something," said Richardson.

"I'll talk with my contacts," said Dr. Worthington. "There's a lot of money involved. They may want to do something about this. Politically, I mean."

"Like call off the audit?" asked Richardson, suddenly hopeful.

"Possibly," said Worthington. "They may think you've tipped our hand, though."

"What, me? No," he said.

"So how would he know where to look?" asked Worthington.

"I'm not sure. But I feel that he needs to be stopped."

"Will he find anything in the files he's auditing?" Worthington asked, snapping his suspenders in thought.

"Only trends, I think, if he's looking for them. It's been going on for years, though," said Richardson. "He's already talking about the loan default rates being higher than average, as well as the student dropout rates."

"Sounds like he's getting too close," said Worthington. "I'll mention that, also."

* * *

"I'm done," said Susan as she slid into the passenger seat of the black Cadillac and pulled the door shut behind her.

The driver, a tan man in his thirties, with the top three buttons of his white dress shirt unbuttoned, grunted and put the car in gear. He eased it away from the curb and headed south to the highway east. Then he shook his head and said, "Geez, I don't know how you stomach that stuff."

Susan changed the subject. "Did you drive up from Phoenix?"

"Yeah, pretty boring drive, Phoenix to Leavenworth."

"What's that, about twenty hours?" she asked.

"The longest twenty hours of my life," he said. "Deserts and mountains, and then the Great Plains."

"What's your name?" asked Susan.

"I'm Luis," said the man. He had black hair cut short and a subtle, indistinguishable accent with certain words.

"Well, thanks for coming, Luis. You're my escape route. Next stop, Dallas."

Luis nodded. "We'll be crossing into Missouri in a few minutes. Then Oklahoma and Texas. Should be about eight hours, and I'll drop you at the airport."

Susan nodded and said, "Thank you. I think I'll catch a quick nap." She turned her face toward the window and leaned into the soft leather seat.

"Where are you heading from there?" asked Luis.

"San Francisco," lied Susan.

Luis nodded to himself.

* * *

It's easy, she thought, *when they don't expect it.* She had spotted Eduardo Diaz returning to his room. She was sitting at a window table at the McDonald's restaurant next door to the motel and sipping her coffee, waiting for Diaz to return. He'd never seen her, didn't know her, so she felt almost invisible.

Susan recognized Diaz from his online mug shot and prison picture, a forty-eight-year-old man of slight stature, who walked back into the motor court and went directly to unit 11. Each room was separated by a carport on each side providing covered parking and privacy to every tenant. There were vehicles in six of the carports, and five other cars in the parking lot, but no one was in sight. The streetlights lit up the parking area.

Susan walked up the side street past the motel and then left the pavement to take a position behind the motel units. The area was dark and scrubby and uncleared, with trash and empty beer cans strewn about, and she was able to see into the units through the small bathroom windows. She looked into unit 11, but the bathroom light was off and the door was closed.

The traffic was light on the side street, Fourth Street. With no trouble Susan stepped through the open carport and knocked on the front door of unit 11. She heard muffled footsteps, and then through the door someone said, "Who's there?"

"Housekeeping," said Susan. "I have fresh towels." The door opened and Susan quickly walked in.

Diaz looked confused. "Yes?"

Susan had raised her right hand, which was holding a .22 pistol, and shot Eduardo Diaz in the face.

* * *

Traffic around the DFW airport was heavy when the Cadillac arrived, and Luis stayed in the "departures" line, slowly inching along. Finally, he pulled over to an open area at the curb and got out. Susan opened the door and stepped to the curb while Luis retrieved a carryon bag from the trunk, set it on the sidewalk and extended the handle with a click and a flourish.

The carryon bag contained old clothes and a small toilet kit procured from a thrift store, and Susan used it as a prop.

"Thanks for the ride," Susan said. She turned and walked across the sidewalk and into the airport lobby.

Once inside, Susan went to the ticket counter and bought a one-way ticket to Chicago. *Going home,* she thought.

It had been a quick trip, taking care of unfinished business for the Diaz boys. She'd settled the score with the snitch in North Utica. *He thought that witness protection would be enough, but he hadn't counted on running into me,* she thought. And then Eduardo Diaz. Now that their father was dead, Benito Diaz was solidly in charge. And she had a good relationship with Benito. He owed her, now.

* * *

"You did well, Susan," said Benito Diaz.

Susan Del Gato, sitting across from the older Diaz brother said, "Yes, thank you."

Diaz looked into her face for a moment. "Was there any trouble?" he asked.

"No," she said. "I was able to handle the Simpsons quickly and then make my way to Leavenworth. It took a few days, but it's done. And there's no trail."

"Did the Simpsons give you any trouble?" he asked.

"No. The wife actually invited me in, when I told her my car'd broken down up the street. It was a rural place, farms in between every house. Lots of corn," she remembered.

"And where is the weapon?"

"I used a kitchen knife. Left it there."

"Clean?" asked Diaz.

"Bleached it," she said.

"Good," he said. "The government was hiding him after he testified against us." 'Us' referred to the Diaz organization.

George Simpson, whose real name was Peter Vandum, had been a low level lieutenant in Diaz's El Paso operation, primarily involved in car theft and loansharking. When he was arrested, he rolled on the organization and identified several people at higher levels. FBI sting operations arrested four of these, and Peter Vandum's testimony had put them in jail. Then, the US Marshals had put Peter and his family in the WITSEC program, and moved him to North Utica, Illinois.

Their fatal mistake came when Peter's wife, Emily's sister, had been in an automobile accident. Emily had contacted her sister, Judy, in the hospital in Richmond to be sure she was alright, and then stayed in touch by phone for a week or so until her sister was discharged. Susan Del Gato, who had arranged Judy's automobile accident, had been watching closely and was able to track the origin of Emily's calls back to North Utica. After that, it was just a matter of time.

"We were fortunate."

"Yes, good," said Diaz. "Was there any trouble in Kansas?"

Susan had wondered about a contract to kill Benito Diaz's father, which seemed as though it could turn into an emotionally-charged event. But both Benito and Raul had assured her that it had to be done.

"No, no trouble in Kansas," she said. Then she added, "It was all over very quickly."

Benito Diaz nodded absently. "Good."

"Thank you for sending the exit vehicle," she said.

Diaz nodded. "We were glad to help."

Susan lit a cigarette and drew a deep breath. Diaz waited patiently.

She said, "You're in charge now."

"Yes. But in fact, I already was," he said. "The killing was retribution for the people he gave up when they caught him."

"I see," said Susan.

"They insisted the score be evened. But the results are the same," said Benito Diaz.

Susan nodded. "You know, I've been thinking," she said.

"Tell me."

"Well, we seem to work together well. Perhaps you can use my, uh, talent more often…"

"Perhaps so," said Diaz.

They were in Mexico, in one of Benito Diaz's homes located in the outskirts of Juarez. The afternoon was hot and humid and there was no protection from the sun. Inside, Susan sipped water and perspired as the air conditioning worked to keep up with the afternoon heat.

"There's something else, though," said Diaz.

"Yes?" she asked.

"I would like you to work with my young cousin, Luis. He's in the same line of work as you are. He gave you the ride to Dallas."

"I pretty much work alone," said Susan, gently resisting Diaz's plan. "I know I can trust myself," she continued.

"Yes," said Diaz. "I know. But I'd consider it a personal favor."

Susan thought for a moment. Then she shrugged and smiled. She let out a puff of smoke and said, "OK. For you, Benito."

* * *

"This view is breathtaking," said Tracy Johnson, standing at the large picture window in Zeke's rented guest house. "I mean, it's the sea, everywhere you look!"

"It is impressive. Even beautiful," Zeke said. He was looking across the room at Tracy as he said it.

She had dropped her carryon bag by the front door and practically ran across to the large window on the opposing wall. The sea was blue-gray in the bright sun. The afternoon breeze had churned up rolling waves that roiled the sea bottom and seemingly disappeared beneath the cottage.

"This alone makes it worth the trip," she said. "And the sky is so, well, so blue!"

"A crisp poleward sky," Zeke said, "in honor of your visit."

"Poleward?" she asked.

"Yes. The bright blue sky you see on a very clear day when you look north or south, toward the poles."

She knitted her brows.

"It has to do with the temperature of the light," he added.

"Oh," said Tracy. She looked at Zeke, then back out the window. "I tend to forget that you remember almost everything," she said, softly, shaking her head in mock dismay. "That eidetic memory..."

Tracy was wearing a short, sleeveless summer dress that fell to mid-thigh. It was simple and the color of white zinfandel, which matched her heels and her nails. Her long legs were bare.

"I'm off to Phoenix again, after this," said Zeke. "To meet with the ICE people."

Tracy nodded, her gaze still riveted on the sea.

"Would you care for a glass of merlot?" asked Zeke.

"Perfect," said Tracy, finally turning away from the window to look at him. Then he saw her look around the room.

"It's a pretty nice setup, pleasantly isolated," said Zeke. "The owners only visit on weekends, and they stay in the big house, next door."

"I could look at this all day," said Tracy, looking back at the ocean, still feeling its hypnotic pull.

Zeke walked to the small kitchen and took a new bottle of wine from the wine rack. He opened it on the small island and set out the bottle and two glasses. "We'll want it to breathe for a few minutes," he said, as he opened an app on his phone. Suddenly, Etta James' mellow voice was softly filling the room.

"What should we do while we're waiting?" asked Tracy, almost innocently.

"I have an idea," said Zeke.

"Does it involve me removing my clothing?" she asked. "Like the last time?"

"It could."

"I didn't bring much to wear," said Tracy, teasing now, glancing at her carryon bag.

"That's all right. I've seen you that way before," said Zeke, introspectively. "And I liked it."

"As did I," said Tracy.

They paused a moment.

"Are you sure you're ready for this?" she teased. "Do you remember what you're getting into?"

"Oh, I remember," he said. "I do remember."

CHAPTER 8

"I don't think you should stop," said Zeke. He was in his hotel room in Phoenix, talking with Clark Hall in D.C. on a secure phone line.

"Well, according to Agent Ramirez, we've put a big hurt on Diaz's pipeline. And on the MS-13 gang," he said.

"I'm sure they've both noticed ICE's presence," said Zeke, politely, "but we don't really know the full scope of their operations. It may be premature to say it was a 'big hurt'."

Clark Hall was silent.

"Ramirez and I talked about Diaz having an insider, perhaps in your organization," said Zeke. "Partly because there were no MS-13's at the first raid at the house in Phoenix. It was like they knew you were coming."

"That's why I wanted to talk with you," said Clark. "What do you know?"

"It's unusual that there were no MS-13's in that raid," Zeke repeated. "Who was watching the refugees?"

Clark didn't say anything for a minute, working things out

in his head. Zeke heard some papers rustle. Then Clark said, "We recovered some refugees, victims, but none of the gang members were in the house when we raided it."

"Right," said Zeke. "Remember what Ramirez said when we asked him about his course of action?"

"He didn't seem to have anywhere to go with it," said Clark Hall.

"He's still interviewing the Nevada brothel refugees, hopeful that they can turn a staff member and get a foothold," said Zeke.

Clark Hall nodded.

"And he said the Phoenix victims were all from the same extended family, never saw their captors and that they were pretty much a dead end."

Clark Hall thought for a minute. "You think Ramirez could be the leak?" he asked. "To Diaz's organization?"

"It's possible." Zeke listened, and let him process the connections.

After a moment, Clark Hall said, "Ramirez is a common denominator. He knew that you were coming to his offices. He was involved in identifying the property for the Phoenix drug raid that went bad, that cake thing."

Zeke nodded and said, "Yes."

"He's been somewhat resistant to accepting help or new ideas," Zeke added.

"The Nevada raid was solid, but it didn't take down any Mara's or any of Diaz's men," Clark added.

"That's right," said Zeke. "Diaz has suffered minimal loss.

It's almost nothing in the scheme of his businesses. Acceptable losses."

Clark said, "Meet me in Phoenix, as planned. I'll be there tomorrow. I need to chat with Ramirez, and I'd like you to be there."

"Sure," said Zeke. "I'm already here, so I'll wait for you to get here."

"Also, I think I want you to take a crack at interviewing some of the Mara's we arrested. The ones that took a shot at you and your partner."

* * *

Clark Hall looked formidable. He stood next to Agent Jorge Ramirez who was sitting at the conference table, and crowded close into his personal space. Ramirez was leaning away from his boss, not certain whether to get up and move or stay where he was seated.

He must be six and a half feet tall, thought Zeke. Probably played college basketball.

"I'm not pleased with this operation so far," said Hall. "You found no bad guys in the Phoenix raid. Is that right, Jorge?"

"Well, yes, but we saved seventeen people," Ramirez replied.

Clark Hall looked down at Ramirez. Then he sat down.

"Jorge, I've been hired to help with the human trafficking, particularly the Diaz situation here in Phoenix," Zeke said. "I think we need to take an aggressive approach and shut down his operation."

Clark Hall nodded, still looking at Ramirez.

"Help me out, Jorge," said Zeke. "There are just a lot of things going on that don't seem to add up."

Ramirez looked up at Zeke. "Like what?"

"Well, how did the bad guys know that I was coming to your DHS offices when they tried to kill me, for one," said Zeke.

"Yeah, I don't know," said Ramirez. "That was strange."

"And two," said Zeke, casually holding out two fingers, "why weren't there any bad guys at the Phoenix house raid?"

"What about that, Jorge?" asked Clark Hall.

Ramirez shook his head. He took a sip of coffee and set his cup on the table between himself and Clark Hall.

Here comes a lie, thought Zeke. He's blocking with the coffee cup.

Ramirez shifted slightly toward Clark Hall and said, "No, I don't know how that happened. It wasn't our guys, I'm sure."

"Also, Jorge," Zeke continued, "the earlier raid on the bakery was your responsibility, too, wasn't it?"

Ramirez looked at Zeke and then back at Clark Hall. "That was information we got from a CI," he said. "It was a while back."

"So far you've got no bad guys in three actions," said Zeke. "Except the four that tried to kill Kimmy and me in the parking lot. Is that right?" He let the words hang in the air as Clark Hall nodded his agreement.

"Exactly my question," said Clark Hall.

"I've been thinking about that," said Ramirez. "I agree, something is going on. It seems like somehow the traffickers know when we're coming. Or at least they know when to disappear."

"You think there's a leak in our organization?" asked Clark Hall.

"I don't know," said Jorge Ramirez, grudgingly. "There's a lot of money floating around. And Diaz's organization is pretty sophisticated. They could have bought someone, it's possible. Not me, but someone."

"How about the Nevada action?" asked Zeke.

"Yeah, we arrested the owners of the Ranch and some illegals. A few of the illegals were underaged," said Ramirez.

"But no MS-13 members," said Zeke.

"Well, no…"

"And no one from Diaz's organization," added Clark Hall.

Ramirez shook his head slowly. "No, that's right."

"So," Zeke said, "how can we improve on that record? Going forward, I mean."

Clark Hall was quiet. He looked at Ramirez.

Ramirez said, "Couple of things, right?"

Zeke nodded encouragingly.

"We can keep the number of people with access to the information smaller."

"I think we have to assume that Diaz has excellent intel," said Zeke. "Looking at his moves in this game, he's avoided losing people, and he contracted a hit on Kimmy and me almost before we arrived in Phoenix." He thought for a moment, and continued, "He's set up an alternative route for his human trafficking, direct to the warehouses in Nevada. He's either ahead of us, or reacting very quickly to everything ICE has done recently."

Ramirez nodded slowly. "OK, I'll work back through the agency personnel files and see what I can find…"

Clark Hall said, "No, I need you on the enforcement side of this, Jorge. I'm going to ask Zeke and his people at The Agency to do the personnel review. We may be too close to it."

"It's possible that there is no leak," said Ramirez, trying to regain control of the situation. "This could be a waste of time."

Clark Hall looked at him. "What are we doing on the enforcement side, Jorge?"

"Well, honestly, we're still finishing up the paperwork and interviews from the raid at the Ranch," said Jorge, suddenly sullen. "We only have so many people to work with."

"Right," said Clark Hall. "And what's the next action?"

"We're hopeful that some of the staff at the Ranch will give us a lead. We've been interrogating them in our Vegas sub-office. We'll flip them and try to work up the food chain…"

"Anything from the refugees you found in the Phoenix house raid?" asked Zeke.

"No, they don't know anything. Their kidnappers wore bandanas and hats, so there's no ID. Most of the time they were locked up in one of the bedrooms. About the only thing we determined is that some of their captors had tattoos on their necks and arms. And possibly on their faces."

"Are we deporting the refugees?" asked Clark Hall.

"We have the paperwork in place for it, but we're detaining them here until we're satisfied that they're all innocents," said

Ramirez. "But it looks like they are. They all vouch for each other, you know family and extended family, all on the same route. And none of them had tattoos."

Clark Hall exhaled. "What's next, then?" he asked, looking at Ramirez.

"Well, we'll finish up with the people from the Phoenix raid and ship them back to where they came from. I doubt they'll share any information." Said Ramirez.

"Sure," said Zeke. "They're scared of La Mara, and they're scared of you, of ICE."

Ramirez looked at Zeke, slightly annoyed, but he didn't say anything.

"Let's focus on the attempt on Zeke's life for a minute," said Clark Hall. "Where are we on that?"

"We have the four survivors in custody," said Ramirez. "No one's talking. They're definitely MS-13, too. One of them needed stitches to reattach his nose." He looked at Zeke.

"Can we make them cooperate?" asked Hall.

"No, not at all," said Ramirez. "They're stonewalling us. They know what the gang will do to them if they talk. And to their families."

"Course of action?" asked Clark Hall.

"We're turning them over to the State Police, and with the FBI's help they'll be prosecuted for attempted murder and a number of other things," said Ramirez.

Clark Hall nodded slowly.

Zeke said, "Where did you get the information that prompted the first raid, the Phoenix house raid?"

Ramirez said, "It was an anonymous tip."

"You said that you'd been surveilling them for a while," said Zeke.

"We had," said Ramirez. "We were tipped off by someone who saw odd activity and shady characters around the house and called it in. The cops sent it over to us, thinking 'human trafficking'."

"Do you have a transcript of the original call? The call to the police?" asked Zeke.

Ramirez looked in his file. "I can get that," he said.

"I'd suggest that we go back to the beginning and take another look. There seem to be some things we're missing," said Zeke.

Clark Hall nodded.

"Let's focus our efforts on the human trafficking, Jorge. We need to find their points of entry and close them down. I want that to be the first priority until it's been resolved. Agreed?"

Jorge Ramirez nodded. "We'll need more resources…" started Jorge.

"Done. Set this up as a task force aimed at the human traffickers, and I'll transfer some resources in to help. Temporary, of course, but we need to shut this down," Clark Hall repeated.

* * *

"What would you like?" the bartender asked.

"Hmm. Give me a Tequila Sunrise," said the man. "That's the 'Arizona' drink, right?"

The bartender, who looked like a college student, nodded slightly to herself, and stepped down the bar to prepare the drink.

Zeke Traynor was sitting at the bar in a restaurant in Tempe, sipping a Sleeping Dog ale and lunching on shawarma.

The man turned to Zeke. "Is that any good?" he asked.

Zeke nodded as he chewed. He was partially watching the room through the large mirror behind the bar, although at this time of day the restaurant wasn't very busy. He swallowed.

"Yes, actually, it's very good," he said.

The man pulled himself up on the barstool and waited until the bartender returned with his drink.

"Tab?" she asked.

He nodded and she stepped down the bar to the register.

"You live around here?" he asked Zeke, after he'd taken a sip of the drink.

Zeke looked at him. "No." he shook his head and smiled politely. He took another bite of the sandwich and chewed slowly.

"I thought you might be a graduate student," the man said, apparently to no one in particular. "Or a professor." He was looking straight ahead at the mirror.

Zeke shook his head and swallowed again. "Here on business," he said.

The man nodded. He was a slight man, wearing a plaid, short-sleeved shirt and black-rimmed glasses. Zeke judged him to be in his thirties. The skin on his face and arms was tanned. He said, "What do you do?"

"I'm a consultant," said Zeke, absently, and he sipped his ale again.

"I'm a software programmer. My name is Jerry. Jerry Sebastian," said Luis Cruz.

"Zeke. Nice to meet you."

"Where are you from?" asked Jerry.

"I live on Cape Cod."

"Wow, nice," said Jerry. "You're a long way from home."

"We have a government contract in Phoenix," said Zeke. "I'm in town for a couple of days."

Jerry nodded. "I interviewed with RMT Systems this morning."

Zeke said nothing.

"I think they're going to offer me a job here," he continued.

"Congratulations," said Zeke. "This seems like a nice place."

"Better than my last assignment," said Jerry.

"Where was that?"

"Detroit," he said simply. "Nuff said."

Zeke nodded. "Where'd you go to school?" he asked casually.

"Carnegie Mellon," said Jerry, warming up to the conversation.

"Oh, Pittsburgh," said Zeke. "I've spent a lot of time in Pittsburgh."

Jerry was quiet for a moment.

Zeke half turned toward the man. "So you studied in the Software Engineering Institute there, I suppose. Downtown on Bayard Street?"

"Yes," said Jerry. "On Fifth Avenue, actually. I should know, I was there for five years." He rolled his eyes.

"Oh, right," said Zeke. "Baynard is one street over."

"What kind of consulting do you do?"

"Well, we do a type of Organizational Behavior work. And we help with communications, sometimes," said Zeke.

Jerry nodded.

"Kind of specialized," Zeke continued.

"Sounds like it. Have you been doing it for long?"

"Maybe five years," said Zeke. "Not too long."

* * *

"I'm on their radar," said Zeke into his secure smartphone. "I was approached by a man who said he was a software engineer."

"Do you think he's a killer?" asked Clive.

"Definitely," said Zeke. "I could tell from a number of things. One was his eyes. They were dead, just empty, flat reflections. And when he smiled, it stopped way short of those eyes."

"You know the type then," said Clive.

"Uh-huh," said Zeke. "Also, his body made it pretty clear that he was lying."

"How so?" asked Clive.

"His blink rate changed when I asked him details about his work history. And he lowered his vocal tone when he was delivering some of the lies," said Zeke.

Clive nodded.

"Plus, he claimed that he's from Detroit, but his tan says something different."

"Is he a better killer than the Mara's were?" asked Clive.

"I'm sure he is," said Zeke. "He looks like an accountant or a...well, a software engineer. But he doesn't wear the disguise well. It's like it's too small for him. His confidence and self-assurance show through. And they seem formidable."

"I see. Next step?" asked Clive.

"Well, I doubt they're planning another attempt like the one in the parking lot. Most likely, this will be a more methodical approach. A planned assassination."

"Yes," said Clive.

"I'll interview the Mara's here. Then I think I'll disappear for a few days, head back east. Then come back here," said Zeke. "There's a lot to do in Cambridge, and if I imply that the project here is over and I'll be leaving soon, it may push him to action."

"What name is he using?" asked Clive.

"Jerry Sebastian," said Zeke.

"OK. Well, keep me informed," said Clive. "And be careful." Then, changing the subject, "How about Ramirez?"

"Met with him this morning," said Zeke.

"And?"

"His boss, Clark Hall sat in on the meeting," said Zeke. "We actually accomplished a lot, toward bringing focus on the human trafficking issue."

"Yes, Clark told me he'd be there," said Clive. "He's a no nonsense guy."

"You spoke with Clark Hall before the meeting then?" asked Zeke.

"I did," said Clive. "He seems a lot more cooperative than Agent Ramirez. Anxious for our help with this."

"It's a matter of tying the victims to Diaz, primarily."

"Right. But since the failed raid, Diaz isn't coming close to the victims."

"Yes, he's distanced himself from everything that might implicate him," Zeke confirmed. "We'll have to try something else."

* * *

"I really didn't know who else to call," said Jerry Sebastian. "And you gave me your number. I'm sorry if this is an imposition."

"No, it won't be a problem," said Zeke. "I'm glad to help."

Jerry was sitting in his car, which was parked in the parking lot of a Walmart, a long block off of South Mill Avenue in Tempe, with the window down when Zeke approached. Jerry'd thanked Zeke profusely.

"It just won't start," Jerry continued. "I thought it might be flooded, but that's not it. The engine won't turn over. It doesn't even try." *But it'd probably do better with the battery wires attached,* he thought to himself.

"I'm not very mechanical, but I'll give you a lift," said Zeke. "Glad to help."

Jerry rolled the window up, opened the driver's side door and exited the car. He turned back and locked it, and then, with a smile toward Zeke, he walked over and said, "Yeah, thanks again."

"Sure. Where you headed?" asked Zeke.

"If you can get me back to my apartment, I can take it from there," he said.

"OK, where are we going?" asked Zeke.

* * *

It turned out that his apartment was in a neat, brown two-story building in a small, respectable neighborhood. The homes in the immediate area were well maintained and the yards cared for. The cars parked in the driveways indicated middle class incomes, but the vehicles were clean and appeared to be functional. The neighborhood was east of downtown and a couple of miles north of Tempe, in Phoenix proper.

"Man, thanks so much for this," said Jerry again. "I'll get this sorted out. I'll call a wrecker and have them take it to the repair shop," he said, jumping out of the car.

"No worries," said Zeke. "You'll be OK from here?"

"I will," said Jerry. His lips smiled, but not his eyes.

"OK, well let me know if you need any more help."

Jerry said, "OK. Well, thanks for the ride."

Jerry turned away and took a step. Then he turned back to the car and said through the open passenger side window, "Let me take you to dinner tonight to pay you back."

"Not necessary, really," said Zeke.

"Well, how about I buy you a beer, then? And we can split dinner. Gotta eat, right?"

* * *

They met at a Mexican restaurant in Tempe, Zeke arriving first and grabbing a table. It was early, and the place was just gearing up for the dinner rush.

"May I order a Dos Equis and some salsa and chips?" Zeke asked. He was sitting in a chair where he could watch the front door of the place.

"I'll get that for you, sir," said the server, a blonde, blue-eyed college co-ed.

"Thanks," said Zeke. When she returned, he asked, "Do you speak Spanish?"

The girl looked at him and cocked her head. Then she said, "Nooo...."

Zeke smiled at her and sipped the beer. "Just curious," he said.

About three minutes later, Jerry Sebastian stepped into the dark room and waited for his eyes to adjust. Then he spotted Zeke and walked directly to the table, followed by their co-ed server.

"Hola," Jerry said in a fake Spanish accent and stuck out his hand.

Zeke stood and shook it.

He sat and the server took his order for a draft beer.

"Did you get it taken care of?" asked Zeke about the car.

"Yeah, it's in the shop now," said Jerry. "Overnight."

"How'd you get here?" asked Zeke.

"Uber. I should have thought of that earlier," he continued, "instead of bothering you."

Zeke sipped his drink.

"So you said you're a consultant? You're in town on a job?" asked Jerry.

"Yes," said Zeke.

"How's that going?"

"Actually, not well. I'll probably be out of here in a day or two. Sort of wrapping things up now," Zeke lied with a credible smile. "Then it'll be a couple short trips back to finish it all up, and I'm outta here."

"Sorry to hear that," said Jerry. "I don't know many people in Phoenix."

"Did you get the job with RMT Systems?"

"Yep, just pending a background check," said Jerry.

"Congratulations," said Zeke. "Sounded like the work was right up your alley."

"It's what I do," agreed Jerry. He thought a moment. "Hey, we should get together before you go. Climb Camelback Mountain or something."

"Sure," said Zeke, acting distracted.

"We could start early and avoid the afternoon heat…"

Zeke nodded slowly and said, "That might be fun."

* * *

"You dined with the killer?" asked Clive when Zeke reached him on the secure line.

"I did. Mexican food," said Zeke.

"Anything new?"

Zeke thought for a moment. "He's building rapport, trust and, maybe some sort of bond. He wants us to climb Camelback Mountain together one day this week."

"He goes slowly, doesn't he," said Clive.

"So far," said Zeke, thinking about Jerry Sebastian. "What do we know about him?"

"Sally's been busy with her research," Clive said. "We think he's responsible for a half dozen, maybe eight other killings. All around the country. She said his real name is Luis Cruz."

"I'll be careful," said Zeke.

"Good. He's rather crafty, and as best we can tell he works for several clients. Moves around quite a bit. We don't know where his home base might be," said Clive, clearly reading the file as he spoke.

"Do we know who his clients are?"

"Some," said Clive. "He's supposedly responsible for several deaths of people who crossed the Sinaloa Cartel, and for some who testified against Benito Diaz's organization. He's also responsible, we're pretty sure, for the death of two people who were in the Federal witness protection program. WITSEC."

Zeke thought for a moment. "Can we follow up with the witness protection people and see if they've lost any more of their charges recently? Say within the past three or four years, and nationally?"

"Yes, certainly," said Clive. "I'll ask Sally to initiate that."

"Good. He may have been busier than we know," said Zeke.

"Yes," said Clive. "Are you heading back, now?"

"I am," said Zeke. "Direct to Cambridge this time."

CHAPTER 9

"Man, where did you get this dope car?" asked the taller boy, Eddie George.

"You like it? It's brand new, man," said Peter Vartis. He had pulled the red Porsche 911 to the curb in front of Eddie's apartment near the Raleigh University campus and it was immediately surrounded by curious boys.

"Like it? I love it, man! How fast does it go?"

"The speedometer maxes out at 350 kilometers per hour," Peter bragged.

"What's that, 220 mph?" asked someone, probably an engineering student.

"About that," said Peter. "But the guy at the dealership said it'll go faster than that."

"Wow," said a couple people in unison.

"This had to set you back a bunch," said Eddie.

"Yeah, almost a hundred grand," Peter said under his breath. He liked the attention.

* * *

"Man, do you think it was smart to buy that car?" Eddie asked Peter once they were in Eddie's apartment. "I mean, we're supposed to be inconspicuous, you know."

"I know, man, but it's a sweet ride. And I got that money, so…I had to have it."

"I know, I've got mine, too," he said. "Can't really put it in the bank, so I've got it stashed in my apartment." Eddie thought for a minute. "I guess I'll rent a safe deposit box and keep it there."

They were referring to the money they'd received for helping to arrange the student loan scam during the past few semesters. Working with some of the university staff, Peter and Eddie routinely identified students who might be more interested in making an easy buck than completing four years of an Ivy League college. It was the grass roots foundation of the scam.

"No one's going to notice," said Peter. "Look around. This town is full of rich kids who get new cars from their parents all the time."

"How did you pay for it at the dealership?" Eddie was curious now.

"I wrote them a check," said Peter. "I deposited the money the last couple weeks, nine thousand dollars a day, like they told us, and today, I wrote a check for the car."

Eddie nodded. "OK, man, that's cool." Then, changing the subject, he asked, "Who do we have lined up for the fall semester?"

Peter said, "Right now we've got the English guy, and the two brothers from Indonesia. We could use two more."

Eddie said, "I've been talking with a girl who may be interested. Lindsay Sommerset. Sounds like she's here because her Dad wants her to be, but she's not really into it. I think she'd rather have some cash."

"We'd better wrap that up quickly," said Peter. "School starts pretty soon, and she'll need to get her loan application in."

* * *

The young secretary at the front desk of Huntington College smiled a warm smile when Zeke walked through the entry door.

Zeke smiled back at her and said, "I'm here to see Dr. Adams about the audit. Zeke Traynor."

"Oh, sure," she said. From across the desk, she smelled as though she'd been dipped in Tea Tree Oil. "Just a moment."

She picked up a handset, checked a list of names and dialed a three-digit number.

823, Zeke noticed.

"Dr. Adams? Hi, this is Cynthia at the reception desk." Her voice rose toward the end of the sentence, as if she were asking, not informing.

"There's a Zeke Traynor here to see you about an audit." She winked at Zeke.

She paused. "Yes, sir, I'll show him to the conference room."

She hung up the phone, stood up and half-walked, half-bounced down a narrow hallway, apparently confident that Zeke was following her. When they got to the right room, Cynthia said, "Go ahead and grab a seat. Dr. Adams will be here in a minute." She turned to leave but remembered something and turned back and said, "Can I get you anything?"

"Water?" asked Zeke.

She smiled an 'I can do that' smile, nodded and walked away.

The water and the doctor arrived at about the same time.

"I'm Dr. Adams," said the plump man. Zeke noticed the added emphasis on the "Doctor." He was about five and a half feet tall and wore a silver suit and a blue pinpoint oxford button down shirt. His gray moustache and eyebrows were untamed, but all other visible hair was trimmed and neat.

Trying to differentiate himself, thought Zeke. *He might have an issue with his height.*

"Hello, Doctor," Zeke said warmly, as if there were no problems in the world. "I'm here for the routine audit and interview. They said they called you about it?"

"Yes, I was contacted," said Adams. "You know, we're audited frequently. In fact, I believe we just completed a student loan audit about four months ago."

"Yes, you did," said Zeke, looking in his folder. "This one is different, though."

"How so?" asked Adams.

"We're looking at trends. Huntington is one of several colleges on our radar that have both a high loan default rate, and a higher than average student dropout rate. We're auditing the school policy and procedures, as well as the money."

"Oh," he said. "Well, we have so many students here, it's hard to keep track of all that."

"Yes, I know. That's why I'm here," said Zeke.

"Well, what would you like to know?" asked Adams.

* * *

"Mr. Traynor, are we almost done here? I'm very busy, you know," said Dr. Adams.

"Well, we can take a break, and get back together for the interview after I've done some preliminary research," said Zeke. "I may have more questions at that point."

"Well, good, because I'm late for an important meeting," said Adams, looking at his watch. He stood.

They had covered the criteria for loan application, the process to provide students the loan information, the steps in the application process, the transfer of funding, and the eventual hand-off to the third party loan servicer.

"I'll work through my audit process and get back with you in a few days," said Zeke.

"Sure, yes, that's fine," said Adams, obviously thinking about something else.

"I have a list of the files we'd like to review..." said Zeke.

"Oh, well, yes, Cynthia can get those for you. And you can use this conference room."

"Thank you, doctor," said Zeke.

"I'm sorry, I need to leave now," said Dr. Adams as he rose abruptly, opened the door and walked through it.

* * *

Zeke found Cynthia at the reception desk and gave her the list. Apparently, Dr. Adams had given her approval to help Zeke, or else she wasn't hung up on authorizations, because ten minutes later she showed up in the conference room with a stack of file folders marked "Huntington College."

She plopped them down on the table, gently pushed them over toward Zeke, and said, "What else do you need?"

"Nothing," he replied.

She looked at him with a long glance, almost staring at him, and then she said, "OK, well, let me know if I can do anything else for you."

For the next two hours, Zeke reviewed the file folders and compared them with the data that The Agency had assembled. With few exceptions, they were identical. Then he stood and packed his notes in his small backpack. On the way out, he found Cynthia in the break room and said, "I'll be back tomorrow morning. OK to leave the folders on the conference table?"

"Sure. I don't think it's booked tomorrow," she said. "How long will you be auditing here?"

"Oh, a few days," said Zeke. "Probably most of this week."

"Well, maybe we can get coffee or something," she said.

* * *

"Hey, Mr. Traynor, good morning," said the pleasant female voice. "Hi. Do you want some coffee or anything?"

Zeke looked up at the source of the question and saw that Cynthia had arrived in the school offices.

"Coffee would be great," Zeke admitted. "Thanks."

Cynthia, standing in the conference room doorway, hesitated. "I don't come in until ten, most mornings," she said. "But I thought you might want some help." Then she walked toward the break area. She returned with a ceramic cup of steaming coffee.

"You take cream, right?" she said.

"Sometimes."

"Do you need anything else?" she asked.

"No, this is good," said Zeke with an easy smile. Cynthia stared at his blue eyes a moment longer and then turned and walked to her desk, across the open office area. She sat and looked at Zeke again, and smiled a wide smile.

She's confident, he thought.

Zeke returned to reading the file on the table in front of him. He was reading about a student named Judith Henderson who had applied as an undergraduate at Huntington the previous autumn. She'd been accepted in the school of arts and had signed up for a full course load. She'd attended classes for three weeks and then dropped all but one class.

Simultaneous with her acceptance at Huntington College, Judith had applied for the maximum amount in student loans through FAFSA, the Federal Student Aid application process. Through that process, Zeke read, she had been offered student loans in the amount of $45,000, which were intended to cover her tuition, room and board. She'd accepted the entire amount and it had been wired to the college's bank.

The timing of her withdrawal from the college was suspicious, occurring in the narrow time frame where her "add/drop" timing intersected with the loan funding. Once she'd dropped the classes—her entire schedule save one class—she moved out of the dormitory and apparently disappeared from the school grounds.

In the meantime, Zeke read, the Student Aid money was credited back to her account by the school and was to be returned to the loan originator by the loan servicer. But this is where the system broke down. The money had sat in a refund account with several million other dollars for several months, and then it had disappeared, never making it back to the originator. The loan was an FISL, a Federal Insured Student Loan, and so the loan originator took no risk in making the loan. If it wasn't paid back, the Federal Government would make good on the obligation.

There's the pattern, thought Zeke. *I need to talk with Judith Henderson.* He read on.

Apparently, according to the documentation and the bank statements Zeke had reviewed, the Feds had sent several requests to the loan servicer, with copies to the school and to Judith Henderson, for the return of the monies. Technically, since Judith was still enrolled in one class at the college, her loan had been marked as a 'low risk,' and the collection efforts were deferred.

* * *

"Goodbye, Benito. Thanks," said Freddy Hanson, and he hung up the phone.

"How did you get involved with the Diaz brothers, boss?" Roy Calhoun asked Hanson. Roy was sitting on a folding chair in Freddy's office, chewing on a toothpick. Hanson was sitting at his desk.

"My dad used to have business with them in Vegas," said Hanson. "With Diaz's old man. That's why we buy prostitutes from them. They bring them in from other countries and ship them to us. I think he sells all over the northeast."

"And since you run the rackets in Boston…" started Roy.

"And surrounding area," smiled Hanson.

"… you kept the connection. After your dad stepped down, I mean."

"Sure. We're diversified, you know?" said Hanson.

"Yeah," said Roy. "Sports betting, money lending, prostitution, muscle for hire…"

"Just about whatever you need," said Hanson.

The office was actually a small, shabby back room with brick walls in a building that housed a bar. The desk was metal and there was a filing cabinet next to it and a couple more chairs along the walls. There was a low upholstered loveseat facing the front of the desk along the wall near the door.

"So I have two jobs for you. I need you to be the muscle for hire," Hanson continued. "You and Louie. And I need you to take care of a problem with a student."

"Sure, boss, what's the assignment?" Roy knew that Freddy Hanson would pay him well for the job. And, as 'extra money' is an obvious oxymoron, he could use the additional pay. *Sort of like overtime,* he thought.

"It's from Worthington, the queer guy at Raleigh University," said Hanson.

"Yeah, what's he want?" asked Roy, slightly bothered by the source of the request.

Hanson said, "There's an auditor up from D.C. who's looking into the student loan defaults at Raleigh. Worthington's nervous, thinks the guy may be finding something…We need to scare him off."

"We're involved with that stuff? Student loans?" asked Roy Calhoun.

"No, only as local muscle. They've got me on retainer in case they need help keeping people in line. Or with something…like this," said Hanson.

"Gotcha, boss," said Roy. He looked across the room at Louie Brennan who was sitting on the small loveseat. The man was a giant, at least six feet five inches tall and over 250 pounds. Roy Calhoun had worked with Louie for several years. Louie Brennan didn't say much, but his presence was a huge factor when intimidation was required.

"And there's another problem. One of the students in the student loan thing is showing off, bought a new car and is bragging about the money he's been making. Bad timing."

"Uh-oh," said Roy.

"Yeah," said Hanson. "This isn't the first time, either. They need him out of the picture before he gives it all away."

Roy looked back at Hanson and said, "So, what do you want us to do, boss?"

* * *

"So I've got my guys on it," Freddy Hanson said to Jobare Worthington. "They should have this situation cleaned up this week."

"Well, OK, but I'm telling you, they're snooping around. They're scaring everyone, and everyone's nervous. I'm afraid they'll upset the proverbial apple cart…"

Apple cart? thought Hanson, and he shook his head. He said, "Just hang on. We'll handle it."

* * *

"As I told the young lady who called to set up the appointment," said Dr. Harrow, "I don't know how I can help you."

Dr. Henry Harrow was a large man. He stood over six feet tall and his girth was impressive. Dressed in a blue blazer with an Exeter University patch over the breast pocket, a dress shirt and tie, he resembled a schoolboy in uniform. Only much, much bigger.

"Yes, sir," said Zeke, easily. "We're looking at some disturbing trends we've found in last year's student loan applications. The ADD of the Department of Education, Cy Stiles, has asked for our help with this. We're auditors."

"I see," said Dr. Harrow, but clearly he didn't.

Dr. Harrow was the Director of Finance at Exeter University, the third of the Cambridge-located Universities in which Sally had arranged an appointment for Zeke. His school also had an unusually high delinquency rate on their student loans, as well as an above average dropout rate.

"What firm are you with?" asked Dr. Harrow.

"It's a D.C. audit firm, very specialized," said Zeke. "I'm sure you haven't heard of us. Greene and Company." Then he added, "Do you have any opinions about these trends, Doctor?"

"Um, well, actually, no."

"Let's start with the files on these students," said Zeke. He handed Dr. Harrow a list of student's names and social security numbers.

"Wait here. I need to make a phone call to verify this," said Dr. Harrow.

"Certainly," said Zeke. Then he pulled out a business card. "Here's ADD Cy Stiles' direct line in Washington. He's expecting your call."

* * *

"Jobare, you've got to do something," said Dr. Henry Harrow into his phone. "It feels as if they're closing in on us. Getting too close, anyway."

"Relax, Henry. It's being taken care of," said Jobare Worthington in his high pitched voice. "The people who need to know about this already do."

"You weren't in the interview with the auditor. The questions were, well, telling. They know something…"

"I believe it's under control," said Jobare.

"Is this legitimate? Does it actually come from the ED?"

"From what we understand, there is some discussion at that level. But our contacts assure me that it's under control," Jobare repeated.

"Under control?"

"Yes, appropriate, uh, actions are being put in place," said Jobare, aware that they were talking on an unsecured phone line. "I've talked with our local muscle."

"What do you recommend, then?" asked Dr. Harrow.

"Make yourself scarce," said Jobare Worthington. "Take a couple of sick days."

Dr. Harrow was silent, uncertain.

Jobare could feel the tension over the phone. "It will all work out, Henry. We've talked with our, eh, resources. They view this as a simple annoyance, you can be sure. Steps are being taken."

Dr. Harrow said, "Alright, then, Jobare. I'll leave it to you."

* * *

It was an unseasonably brisk day; the wind was gusting off the Charles River and across the open campus in front of Dover University's School of Engineering building. Zeke walked across the lawn and toward the domed building, zipping his jacket against the chilly breeze coming off the River. Kimmy walked with him.

"Thanks for coming to Cambridge," Zeke said. "I think I'm pushing the right buttons, and it's only a matter of time before we get a reaction."

Kimmy nodded. "I'll just hang around for a while and watch your back."

Zeke held the heavy glass door open and Kimmy preceded him into the stately building.

"I'll wait outside in the lobby area," she said.

"OK, good," said Zeke. "This shouldn't take very long. Just a preliminary contact."

They walked into the building and Kimmy turned and found a comfortable chair in an open sitting area. She took out her phone and started swiping.

Zeke stepped up to the information desk. "I'm here to see Dr. Halpern," he said. "She's expecting me."

The girl at the information desk was a student, and Zeke waited as she looked up from her textbook, obviously bored. But then her glance settled on Zeke and she looked confused.

Zeke smiled at her and said, "Is Dr. Halpern in?"

The girl, brown haired, brown eyed and thin, looking like a young grade-school teacher, said, "Oh, sure. Sorry. First right down there." She pointed down a hall. "Second door on the left."

"Thanks," said Zeke. He took a couple steps, then turned back. The girl was reading again. He turned and shook his head and continued to Dr. Halpern's office.

At the door, Zeke knocked lightly.

"Yes?" said a rich, throaty female voice.

"Dr. Halpern, hello," said Zeke as he opened the door. "I'm Zeke Traynor."

"Yes, come in," she said.

Zeke did, and walked into an academic's office like many others, with a wooden desk, chair and cabinets against one wall, below the windows. The space was sparse and every conceivable surface was covered with stacks of paper or books or notebooks.

He paused and closed the door quietly. "You're Dr. Halpern?" Zeke asked, extending his hand across the desk.

"Please, call me Katherine, Mr. Traynor," she said. "Good to meet you."

"I'm Zeke, then," he said.

"I must say, you're younger than I expected, Zeke," said Katherine Halpern. "Mostly, our government auditors look like retired people."

Zeke smiled. "I'm here to look over some of the student records."

"I see," said Dr. Halpern. "You're here from the Department in Washington? ADD Styles' office?"

"I am," said Zeke with a smile. "I'm actually reviewing some anomalies with the Federal Student Loan program."

"Yes, well, this is an expensive institution, one of the highest tuitions in the country," she said. "As a result, most of our students have student loans. It can be a confusing process, but most government programs morph in that direction. Confusing. Think 'Health Care Marketplace...'"

Zeke smiled. "That's why I'm here. Can I ask you a few questions?"

"Sure, let's see if we can help."

* * *

"There are two of them, at our seven o'clock," Zeke said to Kimmy as they walked down Vassar Street, from the Dover University building back toward the parking garage that housed their rental car. The street was fairly deserted in the late afternoon, with just a random student or two walking along while reading their smart phones.

"I've got them," said Kimmy without looking. "Big guy and a little guy. Thin-little, I mean."

"They followed us from the Dover University meeting," said Zeke. "Too old to be students and probably too rough looking to be teachers."

"Let's find out what this is about," said Kimmy.

"You ex-Mossad agents are always spoiling for a fight," said Zeke with a grin.

Kimmy loosened her jacket for better access to her weapon, a Jerico 941. The semi-compact model she carried in her belt weighted about two pounds fully loaded. She was able to check it through on the flight from D.C., not a small task given the current state of TSA. But Clive's FBI and TSA connections worked like magic.

Zeke nodded and pointed to something in the distance. Kimmy nodded, too, then gestured and said something innocuous. She took his arm in hers.

"No time like right now," said Zeke, under his breath. "I've got Mr. Big," he said.

They turned suddenly, as if they'd forgotten something. Chatting to each other, they walked briskly back the way they'd come, along Vassar Street. The men stopped for a moment, looked around for an escape route, and then decided to stand their ground. They turned and pretended to be talking with each other on the sidewalk.

"Excuse me," said Kimmy with a smile as they drew near. "I think we're lost."

The thin man looked down at her and said, "What?"

"Well, maybe not lost," said Zeke, "more like curious. We want to know why you're following us."

"What?" said the thin man, again.

His friend remained mute.

"Following us. Why?" said Zeke, and he stepped in closer to both men.

"No, we were going to get our car," the big man started, taking a small step back, followed by Zeke stepping forward to crowd him. Unnerved, he pulled out a gun, a Glock 19, and pointed it at Zeke.

With little motion and seemingly no effort, Zeke wrapped the gun in his right hand, his fingers blocking the cocking mechanism of the Glock's triple safety, the man's index finger stuck in the trigger guard. Zeke ducked under his right arm and twisted, and the big man said, "Ow, hey, hey," and then Zeke was holding the gun. The big man was cradling his right hand in his left.

"You know who we are?" asked the thin man. "You don't wanna mess with us."

"That's just it," said Zeke in a conversational tone. "We don't know who you are." The gun was steady on the thin man, now, obviously the man in charge. Mr. Big was probably just muscle.

Kimmy watched the thin man's hands while she held her Jerico loosely, pointed at the ground.

"I'd leave your weapon holstered, if I were you," said Kimmy, bouncing slightly on the balls of her feet.

He looked at her for a minute, but left his gun where it was.

"So you're the enforcers?" asked Zeke. "For the Boston mob?"

The men were both mute, but the thin man had fire in his eyes. Then he said, "What Boston Mob?"

Zeke looked at him.

The thin man said, "Let's go, Louie," and he turned and walked away. The big guy, Louie, growled at Zeke and then turned and followed his friend, apparently willing to give up the Glock to avoid further embarrassment.

"Bet they didn't expect that," said Kimmy. "Now they've got to make a decision. Report the encounter to their bosses, and admit they lost their gun and were humiliated…"

"…Or keep it to themselves," said Zeke. "Seems like someone involved with the Student Loan fraud might be starting to pay attention to us. Good."

"What do we do?" asked Kimmy.

"Let's see what kind of a reaction we get," said Zeke. "If we keep pushing, they're bound to try again. Then we can see who we're dealing with."

"OK with me," said Kimmy.

"Meantime, I think I'll see if Deputy Chief O'Malley will set us up with a Boston PD sketch artist. Let's see if we can ID those two."

CHAPTER 10

"They've got to be local muscle," said Zeke.

Deputy Chief O'Malley nodded. "Most likely," he said. "We'll set you up with an artist, see if anyone recognizes either of them."

"OK," said Zeke. "Also, can we check for prints on the Glock and the bullets? That might confirm it."

"Well, sure. From what you said, they didn't break any laws except pulling the gun on you. And they'll probably claim that they were scared and thought you had guns or something," said O'Malley. "That's what usually happens."

"Sure," said Zeke, "but it'll shake them up a little, knowing you're looking at them."

"Most of these shooters have a concealed carry permit these days," O'Malley continued. "Makes everything legal. Unless they have a serious record."

Zeke nodded. "Here's the gun." He handed the Glock barrel first to the Deputy Chief. It was enclosed in a clear plastic zip lock bag.

"How'd you get that in here?" asked O'Malley, referring to the police station.

Zeke shrugged, and O'Malley shook his head with a wry smile.

"OK, we'll check it," said O'Malley. "And we'll circulate the sketch here, and with our OC guys as soon as it's finished. I'll get someone in here to work on that." He paused a beat, then he picked up his desk phone and dialed.

* * *

"That's Roy Calhoun," said O'Malley. "I recognize him myself."

Zeke had worked with an artist from one of the local liberal arts colleges. O'Malley had seen the results and spouted the name immediately.

"Local?" asked Zeke.

"Yes, sir," said O'Malley.

"And the other one?" asked Zeke.

"That's gotta be Louie Brennan," he said. "He's a big boy. Let's see it."

The artist handed the second picture to O'Malley, who confirmed the identity with a nod. "Yep, those are the boy-o's," he said.

"What's their affiliation?" asked Zeke.

"Oh, they're just local muscle, like you said. They work for Freddy Hanson, one of the local mob bosses. He took over from his father a few years ago."

"Why would they be following us?" asked Zeke. "Is Hanson involved in the Student Loan problem?"

"Well, from what you said that's very big money, so somewhere along the way, someone had to organize it. Hanson's dad might have been involved at some point."

"Why do you say that?" asked Zeke.

"He was plugged in with the local power structure," said O'Malley. "He grew up with the mayor and a lot of the local politicians. Old Doc Hanson would have the connections to pull off something that big. At least to be involved."

"Doc Hanson?" asked Zeke.

"Just a nickname," said O'Malley. "He ran half the town for years. Stepped down after his wife died, like I said, a few years back."

"And junior picked up where Doc left off?" asked Zeke.

"He did. They'd made their way into the upper echelon of crime by then. Federal construction contracts, bridges and roads, garbage collection, the unions, like that," said the Assistant Chief.

"And student loan money," said Zeke.

"Possibly. But be careful. These guys play rough," said O'Malley.

* * *

"Word is that your auditor will be taken care of soon," said Jobare Worthington.

Dr. Paul Richardson looked up at him. They were walking across a courtyard toward the Dean's offices located in the Raleigh University campus administration building.

"You said that last week," said Richardson. "But he keeps showing up in my offices."

"Can't be helped. They sent some boys to scare him off, but apparently they weren't, well, stout enough to make it stick," said Worthington.

"Who did they send?"

"Roy Calhoun and Louie Brennan," said Worthington. "Two of their best."

"What kind of auditor is he?" asked Richardson. "I've seen Calhoun and Brennan. They seem formidable."

Worthington shrugged. "Well, it won't be long now. No worries. Just keep your mouth shut and go along with the audit." He thought for a moment. "Actually, you should make yourself scarce. You don't want to be around when it goes down. And if you're not available, he can't ask you more questions about the, ah, loans. I've told others the same," he added cryptically.

"I suppose this is what they pay us for," said Richardson, looking furtive.

"My dear fellow, we're talking about millions and millions of dollars, here. What they pay us is a pittance compared to what they keep…"

"I don't know…"

Worthington stopped and looked at Dr. Richardson. He said, "Yes, you do. Don't give them a reason to doubt you, Paul."

* * *

"We don't get that many shootings in Cambridge," said the detective. "Last year we had three murders, and they were all domestic issues."

Zeke nodded, looking at the crime scene.

The police detective, who introduced himself as Feltman, was standing in the street about fifteen feet from an area that was marked off with police tape. Several men and women in dark blue clothing marked 'CSI' were packing up their equipment. Some wore matching blue hats. They all wore protective booties on their feet.

The body had already been removed, but there was still a pack of onlookers, mostly students, standing behind the police line and watching and taking video footage with their smart phones.

"So what happened was this kid, ID says his name was Peter Vartis," said Feltman looking at his notebook, "he was in his car, stopped at the light," he pointed up at a traffic light, "here on Monsignor O'Brien Highway. That's Lechmere Station, by the way," he said, pointing across the street. "He was sitting here when someone pulled up next to him and shot him through the driver's side window."

"Any cameras in the area?" asked Zeke.

"Sure," said Feltman. "On the poles. I've got guys checking the recordings."

"But..." said Zeke.

"But I'm not optimistic. From here, street level, it looks like someone sprayed black paint on some of the cameras."

"Was this the car was he driving?" asked Zeke.

"Yeah. Nice car. A brand new Porsche 911 in red. Some people have no respect. A shame to shoot up a car like that."

"Sure," said Zeke.

"All the blood ruins the leather interior," continued Feltman.

"What do we know about the victim?" asked Zeke.

"He's a student at Raleigh University. Had his student ID with him."

Zeke had just left the offices at Raleigh University, still pretending to work on the audit, when he'd received a call from Sally at The Agency.

"The Cambridge Police just reported that there was a killing not far from where you are right now," she said. "Four hours ago. It's unusual to have a violent crime in Cambridge. Clive thinks it could be connected to the student loan thing, thought you might want to talk with the people in charge."

"That's quite a coincidence," said Zeke.

Sally gave him the details, and agreed to have Clive call both Assistant Chief O'Malley and the Cambridge Police Chief. By the time Zeke arrived at the site, Feltman was expecting him.

"How old was he?" asked Zeke.

"License says he was about to turn twenty-two," said Feltman. "Shame."

"Anything stolen?"

"Doesn't look like it. But we're still investigating," said Feltman.

Zeke looked around the crowded street. "Seems like someone would have seen something," he said.

"My thoughts, too. We're checking."

"I understand there's a lot of wealth in this part of the country," said Zeke. "But that's a ninety-thousand dollar car. Was the victim's family wealthy?"

"We don't know yet. This just happened a few hours ago," said Feltman, suddenly defensive.

Zeke paused a moment. "Here's my card. Call if I can help."

"Yeah, sure," said the detective.

* * *

"Any witnesses?" asked Jobare Worthington.

"No, no one that matters. And no cameras," said Freddy Hanson.

"So it's done?"

"Sure. You'll read about it in the morning paper."

"I assume you mean the Globe."

Hanson said nothing. Worthington was sitting alone at his desk in his office at Raleigh University, his door closed. He was whispering into the phone.

"So we don't have anything to worry about?" Worthington added.

"Not as far as the kid goes. Pretty stupid buying that car, though. Can you keep your people in line?" said Hanson. "We talked about this."

"I know. I had no idea," said Worthington, again.

"This is too big to have it screwed up by some pot head students," said Hanson.

"I know," said Worthington, his voice pitched even higher than usual.

"Keep your people in line, then," Hanson repeated.

* * *

"Hey, Zeke, how are you, man?" asked Jerry Sebastian when Zeke answered his mobile phone. "Been a while."

"It has, Jerry," said Zeke. "I've been bouncing around the country. My boss had a new assignment for me, and we'd finished up in Phoenix, so…"

"Yeah, I figured it was something like that," said Jerry. "Last time we talked, you said you were wrapping things up."

"Sure did."

"Are you back on Cape Cod, now?" Jerry asked.

"No, Boston," said Zeke. "I have a new consulting assignment here in Boston."

"Boston's a nice city. I used to go there for long weekends when I was in college."

"In Pittsburgh, you said," remembered Zeke.

"Right," said Jerry. "Well, do you have any more business out this way? Are you coming to do any follow-up in Phoenix?"

"I will need to visit Phoenix again soon, Jerry. I need to debrief our client and turn in a final report," Zeke said.

"Well, I've officially got the RTM systems job," said Jerry.

"Congratulations," said Zeke. "Are you liking it?"

"Uh, yes, I am enjoying it. I like what I do," said the killer.

"I'll let you know when I'm heading out your way, and

maybe we can get together," said Zeke.

"I'd like that," said Jerry. "Yeah, let me know."

* * *

"I just spoke with him yesterday," said Luis Cruz. "He said he's in Boston, said he's working."

"And?" asked Benito Diaz. They were in Diaz's back yard, sitting in the afternoon heat.

"And he says he's coming back to Phoenix to close out with his last client."

"That would be ICE," said Diaz. "Jorge Ramirez. Was he telling you the truth?"

"Most likely. No reason to lie," said the killer. "Either way, we'll get close to him. Here or there."

"Yes," said Diaz.

"I don't see him as a problem. He trusts me."

* * *

Zeke dialed the phone.

"4273," said the female voice, answering on the second ring.

"Hello, Tammy," said Zeke, using the word code. "Can I get a message to Eric?" Eric was The Agency's code name for Clive Greene, used on an unsecured line.

"Hold on, please," said the woman's voice, almost wispy in its now-soft tone.

Zeke held.

There was a click on the line. "He'll call you back in an hour," she said.

* * *

Zeke's secure phone rang exactly ten minutes later, and Clive said, "Have you been consorting with killers, then?"

"I have," said Zeke with a smile. "I think I'll need to meet him in Phoenix and finish it."

"You still think he's gunning for you?" asked Clive.

"It's a continuation of the refugee raid, retaliation by Diaz for my interference, or something like that," said Zeke. "The Mara's tried to take us out before we got started."

"So this will be more subtle, I suppose," said Clive.

"I think so. And while I'm out there, I'll deal with Ramirez. He needs to be taken out of the SAC position."

"If Ramirez is the leak, Clark Hall agrees," said Clive. "If that's true, Ramirez is too dangerous and disruptive to stay in place. But be careful. If he turns quickly, he'll be like a trapped animal," said Clive.

"Do we have enough evidence against him?" asked Zeke.

"ICE went through phone records going back six months. Not only do we suspect that Ramirez is somehow involved in the human trafficking, but they've got him directly connected with Diaz's phone number on several occasions."

"Sounds circumstantial," said Zeke.

"Sure, but his phone records also include multiple calls to the WITSEC group headquarters."

"Using his influence to arrange reassignments?" asked Zeke.

"Maybe, or calling to find out where certain witnesses are being moved to. Either way, it puts him in the middle of it," said Clive.

"Do we know who he spoke with at WITSEC?" asked Zeke.

"We do," said Clive. "And as you'd expect, it was someone in the U.S. Marshal Service in Arlington."

CHAPTER 11

"Ramirez sent over a copy of the original call," said Sally, over the phone line, "of the anonymous tip that led to the raid on the house in Phoenix."

Zeke nodded, sitting in an overstuffed chair in his Cambridge hotel room. Then he said, "OK, good. And…"

"And there was nothing there. Just a whispered male voice, Hispanic accent, speaking in semi-broken English. He called the Phoenix police tip line and said, 'Note this address,' and gave the address and then he said, 'Prisa.'"

"'Prisa means hurry," said Zeke. "But they didn't hurry. According to Ramirez, they passed the call over to ICE. Then ICE 'surveilled' the place for quite a while before the raid."

"Quite right," said Clive Greene, also on the call. He was glancing through a paper file. "How would the police know that it wasn't an emergency? Why didn't they respond themselves?"

"The house was in the Glenwood neighborhood," said Zeke. "That's a dense, populated area of Phoenix. If there was commotion or screaming from the house, it would probably have been heard by the neighbors."

Sally said, "It would have."

"What about the personnel search?" asked Zeke.

"We're pretty much through all of the personnel files," said Sally.

"What did you find that looks interesting?" asked Zeke.

"Well, we did a check on each of the ICE personnel who could have been involved somehow in deflecting or steering the investigation. It seems like there are just a few that have the rank and the authority to do so."

"Let me guess," said Zeke. "Ramirez is at the top of the list."

"And Jose Fernandez, his ICE Unit Commander. Fernandez organized the takedown in Phoenix."

"That was the raid that scored 17 refugees and no bad guys," said Zeke.

Clive made an affirming noise.

"What's Ramirez's service history?" asked Zeke.

Sally opened a file. "He was a Sergeant in the Border Patrol up until six years ago. Then he transferred to ICE and has worked his way up since then."

"Both organizations are part of Homeland Security. That was probably a pretty easy move for him. A transfer. How long did he work at Border Patrol?"

"It says he was there for five years," said Sally.

"How about before that? Was he in law enforcement?" asked Zeke.

"Before that, he was a prison guard in the U.S. Penitentiary at Tucson, Arizona," said Sally. "He worked there for four years, after he was discharged from the Army."

"Then he knew Raul Diaz," said Zeke. "Raul was housed in the high security wing of that prison for seven years, the same time Ramirez worked there. He was in for selling drugs and participating in a child pornography ring."

"Really?" asked Clive. "You remember that?"

"Well, we are dealing with the Diaz cartel. So I did a little bit of research," said Zeke.

"Hmm," said Clive.

"There are actually quite a number of child pornographers and sex offenders in that prison. They have a special program for them there," Zeke continued.

"Ew, gross," said Sally. "That's way too much information."

"Back to Ramirez," said Zeke. "Federal prison guard, then Border Patrol, then ICE and now an Agent in Charge."

"Right," said Clive.

"So, what did he do in the Army?" asked Zeke.

"Says here he was a helicopter pilot. Served in Afghanistan," said Sally. "You were in Afghanistan," Sally said to Zeke. "Maybe you ran into him there?"

"I was in counterintelligence. We didn't spend much time with the fliers," said Zeke.

"It does look as if he may have had continuing contact with Raul Diaz, though," said Clive. "That's something."

Then, to Zeke, "Come on back to D.C. and we'll sort this thing out."

* * *

A few blocks from the office, Clive had just ordered a Sunday Roast at the Elephant and Castle, his favorite D.C. restaurant. Zeke walked into the restaurant, looked around, and joined him at the table.

"It's got to be Ramirez," said Zeke without preamble. "He's the common denominator."

"Join me for a draft," said Clive. "I just ordered."

Zeke waved the server over and ordered a Black and Tan. When she was gone, he continued. "The key is the location, Phoenix and surrounds."

Clive sipped his gin and tonic. He tasted the Boodles and nodded to himself.

"It did seem like an odd coincidence, the ICE job, Diaz, the refugees and the killer, all converging in Phoenix…"

"Right? So tracking backwards, there had to be a reason. Then I realized there had to be a connection between Diaz and Ramirez. That connects everyone, the killer Jerry Sebastian, Benito Diaz his boss, the refugees, and," Zeke paused, "and the WITSEC guy who died in the canyon. I'm wondering whether it was Ramirez or Diaz that had him reassigned to Phoenix after he testified. One of them probably influenced the WITSEC guys to move him there."

"Logical," said Clive.

The Sunday roast arrived just then, a plate full of roast beef, roasted potato, Yorkshire pudding, sausages, stuffing, vegetables and gravy.

Zeke scanned the plate. "You must be hungry," he said.

Clive, his mouth full of roast, just nodded.

"It also explains why Ramirez has been so ineffective against the traffickers, and against the MS-13 gang. He didn't want to catch them in any of the raids," said Zeke.

"So he's Diaz's man?" asked Clive, as he took another bite.

"Pretty much has to be," said Zeke. "He's been obfuscating the ICE investigation from the beginning."

Clive nodded. "It's time for another conversation with Clark Hall, then."

* * *

"Witness Protection, WITSEC headquarters, says they've lost eight people in the past three years," said Sally without preamble.

They were seated in Clive Greene's D.C. office, now, overlooking Pennsylvania Avenue through the wide floor to ceiling windows. Sally had joined Zeke and Clive, and they were discussing their findings about Jerry Sebastian. It was a warm afternoon outside, an Indian summer Saturday, and traffic was light in the capitol.

"How many people have been in the program? WITSEC?" asked Clive.

"Hard to say," said Zeke. "But best guess is about 9,000 to 9,500, plus another 12,000 family members."

"And they've had eight killings in the past three years?"

"Yes," said Sally, nodding.

"Unsolved?" asked Clive.

"Totally," said Sally. She was dressed in blue shorts and seamed nylons that ended in classic pumps. Her short-sleeved blouse was a swoop necked affair that looked as if it were made of beige satin. She wore her hair up.

"Did they share anything else?" asked Zeke. "Anything similar about the killings? The weapons? The locations?"

Sally said, "They're not in the habit of sharing much, even when their bosses tell them to share with us. But they did say that almost all the killings were former gang members and their families."

"What else?" asked Zeke.

"All the killings were quiet," said Sally, she opened her file. "Knives were used in a few, a garrote in one, poison twice." She looked at her notes. "And one was beaten to death. They thought that one was a mugging, initially, but it wasn't."

"Any others?" asked Clive.

"The most recent victim fell off a ledge in the Grand Canyon."

* * *

"We'll need to take this Luis Cruz out of the picture," said Clive. "He's too dangerous."

Zeke nodded.

Sally had left the room, and now returned with a serving cart carrying an insulated coffee pot, cups, tea and the appropriate condiments. Zeke was looking through her WITSEC file while she was gone.

"Former gang members. Silent killings. How about geography? Says here the killings took place in Jackson, Detroit, Oklahoma City, Tuscaloosa, and Portland. That's Portland, Maine. And the Grand Canyon National Park."

"Right. Two killings were double homicides," said Sally.

"Where did the fellow live? The one killed in the National Park?" asked Clive.

"He'd just gotten into the program and had been moved to Phoenix," said Sally.

"That seems like quite a coincidence," said Zeke.

"Considering the human trafficking work we did with ICE in Phoenix, it still seems unlikely that we'd all end up in that city at the same time."

"It does. That's too big a reach," said Clive.

"Unless there are some relationships here that we haven't seen yet. Some common denominator," said Zeke.

"Like what?" asked Sally.

"Mostly connections in Phoenix. We have the traffickers, the Mara's. We have Diaz with his house there. We have Ramirez who transferred into ICE. We have Luis Cruz, who's just arrived and is likely here at Diaz's request to stop us. And Ramirez knew Raul Diaz in prison. Sally said that Raul Diaz lives with his brother in Scottsdale, now."

"So the geography is a common factor?" asked Sally.

"For some reason, it seems to be," said Clive.

"I'll take a look at the WITSEC killings. There may be something there that explains it," said Zeke.

* * *

"I've studied the files, " said Zeke. "There doesn't seem to be a lot of overlap in the M.O.'s." He was talking about the methods the killer had used to dispatch his eight WITSEC victims, his modus operandi.

"Right," said Clive. "Different methods, different weapons, and different locations."

They were back in Clive Greene's offices, taking another look at the WITSEC files Sally had acquired.

"These were all bad guys," said Clive, leafing back through the crime scene photos. "All criminals and gang members who the Feds turned. They all testified against someone in Diaz's organization, or an MS-13 member, before they were killed. But they were all involved with drugs and kidnapping and armed robbery at some point."

"If we look more closely, I'll bet we find that some of their distant family members were killed or went missing, too," said Zeke. "Probably the family members first, to extract the most pain and create the most fear."

"Makes sense," said Clive. "Bloody gruesome, though."

"So I ranked the killings a few of different ways. Chronologically, by weapon, and by city. Looking for patterns and common characteristics.

"What have you found?"

"A couple patterns. All of the killings were up close and personal," said Zeke. "The killer had to be within arm's length of the victim in every case."

"So he likes it personal," said Clive.

"Appears to. Also, they took place mostly in the warmer months. April through October. Only two of the eight victims were killed during winter months."

"That's interesting. Do you think it was intentional?"

"Possibly. The two killed during winter were in Detroit and Portland, Maine," said Zeke.

"Coldest cities on the list."

"Yes, they are," said Zeke. "Each of the victims had been relocated to the city they were killed in for between six and eighteen months. Enough time for them to acclimate and get established and familiar with their new cities. And enough time for their Marshal detail to leave them mostly on their own."

"And, apparently, enough time to let their guard down..."

"Right. The other thing that stands out is the progression of the weapons used," said Zeke.

"Chronologically?" asked Clive.

"Yes. First was with a knife," said Zeke. "Took place in Detroit. That was two and a half years ago, one of the winter killings."

"OK," said Clive.

"Second was in Oklahoma City, eight months later. The vic was bludgeoned to death."

"Sounds messy," said Clive.

"Yes, but it's possible that one got out of hand and he had to finish the job without his weapon," said Zeke. "The third killing was also with a knife, it was a husband and wife."

Clive nodded.

"Seven months after number two, in the spring of the next year, that killing was in Tuscaloosa," Zeke continued. "Number four was in Jackson. In Mississippi."

"Also a knife?" asked Clive.

"No, that one was the garrote. The vic was strangled with a wire hanger," said Zeke. "Only five months after the third killing."

"Also possibly a weapon of convenience," said Clive.

"Then, five months later, in February, another double homicide in Portland, Maine. Another husband and wife. He was on a roll."

"Weapon for that one?" asked Clive.

"They suspect poison. But that file had been closed as 'accidental deaths' until we started looking for trends, you know… dying witnesses."

Clive nodded. "And then the tumble in the Grand Canyon," he said. "This summer."

"Correct," said Zeke. "I feel like we're playing the game Clue. Mrs. Plum in the library with the candlestick…"

Clive chuckled. "It's more deadly than that," he said. "It's good that you spotted the trend. We've had a killer picking off witnesses under protection of the Marshals, and no one connected the dots."

"I don't know how they could have, actually," Zeke said. "The Marshals' organization is set up geographically, which works well for most things. But you don't always get a cross section of related events with that hierarchy, particularly when there are so many differences in the killings."

"And you think you're this killer's next victim?" asked Clive.

"He seems to think so," Zeke said.

* * *

"So who were Luis Cruz's murder victims?" asked Clive.

"Like we said, mostly bad guys," said Zeke. "In fact, most of the people in WITSEC are bad guys who rolled over on someone else."

"And they got a free pass," said Clive.

"That's the way the Feds work, right?" said Zeke. "OK, so the first one we found, two and a half years ago, was an enforcer. Low level thug, actually. The WITSEC guys say he was a CI, a confidential informant, before he was put in the program. They say he killed two people, but it was never proven. He turned on Benito Diaz, gave up a couple of Diaz's lieutenants, testified and got the free pass. As you mentioned."

Clive nodded. "Was he heavily marked?"

"No, no Tats on that one. The Mara's have actually been moving away from that, so that they blend better."

"Do you have a name?" asked Clive.

"Feds say that his real name was Renaldo Juarez, but his street name was Paulo," said Zeke. He hadn't looked at his file notes yet.

"You said he was killed with a knife...?"

"He was cut several times. Across the forehead, probably to blind him with blood flow, and his vagus nerve was severed at his neck."

"That's pretty extreme," said Clive. "And an expert move."

Zeke nodded. "That move would immobilize him. The kill shot was a slice across his femoral artery. He bled out."

"In Detroit," said Clive. "Seems like a dismal place to die."

Zeke thought for a moment. "It seems like it would be difficult for an individual to commit these killings," he said after a minute. "Especially the double homicides. Too much risk, I'd think. I suppose we need to look into each of these murders. We should see if there's anything more to it."

"Like…?" asked Clive.

"Like, was Luis Cruz acting alone? Did he kill all the victims, or might there be someone else involved?"

"An assistant?" asked Clive.

"Or a second killer," said Zeke.

* * *

"I received an interesting call this morning," said Clive Greene, in a preface to their discussion. He, Zeke and Kimmy were gathered in Clive's library-like office after a short break. They were there to discuss Ramirez and the WITSEC killings. And a possible connection between the two.

"What was that?" asked Kimmy.

"George Farmer, head of the U.S. Marshal's Service here in D.C. called. He mentioned that they're looking into the Grand Canyon killing—the WITSEC guy, the last one—and noticed that we were already investigating. It was noted in the file that we'd been given copies."

Zeke sipped his cup of Ethiopian coffee and waited for Clive to explain. The coffee was very hot, and he blew across the surface lightly.

"Said they have an agent, a Marshal David Brown. He's with their internal investigators. He's looking into the killing, also, and Farmer suggested that we share information," Clive continued.

"Where is Marshal Brown?" asked Zeke.

"In Phoenix, well, central Arizona right now. Do you want to join up with him?"

"Probably be a good idea," said Zeke. "I'll get Sally to book a flight out tomorrow. Let me have Brown's phone number."

"OK, will do," said Clive. "Luis will be looking to connect with you soon, I'd think."

"Most likely. He thinks I'm on Cape Cod now, but he'll want to take his shot. He's been courting me long enough," said Zeke. "I'll work that out."

"There's overwhelming evidence that Ramirez is on the inside for Benito Diaz," said Clive, getting the meeting back on track. "The question is, how implicated is he in the WITSEC killings? And, was he directly involved?"

CHAPTER 12

"You can take care of this problem, then?" asked Benito Diaz. "I'm growing impatient with these interruptions."

Luis Cruz looked at him across the table and slowly nodded.

"I've suffered raids on my warehouses and my ranch," he said, referring to Susie's Ranch in Pahrump. "It is a nuisance."

"Yes," said Luis Cruz, respectfully. "We're very close to finishing, to eliminating the problem."

"I don't know why it takes so long to kill someone," said Raul Diaz, sitting next to his brother. "Just bang and they're gone. What's wrong with that?"

Luis looked at him patiently. He noticed that Benito Diaz was ignoring the interruption, so he did the same.

"Very well. We need to reestablish our operation in Nevada quickly," said Benito.

"I agree," said Luis Cruz. "I would prefer another week or two, but my target is leaving town soon and I believe it will be prudent to act quickly."

"I also received a call from Freddy Hanson in Boston," said Benito Diaz. "We do business."

Luis waited.

"Apparently, they're having some sort of trouble with this Zeke Traynor up there, too. He's looking into one of Hanson's client's operations, I think."

"Why did he call you?" asked Luis.

"He's a buyer in my supply chain, so to speak," said Diaz.

"Yes?" asked Luis.

"And there are only so many places you can find your kind of talent," said Diaz, referring to the killer. "Only a few. And we've helped Freddy Hanson before, when the problem was too large for him."

"So he also needs a permanent solution?" asked Luis.

Benito Diaz nodded. "We would like this done before the end of this week," he said. "I have another shipment arriving soon."

Luis Cruz said nothing while maintaining respectful eye contact with Benito Diaz. Then he nodded.

Diaz watched him carefully, as if reading the man's thoughts. Then he said, dismissively, "The end of the week."

"Yes," said Cruz. He stood to leave.

* * *

"I do not trust him, Benito," said Raul Diaz, once he had shown Cruz out.

"Good," said Benito. "You should not trust anyone. You'll

live longer if you follow that rule."

Raul, again sitting at the table, nodded. "I know," he said.

He knows very little, thought Benito Diaz. *He is too emotional and too proud. He's lucky that he's my brother.*

"When do you expect the next shipment?" Raul asked, referring to Central American refugees. Benito Diaz's organization reached from the slums of El Salvador and Nicaragua, along the escape routes that wound through Mexico and into the southern *Estados Unidos.*

"It is supposed to arrive this weekend on Saturday night," said Benito Diaz.

Raul nodded sagely. "I see," he said.

* * *

"I talked with Diaz," Luis Cruz said. He was standing calmly in an aisle between two bookshelves in the Phoenix Public Library, apparently browsing. "He said 'this week'."

In the next aisle, Susan Del Gato stood alone, facing the same shelves. They could hear and see each other between the books. She said, "I'll bet."

"Traynor's heading back here," continued Luis. "He'll be here tomorrow afternoon, around six."

"How do you want to do it?" she asked in a quiet voice.

"I'll take care of this one," said Luis. "Can you get me what I need?"

"Sure," said Susan.

"Put it in a small glassine envelope, like we discussed?"

"Sure can," said Susan.

"Bring it by tonight, later?"

"I will," said Susan. They had separate accommodations, Susan staying in a local hotel while Luis used his rented apartment.

"You should plan to stay with me a while," said Luis.

"Thanks, no," said Susan. "I don't mix work and pleasure. You know that."

"You can't blame me for trying. You're a package," he said.

Susan smiled to herself.

Changing the subject, Luis said, "I think this will go smoothly. No reason to worry."

* * *

The plane landed at Phoenix Sky Harbor Airport and Zeke deplaned with his carryon bag. He stepped outside the terminal and walked toward the area marked 'ground transportation'. Outside it looked hot and dry.

Marshal David Brown was a nondescript man wearing a cowboy hat that looked too big and out of place on his head. He looked at a picture he held, nodded to himself and greeted Zeke as he walked through the TSA security exit.

"I'm David Brown," he said and held his hand out to shake with Zeke.

"I'm Zeke."

"I saw that you boys have been looking into the WITSEC deaths," Brown said as they continued through the terminal toward ground transportation. "How's that going?"

"We've isolated some patterns," said Zeke. "We think the killings were probably done by the same assassin. Or assassins."

"More than one?" asked Brown.

"Most likely. I've examined each file, and there's too much risk if only one man was involved. The chances of the killings getting out of control are too high." Zeke paused.

"And, all the killings were in close. And violent. Not the signature of a professional."

"But possible with two killers?" asked Brown. He seemed to be a plain spoken man, and Zeke liked him immediately.

"Yes, with two, the risk would go way down." Zeke paused inside the terminal exit door. "I need to separate now. One of the killers is picking me up."

Brown said, "OK, give me a call as soon as you know what the plan is," and handed Zeke his business card. "We'll be ready."

* * *

Zeke exited the terminal alone at the 'Ground Transportation' sign, and emerged pulling his roller bag near the curb.

He heard a car horn and saw Jerry Sebastian wave at him from his spot at the curb. Zeke walked down to the car.

"Hey, Zeke, welcome back to Phoenix," said Jerry with some enthusiasm.

"Good to be back," said Zeke. "Congratulations on your new job."

"Yeah, thanks," said Jerry.

"So you got your car fixed," said Zeke.

"I did," Jerry agreed. "It was something electrical, I don't know... But it works now."

"Great," said Zeke.

"Where are we going, then?" asked Jerry Sebastian.

"Let's stop by the hotel so I can check in, and then we'll grab some dinner. I'm staying at the Holiday Inn by the airport."

"OK. Where would you like to eat?" asked Jerry.

"Let's try that place you mentioned. The Mexican restaurant" said Zeke. "What's it called?"

"It's called the Barrio," said Jerry.

The Ghetto, thought Zeke. *OK...* "Food's good?" he asked.

"Yep. I had the Carne Asada last time. It was very good!"

"Are you still living in the apartment?" asked Zeke, idly.

"When did you... Oh, I remember, you dropped me off when my car broke down. Yeah, I'm still there."

* * *

Jerry pulled under the hotel's port-a-cache and Zeke got out. He opened the back door, took his carryon bag out and said to Jerry, "I'll just be a minute."

"Sure," said Jerry.

Zeke stopped at the front desk and retrieved a card key, and then went directly to room 212 using the interior stairs. One of Marshal Brown's people had rented the room in Zeke's name the day before.

The door opened easily and he dropped his bag on the bed and went into the bathroom. There he opened the toilet tank and retrieved his package. In it were the Walther PPK, a Walther TPH, a smaller, lighter gun, and several extra clips of ammunition, all sealed in a plastic freezer bag.

Zeke removed the guns and tossed the bag into the trash. Then he picked up the room phone, dialed the number Marshal Brown had given him, and said, "It's going down at the Barrio restaurant, now."

* * *

"Sorry for the delay," said Zeke, as he slipped back into the passenger seat.

"No worries," said Jerry. "You're gonna love this place," he said, referring to the restaurant. And he pulled the car smoothly into traffic.

The drive to the Barrio was slow, as the downtown Phoenix traffic hadn't yet cleared out after rush hour. When they arrived, Jerry parked his car behind the busy restaurant. At the hostess station they were told there would be a fifteen-minute wait.

"We'll wait at the bar, ok?" said Jerry.

"Sure," said Zeke. The eleven and a half ounce TPH was comfortably holstered above his right ankle. He'd left the PPK and the extra clips hidden in his room.

The men found two empty wooden stools at the small, ornate bar and eased themselves onto them. The restaurant was noisy, with families and children laughing and talking. It smelled of Ropa Vieja and spicy grilled beef.

Zeke ordered a dark Dos Equis in a frosty mug, and Jerry opted for a classic Margarita. While they waited, Zeke said, "I think I'll wash my hands."

"Sure," said Jerry. "I'll hold your seat."

As soon as Zeke was out of sight, Jerry reached into the chest pocket of his green plaid shirt and took out a small glassine envelope. He waited until the bartender set their drinks on the bar and turned his back before he spilled the powder into Zeke's beer mug.

Wolfsbane. Actually, aconite. Five milligrams will be more than sufficient.

Jerry knew that the symptoms would appear quickly, starting with a burning in Zeke's mouth, then progress to vomiting and diarrhea. He figured to call 911 at that point, and request an ambulance, although it would already be too late. And when Zeke died a short time later it would be from paralysis of the heart.

It's the perfect poison, Jerry thought. *So quick, and the only post mortem signs are those of asphyxia.*

* * *

Zeke slid onto the stool to Jerry's left and settled himself back into the seat at the bar.

"The food smells great," he said, looking at Jerry.

Jerry nodded enthusiastically. "Yeah, it is," he said. "This is my favorite place in Phoenix, so far." He smiled, waiting for Zeke to sip his beer.

He felt, rather than saw, a presence over his right shoulder. Jerry turned his head, just quickly enough to see the man. He was large and animated, making eye contact with the bartender over Jerry and talking loudly across Jerry, ordering drinks. Jerry categorized the man as a non-threat and then turned back to the bar. Zeke was gone.

"Hey, what…" he started, looking around the small bar area.

Jerry sensed it first. Then the waving arms of the man behind him suddenly encircled his arms and chest, and the hands locked together, securing him to the chair in a bear hug. The bartender, small and wiry, quickly reached across the bar and, with two fingers encased in a plastic glove, extracted the glassine envelope from Jerry's shirt pocket. A moment later, Jerry's wrists were manacled behind him and he was flat on the floor on his stomach, the large man, gun in hand, kneeling on his back.

* * *

"You cut it pretty close," said Marshal David Brown.

"I was OK," said Zeke. "I had my weapon in my left hand, down at my side. There was no danger."

The Marshal shook his head.

"Besides, your guys had it under control," said Zeke.

"You think this guy is linked to a number of the WITSEC killings?" asked Brown.

"We do," said Zeke. "He's Benito Diaz's favorite go-to killer. His real name's Luis Cruz."

Brown nodded. "Can we connect those dots and put him away for the murders?"

"Maybe some of them. But you've got him for attempted murder," said Zeke.

"And on camera," Brown added. "This'll take some time to clean up," he said, looking around the restaurant. "But how about we catch up tomorrow?"

"Works for me," said Zeke.

"Think we can roll him?" said Brown, referring to Luis Cruz.

"Don't know, but from what we've seen, Benito Diaz is a serious threat with a long reach. If Cruz turns against him, I wouldn't give him good odds of staying alive in prison," said Zeke. "And he knows that."

"If he rolls on Diaz, we'll just have to put him in the WITSEC program," said Brown with an ironic smile.

"Sure, because we all see how well that's been working," said Zeke.

* * *

The Uber driver dropped Zeke at the door to the government complex where the ICE offices were housed. There were no visible signs left from the Mara's attack on Zeke and Kimmy. The place seemed quiet and unassuming.

Zeke passed through the metal detector at the entrance,

and found his way to the ICE offices. Marshal David Brown had suggested they meet in the DHS building. He was based out of Dallas and didn't have office space in the area.

Zeke climbed the stairs to the second level and navigated a long hallway to an open bullpen area with several cubicles. It was quiet in the room, except for a man in his cowboy hat, standing, speaking into his cell phone. He saw Zeke and waved his free hand, inviting him over.

"They called up and said you'd arrived," said Marshal Brown, hanging up his phone. "Good. Good to see you again."

"You, too," said Zeke.

"That was something, yesterday," said Brown.

"Sure was. I appreciate the support. And, yes, I had a dual purpose in being here," said Zeke, "but one is to work with you, to help any way we can."

"The witness deaths seemed random to us," said Brown. "But we don't really have a way to watch those particular trends. There's so much secrecy involved in the WITSEC program, you know."

"Sure. You guys probably would have seen it if they were all shootings, or all poison," said Zeke. "But from what I see, the killer was good at changing it up."

"He must be good. He's killed some pretty bad hombres."

"He's very good," said Zeke.

"Well, we're going back through each death, now, looking at them with new eyes. Killings, not accidental deaths."

"The last one was in the Grand Canyon. What do you have on that one?"

"Have you read the file?" asked Brown.

"I have," said Zeke. "Most of that was written when they thought the fall was an accident. It dealt mostly with the body recovery and the autopsy. Not much about the cause of the fall."

"I guess everyone just assumed that he got too close to the rim. His real name was Steve Cowlard. He'd testified against a couple of Diaz's guys in Los Angeles, and they moved him to Phoenix and changed his name after the trial was over," said Brown.

"How long have you been with the Marshals?" asked Zeke.

"Started out with the Texas Rangers a long time ago. Then the Marshal Service had an opening for an investigator, and my wife was interested in having me home more and out of the line of fire. So I made the move. It's been eight years, now."

"Is your wife happier?" asked Zeke.

"She is. She divorced me along the way and married a dentist. I think she's very happy, now," said Brown.

* * *

"So, what else can I tell you?" asked Zeke. They'd been talking for the better part of an hour.

"That should do it, Zeke," said Brown. "We've got a killer who was crisscrossing the United States, knocking off former Federal witnesses. Wow."

"And we're not certain he's been working alone," added Zeke.

"What're you saying?" asked Brown. "You think there's still a killer out there?"

"I do," said Zeke. "It's about all that really fits. A couple of the killings had to be two-man jobs."

Brown was quiet, thinking.

"I'm heading back east tomorrow," said Zeke. "Now that you've neutralized Luis Cruz."

"Sure," said Marshal Brown. "We'll be in touch."

* * *

"Are we still on for tomorrow?" asked Tracy Johnson.

"We are," said Zeke. "My flight arrives mid-afternoon. Let's meet at Logan airport and we can drive to the Cape together."

"You driving?" asked Tracy.

"After Atlanta's traffic, I think you're probably the expert in that department," he said. "Just kidding. I'd be glad to drive."

"Oh, good, a real vacation," Tracy laughed.

They coordinated their flights and Zeke said, "Great, I'll see you there."

* * *

"So how long can you keep up this charade?" asked Tracy.

"Charade?" asked Zeke. They were cooking dinner in his small Cape Cod kitchen, moving around carefully, occasionally bumping each other and laughing as they passed. A jazzy Ronnie Laws tune was playing in the background.

"Pretending to be the perfect boyfriend," said Tracy. "How long do you think you can keep it up?"

Zeke smiled and kissed her as she passed him on her way to the refrigerator.

She paused for the kiss, then reached around his waist and gave him a hug.

"OK, that's enough of that, young lady," he said. "Get the asparagus."

She smiled and opened the fridge.

Zeke took a cast iron skillet from the cabinet and set it on the island. He rubbed it with garlic and olive oil and put it in the broiler.

"I need to sear the steaks first," he said.

A plate of grape tomatoes, skewered with mozzarella cheese and anointed with balsamic vinegar sat on the island. Zeke popped one in his mouth.

"I'll get the veggies going," said Tracy. "Can we eat on the back deck? Looking at the ocean?"

"That's the plan," said Zeke. "You read my mind."

"That's my superpower," said Tracy with a smile. "You finally guessed it."

Zeke poured some more merlot into their wineglasses. Then he sipped his and smiled.

"No, that's just one of your superpowers," he said.

Tracy gave him a cryptic smile but said nothing. She was wearing one of Zeke's white dress shirts with her sleeves rolled to her forearms. Her thick black hair was pulled back in a ponytail. She was barefoot.

"You are special," he said. He watched as she arranged the asparagus on a flat pan, added oil, salt and pepper, and slid it into the oven.

"I'm glad you think so," Tracy said. "We'll probably need a nap, after we eat."

"No doubt," he said, opening the broiler and putting two room-temperature filets on the iron flat skillet. They immediately sizzled and a small billow of fragrant smoke floated into the room.

"Yum!" she said. "So tell me about the witness protection killings."

"Not much to tell," said Zeke, looking at his watch, timing the steaks. "It appears there's a killer or killers, taking out witnesses in the program. Maybe eight killings over the past three years."

Tracy nodded. "That sounds significant," she said. "Was that who you caught yesterday?"

"One of them," he said.

Zeke nodded at his watch, opened the broiler and pulled the shelf toward him. He flipped the two steaks, now seared on the bottom, and brushed some olive oil on the top. Then they went back into the broiler.

"Smells heavenly," said Tracy.

"Better than El Nihilo?" Zeke asked her.

"Different," she said, thoughtfully. The asparagus was done, and Tracy shut off the oven and slid the pan out.

Then she added, "Do you think the witness killings are related to those Mara guys and their attempt to kill you?"

"Perhaps," said Zeke. "The deeper we go, the more connections we find. But I think we'll wrap it up soon." He had the broiler open again, flipped the steaks, applied more olive oil and closed the broiler door again.

"That's good. I don't like the idea of someone trying to kill you," she added.

Zeke smiled at her.

"I mean, if something happens to you, who would I stay with on Cape Cod?"

"No worries. The rent's paid through next month. Just take a key when you leave," he joked. Then he opened the broiler, took out the skillet and set it on the island to cool.

"Oh, alright. I didn't want to lose the ocean view, just when I was getting used to it," she said with a twinkle in her eye.

"The steaks need a couple minutes to cool off," said Zeke, stepping around the island. He reached up and unbuttoned the top three buttons of Tracy's shirt, kissed her, and then took her hand. "Let me show you the view from the bedroom."

CHAPTER 13

He watched the woman enter the hotel restaurant and look around. Then she saw him and smiled and walked briskly to his table.

He stood as she approached, pulling out a chair and holding it for her. She paused a moment and looked in his eyes before giving a short nod, as if to herself. Then she sat, and he eased her chair back in.

"You're Susan. Your picture doesn't do you justice," he said.

"Oh?" she asked.

"You can't catch some things in a photo," he said.

She inclined her head slightly, a signal for him to continue.

"Attitude. Posture. Bearing. Directness. Like that."

"Ah," she said. "You appear to be different than I pictured, also." She had a slight continental accent.

He waited.

"Things you can't see in a photo, Jonathan. Manners. Stature. Confidence. Good eye contact."

"Thank you, that's very kind," he said.

"And the Boston Harbor Hotel. Very nice."

Although they had never met, they had been in secret communication for several days. They'd both said they were married, but not to each other.

"Is it always Jonathan, never Jon?" she asked.

"I was Jon until I graduated Prep School," he said. "But never since then."

His pedigree included Phillip Exeter Academy in New Hampshire, followed by a graduate education at Yale University. On a recent phone call, he'd told her that he held a government job, something inside the beltway, and she had made a small, sexy joke of things "inside the beltway," and they'd laughed together.

"I must say, Madison Ashley certainly delivers on her promises," he continued. "You seem to be 'as advertised,' maybe better."

"Thanks for the compliment. I appreciate it." She smiled at the table for a moment. Then she looked at him and said, "Are you hungry?"

"Well, no, but a cocktail might be nice," Jonathan responded. "What would you like?"

"Well, I think I'd like a Blanton's Single Barrel," she said. "Neat."

"Carmel and citrus, from Kentucky," he said. "That does sound good. Nice choice."

"And you?" she asked.

"Oh, perhaps a dram of Writers Tears."

"You prefer Irish Whiskey?" she asked.

"No, but I do like Writers Tears." He smiled easily at her.

The waiter approached and Jonathan ordered their drinks.

When he'd left with a "Very good," Jonathan said, "What drew you to Madison Ashley? Why a dating service?"

Susan paused for a moment, thinking. "I think it's the adventure," she said simply. "And meeting new people. I'm very social."

The waiter arrived with their glasses and carefully set them on the table. Jonathan nodded to him, and he withdrew. An instrumental version of "Masquerade" was playing in the background.

"Social," he said. "Yes, I can see that."

"I don't have much opportunity to meet new people," she lied. "My husband works constantly, and then we have to attend the company dinners and such. But it's mostly the same crowd. And I'm the boss's wife."

"Sure," said Jonathan. He sipped some whiskey.

"So from there, it's tough to form real relationships," she said. "Too many strings attached."

Jonathan nodded.

"But let's not talk about that right now," she continued.

"All right. What do you prefer?"

"I prefer that we finish these drinks and go to your room," she said. "We can continue to get acquainted there."

Jonathan nodded slightly, looked at his drink and took another sip.

"What color are your underwear?" he asked politely, with a gentle smile.

She raised an eyebrow. Then she said, "You'll see."

* * *

The heavy, wooden door closed slowly and with almost no sound. Susan looked around the room for a moment, and then walked to the King-sized bed and set her purse on the bedside table.

Jonathan smiled.

Susan looked at him for a moment, and then reached back over her shoulders with both hands and pulled the black dress up over her head. She then laid it over the winged back chair near the window. She was dressed in high heels, seamed hose, a garter belt, and a bra and matching Brazilian-cut panties. "They're red," she said.

He admired her taut body and her firm stomach. "Are you claiming that side of the bed?" he asked.

She smiled. "I'm claiming the whole thing," she said.

* * *

Susan Del Gato leaned forward, hunching slightly, and dropped her small breasts into the red bra she was holding, then she hooked it with the clasp. She sat on the edge of the bed, her back to Jonathan. She smiled to herself.

"That was delightful," he said.

Susan said nothing, but began to slip the short black dress over her head, her back to him.

Jonathan shrugged to himself and sat up, looking around for his suit. It was folded neatly on a chair near the bed. He stood and went over to it.

"Are you interested in meeting again?" she asked, still facing away from him, toward the window.

"Yes, I think so," he said. He was nodding.

She fitted and smoothed her dress, and ran her fingers through her hair. Then she took her jewelry from the bedside table and began to put it back on. She turned and looked toward him.

"There was a certain fit to it," she started. "A good experience for all, I hope." She said it as if they had been test driving a new car, possibly a Lamborghini.

He nodded, buttoning his shirt.

She slipped on her shoes. "I'll be going, now," she said, unnecessarily.

"Let's stay in touch," he said, absently.

* * *

Zeke knocked on the door of the apartment and heard a scampering from inside.

"Who's there?" A male voice, raspy and young sounding, came from inside.

"I'm here to talk with Judith Henderson. I called ahead, and she's expecting me," he said through the door.

Silence. Then, from inside in a louder voice, "Judy. There's someone here to see you."

The door remained closed for about twenty seconds, and then it was pulled open by a young girl with short brown hair and a green and red tattoo on her neck.

"Yeah?" she said.

"I'm Zeke. I called you earlier," he said with a big smile. "About the student loan thing." Discounting it as if it were a small matter.

"Yeah. I'm Judy. Come on in, I'm cooking bacon. We can talk in the kitchen."

Zeke followed her through the small living area and into the galley-style kitchen. He noticed two prescription drug bottles on an end table and an ashtray full of cigarette butts and a few smoked joints on the coffee table. The owner of the male voice was nowhere to be seen.

"Who're you with, again?"

"I'm an auditor," he said. "Independent."

"But Dr. Richardson said there wouldn't be any trouble. That I wouldn't have to pay it back." She sort of whined when she talked.

"Paul Richardson, at the college?" asked Zeke.

"Yeah. They sent me to talk to him when I dropped out of my classes. He's in charge of the money," she explained.

Zeke nodded.

The smell of hot bacon grease and hemp was strong in the small kitchen. Judy started turning the bacon. There was bacon grease splattered on the stovetop and on a burning joint resting on the edge of the plate that held the cooked bacon.

"Why'd you decide to drop out?" Zeke asked, pleasantly.

She paused and looked at him. "You don't look like an auditor," she said.

"I'm just helping out with this one," said Zeke disarmingly.

Judy thought for a moment and then nodded to herself. "So what do you want to know?" she asked.

"Why you dropped out this semester."

"Oh, school's a drag," she said.

"How did you find out about the student loan money?" Zeke asked with a sincere expression.

"Um, I think someone at the school brought it up." She thought. "Yeah, it was Eddie George. We call him 'Fast Eddie' because he's always got an angle going. You know?"

"You buy your weed from him?" Zeke asked.

"Sure," said Judy. "Everybody does. Well, things slowed down a little when Peter was shot."

"So Eddie approached you about this?"

"Yeah," she said, and took a drag on the joint. "I got hungry from the weed, so I thought I'd cook up some bacon." Then she shouted, "Hey, Hank, you ready for some breakfast?"

She took the bacon out of the pan and turned and blotted it on a paper towel and set it on the plate. Then she put the last of the raw bacon in the pan.

"A cast iron pan works best," she said. "My grandma gave me this one."

"What did Eddie tell you about the student loan thing?" asked Zeke, again.

"Well, he was at my dorm and we got to talking about how my Dad really wants me to go to Raleigh College. It's where he went. He calls it his 'alma mater,' really sappy-like."

Zeke nodded.

"But I'm not really into it. Maybe in a few years, I guess."

"What happened?"

"Well, I was saying, you know, that I wasn't really into my classes this year, and that I was probably going to drop one or two, or even withdraw," she said. "Eddie said that I could do that and make some money, too. That sounded good."

"How did it work out?" asked Zeke.

"Well, I was already enrolled for this semester, and I had my Student Loan papers in to the school. But you have a couple weeks at the beginning of the semester where you can add or drop classes, you know," she continued. "So as soon as I got the loan approved, Eddie told me to drop all my classes, all but one. So I did."

"Was there much money in it?" Zeke asked.

"Well, it's a private school, so my tuition was something like fifty thousand dollars a year. That's crazy, right?"

Zeke nodded. *So the loan was probably about $18,000 a semester,* he thought.

"So Eddie helped me with the timing of everything, and he gave me a thousand dollars, cash."

"Was Eddie alone?" asked Zeke.

"Well, sometimes Peter Vartis came with him. He's the one who was murdered in his car," she explained. She shook her head.

"Did you have to talk with Dr. Richardson?" asked Zeke, reminding the girl.

"Oh, yeah, Eddie coached me for that, too. And Dr. Richardson explained how it all works, how the debt will go away."

"Did he say that it would 'go away?'"

Judy bit her lip. "He said, uh, it will be 'forgiven'. That was the term he used."

"Don't you think you'll have to pay the loan back?" asked Zeke.

"No, they don't care about that. The government just writes it off or something. Nobody really loses money or anything," Judy said. "I saw how it works on the Internet."

Hank walked into the kitchen wearing a large football jersey and boxer shorts. He had a scraggly brown beard that refused to fill in and brown eyes, and he wasn't much taller than Judy Henderson. He reached across Zeke proprietarily and took a piece of bacon from the plate on the counter.

"Sorry," said Zeke. "I'll get out of your way. Judy, I'll call your cell phone if we need anything else, OK?"

The girl nodded, still watching the cooking meat.

Zeke let himself out.

* * *

There was a warm breeze blowing lightly across the campus as Zeke entered the University of Raleigh Administration Building. The audit project had been extended a few days and Zeke nodded to Cheryl, who was sitting behind an administrative desk outside of Dr. Richardson's office.

He hasn't been around for the past four days, thought Zeke. He's ducking me.

To Cheryl, he said, "Is Dr. Richardson in today?"

"He had a meeting off campus," the girl replied, checking a

calendar page on her desk. "A lunch thing and then something with some donors, I think."

"I'll just help myself to the coffee, if that's OK," said Zeke.

Zeke set his backpack in the conference room and went in search of the coffee. The break room, down the hall from Dr. Richardson's office, was well equipped. A fresh pot of coffee from the smell of it was warming on a burner.

Back in the conference room, Zeke pulled the stack of files toward him and sat. He retrieved a pad and pen from his backpack and began making notes from the files.

Two hours and fifteen minutes later, the coffee was gone and Zeke stood and stretched, aware that the secretarial pool had full visibility of the conference room through the glass walls. He rolled his shoulders and walked across the hallway toward the area that housed the men's room, not far from Dr. Richardson's office.

Once out of site of the administrative area, Zeke detoured slightly to the Vice President of Finance's office door. It was shut and locked tight, and there was no sign of anyone nearby. Zeke had noted that the staff generally disappeared during the noon hour, and particularly when Richardson was away.

Ten seconds with a lock pick released the door lock. *Almost as fast as it takes with the key,* Zeke thought. He shut the door behind him and pulled the slatted blinds the rest of the way closed.

Zeke started up the desktop computer on Richardson's desk and inserted a thumb drive in the USB port. He copied a file onto the computer desktop and ejected the thumb drive. It went back into his pocket.

A few keystrokes later, the computer's microphone and monitor-based camera were available for outside control. The software deactivated the LED light indicator located near the camera and allowed it to be controlled remotely, via its Internet connection.

Zeke made a mental note, confirming the computer's IP address, deleted the thumb drive file from the desktop and powered down the computer. He wiped the keyboard with a small micro cloth and exited the office, locking the door behind him.

* * *

"I'm looking for Edward George," said Zeke with an ingratiating smile. The girl at the information desk returned it warmly.

"Sure, let me see if he's listed here," she said, tapping some keys on her computer keyboard. "Just a sec."

Zeke was at the information desk in the main Administration Building of Raleigh University. The sign over the desk read, "Student Services."

"Here we go," said the girl. She was rather plain looking and young, maybe a sophomore, certainly an undergraduate. Her blonde hair was clipped back on each side and she wore a print blouse with a bow at the neck. She wore no makeup.

She gave Zeke the requested information and a campus map to help him find Eddie George's current classroom.

Zeke looked at the computer monitor and saw a profile picture of the boy.

The girl added, casually, "We're not supposed to give this information out, really."

Zeke said, "It's OK, I'm an auditor." Which seemed to give her some level of comfort.

"You are?" she asked. "What's your name?"

That was clever, thought Zeke, revising his opinion of the girl. "I'm Zeke Traynor. What's your name?"

"Tina Silverson," she said. "I'm usually here working in the afternoons. So, let me know if I can help you with anything."

Zeke smiled, and said, "Thanks."

She looked as if she'd just thought of something. "Here, take a card. That's my number here, if you need me."

* * *

Eddie George, it turned out, was not in his classroom. Instead, he was in the hallway outside of the classroom, exchanging something with two other students. Zeke recognized him from his picture on the Student Services computer.

When Zeke approached the group, one of the boys immediately drifted away, and the other said to Eddie, "OK, see you around, then." He turned and walked away, leaving Eddie and Zeke alone in the hall.

"Are you selling?" asked Zeke with an innocent smile.

"No, man. No, we were just talking. Who're you?"

"Actually, I'm the guy who's looking into the student loan scam you're involved with," said Zeke.

"Don't know what you're saying," said Eddie, still acting

cool under pressure, but starting to touch his face, often a sign of lying.

Zeke looked at him for a long moment. "Judy Henderson said you helped her with her student loans. And that you paid her to drop out this semester," Zeke said.

"No, man, it wasn't like that. I lent her some cash after she dropped out, you know, until she could find a place to stay and some work. Just helping a friend out."

"How many other friends did you help out this semester?" Zeke asked.

"Look, man, I don't have to listen to this," said Eddie. He turned and started to walk away.

"What about Peter. Peter Vartis?" asked Zeke.

Eddie George stopped walking. He turned around. "Yeah, I knew him," he said, now sounding shaken.

"Judy said that you guys were close. That you both helped her with her loan situation."

"Well, maybe so. She was working against a deadline and asked us for assistance, you know?" It was a question, but he wasn't asking.

"The way this goes, Eddie, is that you end up jammed up for student loan fraud and a few other Federal charges. Repayment plus jail time, I'd expect. Unless whoever killed Peter starts thinking you'll roll over on them, make a deal. Then they'll kill you first," said Zeke.

"Don't know what you're talking about, man," said the student, now visibly shaken.

"Think about it," said Zeke. "You can reach me at this

number." He handed Eddie a card with a phone number on the back.

* * *

The voice was smooth and soothing.

"I know, dear, I can't wait to see you again, too," said Dr. Richardson, seductively. "I have something special for you."

Zeke rolled his eyes. He was sitting on the edge of Clive's hotel room desk, watching and listening to the live feed from Richardson's computer. The Vice President of Finance at Raleigh University was at his desk, chatting up a female voice on his cell phone, all of which was being captured by the camera and microphone located in his desktop computer.

"Well, yes, we can meet tomorrow if you'd like. I'll have to clear a couple things from my schedule... You know that Thursdays are better for me," he said with a small touch of annoyance in his voice. He looked at his day planner for a moment, then picked up a pencil and made a notation.

Zeke heard a tapping sound, knuckles on wood.

"Just a moment," he said. Then, "Yes, Cheryl?"

"Dr. Richardson," the voice echoed from across the room, "Dean Worthington called me. He's been trying to reach you on your cell phone."

He nodded toward the door and said to the woman on the phone, "OK, tomorrow for lunch. Wednesday." Zeke heard a cell phone beep, signaling the end of a call. On the monitor, they watched Richardson as he dialed his phone. In a much more professional voice he said, "Hello, this is Dr. Richardson."

He nodded and waited and nodded again, as if the person he was speaking with could see his physical affirmations.

Then he said, "When will this happen?"

A pause. "Friday," he repeated. "OK."

He listened and said, "Are you sure they'll be able to take care of the problem this time?"

Zeke smiled and pointed to his chest. "I'm the problem, I'd wager," he said to Clive.

Clive smiled and said, "You usually are."

"Alright, then. Thank you," said Richardson in his professional voice.

* * *

"It looks as though we've stirred up a hornet's nest," said Clive.

"Indeed," said Zeke. They sat together at a small table in the Elephant and Castle, the restaurant's Boston location, Clive lunching on Steak and Mushroom Pie. Zeke had a large cup of coffee.

"I expect that you'll queer their pitch," Clive continued.

"Just like last time," said Zeke, nodding.

"The bug in Richardson's office came in handy." Clive tasted some pie and nodded to himself. "Good to be tipped off about these things."

"We knew they'd try again, though," said Zeke. "Particularly with me hanging about at the school like an unwelcome relative."

"And while you're there…" said Clive, wryly.

"I guess I need to talk with Jobare Worthington, also."

Clive nodded, his mouth full of steak and gravy. He swallowed and said, "So your next move is…?"

"I think I'll advance their time line," Zeke said.

Clive raised an eyebrow.

"Today is Tuesday. I don't see any reason to wait until Friday to find out what they're planning. Do you?"

Clive shook his head. "No, I'm not one for waiting around either."

"I'll return to Cambridge this afternoon and chat with Dr. Richardson at lunch tomorrow," Zeke said.

Clive looked quizzical. "But he has a lunch date tomorrow."

"Exactly," said Zeke.

Chapter 14

"Darling, you look stunning."

Sheila Carson was wearing a dark blue dress with white piping accents and black heels. As always, she looked both elegant and distant, and the effect wasn't lost on Dr. Paul Richardson. He stood as she approached the table.

Tuscano's was a discrete restaurant, located on Brattle Street, out of the way and high-end, which assured that he wouldn't run into any of his students there. He always requested a table in the back, away from the windows. He felt that it gave him more control. If Sheila had noticed, she'd never mentioned it.

He gave Sheila a quick hug, putting his hand proprietarily on her derriere for a moment, pulled her chair out to seat her, and sat back down at the table next to her. The maitre d' had followed Sheila across the restaurant, but eased away when he saw their embrace. A waiter appeared discreetly and poured Sheila a glass of Cabernet Sauvignon from the bottle chilling on the table.

"Did I keep you waiting long?" she asked.

"No, no, I just arrived," said Richardson, his eyes sparkling. "It's so good to see you."

"Paul, you'll make me blush," Sheila said, adding in a whisper, "I know you're just here for the sex."

"Oh, no, I assure you there's much more," said Dr. Richardson, the charm turned up to full volume. "I so look forward to these lunches."

"And what follows," she added.

"Of course, of course, but you mean so much to me…"

At that moment, the chair opposite Sheila Carter was pulled out and suddenly occupied. Dr. Richardson, surprised, turned his head away from the woman and toward their visitor.

"You," he said. "The auditor. What are you doing here?" He seemed puzzled at first, and then he became nervous.

"Well, I've completed the audit," said Zeke. He turned to the woman sitting across from him. "Hello. I'm Zeke Traynor."

Sheila Carter looked away and said nothing.

"I'm sorry to interrupt this tryst," Zeke continued. "You both look like you need it. But I believe Dr. Richardson has some information I need."

"Can't this wait?" asked Richardson.

"Until Friday?" asked Zeke. "When they plan to kill me? I don't think so."

Sheila was taken aback. Seeing the stakes rise quickly, she stood suddenly, tipping her chair. She caught it before it fell, then quickly walked to the front door and out onto the street.

"What?" asked Dr. Richardson. Clearly upset, his mouth opened and closed twice. "What?"

"I know the 'what'," Zeke said. "So, what's important now is the who, the where and the when."

"This is ridiculous," said Dr. Richardson, louder, looking around the room for help.

"Hmm," said Zeke. He lifted the wine bottle from the table-top wine cooler and in a quick move, jammed the mouth of the bottle hard into Richardson's diaphragm. Then Zeke replaced the bottle carefully.

Richardson, surprised, coughed and wheezed and clutched his chest. He made breathless noises through his nose and mouth. Zeke waited patiently, a concerned look on his face. A waiter noticed Richardson and came to the table.

"Is he alright?" the waiter asked Zeke.

"I don't know. I hope it's not a heart attack," said Zeke.

Richardson, recovering somewhat, looked at the waiter and started shaking his head and coughing.

"Perhaps he has something in his throat?" asked Zeke.

Richardson flailed and then shook his head again, starting to gain control of his breathing. His face was red and blotchy. Zeke reached over and loosened Richardson's tie.

"I guess he'll be OK," Zeke said.

The waiter said, "Should I call an ambulance?"

Again, Richardson, coughing, shook his head no.

The waiter drifted away, still watching Dr. Richardson from a distance. Richardson was gathering himself.

"You'll need to tell me who, where and when," Zeke repeated quietly.

"They'll kill me," said Richardson, his voice a croak. "You

have no idea," he paused and took a short breath, "who you're dealing with."

"Enlighten me," said Zeke.

"I can't," said Richardson. "All I know is Friday."

"All you know?"

"They didn't say. Just that it will be taken care of. Friday."

"Tell me from the beginning," Zeke said. "You're already in a lot of trouble. The Feds will be looking for you soon, I'm sure." *Because I've arranged it,* thought Zeke.

"No, no, it's them, they caused it. They gave me no choice, you see," he said. "They used blackmail."

"You and Sheila Carson?"

"You know her name? Apparently there aren't any secrets anymore," said Richardson bitterly.

Zeke looked at him.

"They did it. They made me write the checks and they took the money. It was for student tuition, but they made the students quit and they took the refunds."

Zeke thought for a moment. He noticed that Dr. Richardson, typically very self-involved, was beginning to distance himself. *Fewer "I's" and "me's" in his conversation,* thought Zeke, *and more "they" and "them's."* Richardson was lying. Or at least steeply shading the truth.

"You don't go around killing people," Richardson continued, his voice still raspy.

Minimal self-referencing, thought Zeke. *He's lying about his involvement, now. He knows a lot more.*

Zeke nodded expectantly.

"I don't know what else to tell you," said Richardson.

"How much money?"

"Oh, not that much," said Richardson, looking around again. "You have to understand, they've been doing this for years…"

"Who's your contact?" asked Zeke.

"No, I can't say. They'll kill me, too. They're the mob."

Zeke nodded, as if this was an acceptable response.

"You don't care if your wife finds out about Sheila Carter?" asked Zeke.

Richardson looked at him. "No, you wouldn't do that…"

"Every Thursday since last April 6th, with a couple days off when you were out of town. Would you like to see the hotel receipts?"

"OK, OK. It was Jobare Worthington. He's my contact," said Richardson. "I don't know who else is involved."

"Right," said Zeke, empathetically. "Where would I find him?"

"He's the Dean of the Liberal Arts College at Raleigh University. He's the one with the mob contacts. Look, I've told you what I know. Can you let me go, now?"

Zeke stood and said, "Stand up, Dr. Richardson. You're under arrest." Two FBI agents, dressed as servers, made their way to the table and stood Richardson to his feet. One cuffed him and read him his rights as the second frisked him for weapons.

The patrons at Tuscano's were watching now, most uncomfortable and feeling awkward. The FBI agents walked

Richardson out. As Paul Richardson exited the front door, he saw Sheila Carson standing with a female officer just outside the restaurant; she, too, was handcuffed and obviously ashamed.

* * *

"You know about Luis and how it went down?" Susan asked.

"Unfortunately, yes," said Benito Diaz. "He was set up by the police."

Susan shook her head slowly. "And now you want me to clean up the mess?"

"I do," said Diaz. "Both messes." He smiled an insincere smile, which she saw on her side of the Skype connection. "But you and Luis have let me down."

"Luis is in jail," Susan commented. "But he won't give you up."

"No, he won't," said Diaz. "I would much rather talk with you face to face," he continued.

"I remember," said Susan. "But I'm in Boston, and you're, where, Scottsdale?"

"It's a matter of the timing," Diaz continued. He ignored her interruption because he needed her, now.

"You sent me with Luis as backup," she continued. "And now, I'm the primary."

"Yes," said Diaz. "It has to happen tomorrow," he continued. "While he's still in Cambridge."

"He hasn't moved on?" she asked.

"He had one of our academic people arrested today, and he's harassing another. He's getting too close."

"Too close to what?" she asked.

"That's our business. But he's getting too close, and we need to shut him down," said Raul Diaz from off screen.

Pig, thought Susan.

Then she said, "I understand. Give me the details. I'll clean up the mess."

* * *

When Benito Diaz had completed his briefing, Susan asked, "How can I get access to the office building he's working in?"

"We'll arrange it," said Benito Diaz. "We'll set it up for this afternoon. What else do you need?"

"I think that's it," said Susan. She knew the money would be deposited in her account, less than $10,000 at a time until it was all there. Diaz was good about taking care of that.

"We'll want to see you when you get back here," said Benito. "To talk."

"Of course," she said. Diaz' obsession with face to face meetings was well known, and was not lost on Susan.

"How are you returning?" continued Diaz.

"I'll drive to Rhode Island and fly out of Providence," she said. "It's only an hour or so from here. The airlines connect in Chicago, and then it's a quick trip home." She didn't mention where 'home' was, and Diaz didn't ask. "I can get over to see you next week," she said, politely.

"Good, yes, let us know when it's done," said Benito Diaz. The screen went blank.

* * *

"Appreciate you joining me on short notice," said Zeke.

"No worries. Clive told me that this might happen," said Kimmy, sitting across from Zeke at the small table. They were at a popular coffee shop in Cambridge, located near Harvard Square.

"It appears to be moving quickly," Zeke said. "Before Richardson was taken away, he mentioned his contact, a Dean at Raleigh University."

"By name?" asked Kimmy. She was sipping on a cup of organic Assam tea, and balancing her smartphone on her knee while they talked. She looked up at Zeke, then down at the phone again.

Zeke nodded. "Jobare Worthington," he said.

"Jobare?" asked Kimmy. "What kind of name is that?"

"No idea," said Zeke.

"Sounds kind of French…" she continued. Then, "So what's the plan?"

"We should chat with the Dean, I think, before the FBI goes looking for him. Richardson will inevitably give him up again, once they get to the interrogations and all. So we have a small window of time."

Kimmy nodded. "How do you want to do it?"

"He's used to authority, I'd think. Being in charge," said Zeke.

Kimmy nodded.

"So let's take that away from him. I'd bet he's pretty fragile without his academic facade.

"OK," said Kimmy, smiling a little bit.

"Let's visit the Dean. At home, where he's more vulnerable. Sally gave us his address. And she said that he usually works from home on Thursdays and Fridays."

* * *

The doorbell on the brownstone rang deep within the brick walls. Zeke could hear it echo for a moment before it stopped. A minute later, a tall, thin man opened the door and said, "Yes?"

"Jobare Worthington?" asked Zeke.

The man bristled. He'd worked through several possible responses and settled on angry.

"What the hell do you want?" he said. "Why are you bothering me?"

That's quite a reaction, thought Zeke.

The man wore small, round glasses without frames and his longish hair was pulled back into a ponytail, held in place with a green rubber band. His jeans were distressed, and his white dress shirt, worn outside the jeans, was crisp and unwrinkled.

"Jobare, we're investigating some student loan fraud. We thought you might want to talk with us about that," said Zeke, staring directly at the academic.

Jobare Worthington stuttered. "Uh, uh, what?" His face reddened. "Who are you?" He was still trying to work up an attack.

"What we'd like to know is this. Who're the brains behind the scam?" said Zeke. "'Cuz it certainly isn't you."

Standing in the doorway, the door propped open, Jobare Worthington turned suddenly and tried to shut the door.

Zeke blocked the door with his shoulder and pushed the Dean back into his living room. He stepped in, and Kimmy followed, closing the door.

"Hey, you can't do that," said Jobare. "You can't come in here like that!"

"But we did," said Kimmy with a smile. "You should sit, before we make you sit," she said pleasantly. Then she walked around the small residence, confirming there was no one else in the home.

Jobare Worthington looked at Kimmy, and then he looked at Zeke. And then he sat down on the small couch and took out his cell phone.

"I'll take that," said Zeke, holding out his hand.

"I'm not scared of you," said Worthington. He snatched the phone back against his body.

Zeke reached in and grabbed Worthington's nose between his index finger and thumb. He twisted it, and the academic cried out in sudden pain. Tears ran from his eyes as he dropped the phone and reached for his face and Zeke's hand.

Zeke let go of Jobare's large nose and deftly picked up the cell phone from the couch cushion where it had fallen.

"Let's see who you were going to call," said Zeke.

Jobare Worthington visibly pouted as he rubbed his nose. "You can't do this!" he said, sounding more outraged than angry.

The number on the face of the phone was a local number that Zeke didn't recognize, but he knew the associated name. He mentally noted the number and hit 'cancel' on the screen. The phone reverted to its home screen.

"Who's Roy Calhoun?" asked Zeke, feigning ignorance.

Jobare looked away.

"Why would you call him?"

"You'll see," said Jobare, suddenly more antagonistic. He was still rubbing his nose.

"He's your boss," said Zeke.

Jobare snorted. "No, he's not." Then he shut up. Zeke saw his jaws tighten, a rebellious reaction, as Jobare Worthington became determined to remain silent.

"So, who's behind the student loan scam, Jobare? Who organized it?"

The academic shook his head and pressed his lips tightly together. He looked like an eight-year-old refusing to answer his mother's questions.

"Perhaps you'll be more forthcoming with our friends from the FBI," said Zeke. Kimmy smiled at Jobare Worthington and nodded.

Jobare said nothing, but his expression went from smug to cautious.

"I'm sure they'll be by to visit you in a day or two," said Zeke.

No response from Jobare.

Zeke threw the phone back on the couch, next to Jobare. "We'll let ourselves out," he said.

* * *

Deputy Chief O'Malley shook his head.

"Curiouser and curiouser," he said.

"There's a connection between Worthington and Hanson," said Zeke, jumping ahead.

"Looks like it. Roy doesn't work for anyone except Freddy Hanson," O'Malley said.

"That could be the link between the school and the Student Loan fraud," said Zeke. "Someone in the school has to release the funds at some point. At Raleigh it could be Jobare, a Dean, or it could be Paul Richardson, Vice President of Finance."

"Yes. You think Jobare tried to call for muscle when you barged in on him?"

"Seems right. His ego is the size of Cambridge. I imagine he was both surprised and annoyed that we walked right in. Calling Calhoun was a logical reaction, like siccing his dog or dialing 911."

"He's a prize," said Kimmy.

"Not uncommon in this town," said O'Malley. "The big ego, I mean."

"So, do you think that Freddy Hanson is behind the Student Loan fraud?" asked Zeke, guiding the conversation.

"Doubt it," said O'Malley, shaking his head. "He's not organized enough. I guess there could be another explanation."

"He could be aware of it peripherally, I suppose," said Zeke. "Maybe he lets others run the show in return for a cut. It's a very sophisticated scam, and it's being done in his territory."

"That sounds reasonable," said O'Malley. "I could see that. Maybe he supplies the local muscle, protection for a piece of the action."

"So, we need to chat with Freddy Hanson next, I suppose," Zeke said.

"Do what you want," said O'Malley. "But be careful of that group. They'd just as soon kill you as talk with you. And they seem to know how to dispose of the bodies."

* * *

Susan stood at the hotel window, looking down on the Charles River. She knew that her own window of opportunity would be small, and that her accuracy would have to be almost perfect. It didn't bother her.

After the Mara's had failed in their attempt to kill Zeke and Kimmy, Benito Diaz had communicated with the Boston mobster, Freddy Hanson, clearing the East Coast action. Then Diaz had dispatched Susan. She considered Hanson an amateur, and Susan insisted that Diaz keep her identity private. She didn't want or need local backup. She was more comfortable working solo, fending for herself, even in unfamiliar surroundings.

The plan had come to her quickly when she realized this Zeke Traynor would continue his audits at Raleigh University, as Jobare Worthington had told Freddy Hanson, and Hanson had shared with Diaz. She was certain that she could find a moment to kill him. A moment would be all she needed.

The trickiest part would be the escape, as always. She decided to avoid traffic, so she planned for an early afternoon killing, well before the Boston rush hour. Jobare had also provided Traynor's temporary working location in the Administration Building, in the Finance Department's conference room.

Susan entered the building and signed in with the security Guard. Then she walked the floor of the Finance Department Thursday afternoon after confirming that Traynor wasn't in the building. She committed the building's floor plan to memory and found, in a casual way, the restroom and breakroom locations.

She checked out the aging security guard, who was sitting at his lobby post. Then she casually attached a small video camera to the wall near the women's room door, pointing it across the hall toward the entry door to the Finance Office. The camera sent video via 4G and was linked to an app on her cell phone.

Outside, she circled the building on the sidewalk and noticed the electrical panel and utilities access points. The fire alarm system was next to them in a padlocked metal box.

She took out her cell phone and dialed one of the administration offices listed on the building's lobby directory. She made an appointment for the following afternoon at two fifteen PM. By then, she planned to be on her way to Rhode Island. But the appointment would give her credibility, a reason to be in the building if she were stopped or questioned.

Having finished her preparations, Susan returned to her hotel room. She sat on the bed for a moment. Then she dialed a number on her cell phone.

"Hello?" asked a male voice.

"You know who this is," she said. "Are you available?"

"I am, coincidentally," said Jonathan. "I can get out for a little while."

* * *

At one fifteen on Friday afternoon, Susan stepped into the Administration Building along with a small group of women returning from their lunch break. Wearing a visitor's badge, she passed the security guard's desk and walked to a door marked Finance Department. Across the hall from the door were men's and women's restrooms, their doors recessed in an alcove. Through the glass door, Susan visually confirmed that Zeke was in the Finance Conference room, and then she ducked into a stall in the women's restroom to wait.

* * *

"Do you need anything, Mr. Traynor?" asked Cheryl.

"No, I'm good, Cheryl," Zeke said. There had been a time of chaos after Dr. Richardson's arrest, but no one seemed to have put Zeke and Richardson together, so he continued with the faux audit, planning to finish the show this week.

Cheryl lingered in the doorway for a moment.

"You're wrapping it up?" she asked.

"I am," said Zeke, and he turned his attention to her and gave her a smile.

"I thought we might get a coffee or something," she continued, leaving the invitation hanging.

"Sure," said Zeke. "Let me just finish this up and I can take a break. Say thirty minutes?"

"OK, great," she said. Cheryl smiled and started back to her desk.

At that moment, all the lights in the building went off, and simultaneously the burglar alarm and fire alarm began sounding. Zeke immediately took his handgun and flashlight from his briefcase and slid down to the floor near the conference table.

In fact, Zeke had decided to spend most of Friday in the Finance Office in order to provide an easy target for the assassin. The loss of power, combined with the sounding alarms, was an obvious prelude to an attack.

* * *

From inside the women's restroom, Susan waited the ten seconds until the emergency backup power kicked on, then checked her phone again. The wide-angle camera she'd planted just outside the restroom was positioned to monitor the entire hallway, including the door to the Finance Office. She watched patiently while several administrative people and some students walked down the hall briskly toward the outside exit door.

A few moments later, the office door opened and Zeke stepped out, accompanied by a younger blonde woman carrying a laptop computer. They turned toward the same outside exit door, away from Susan, and walked down the hall.

Got him, Susan thought.

She eased out of the restroom and looked around as if confused while smoothing her skirt. She was wearing a box cut dress that was designed to make her look more matronly and blend in with the academic theme of the campus. Her hair was pulled back in a simple ponytail.

The explosives seem to have worked, she thought. Before entering the building, Susan had attached two small charges to the building walls. One was designed to interrupt the power at the service entrance, and the other set off the alarms.

Susan stepped into the hall and walked briskly toward the exit door. Outside, she looked around at the gathering crowd. Most were standing in small groups, away from the building, watching and chatting.

Then Susan walked closer to where Zeke was waiting and stood about six feet behind him and to his left, in a group of people. From an outside pocket, she took a small syringe filled with a clear liquid and concealed it in her right hand.

The liquid was sulfuric acid taken from a twelve-volt car battery. *Sulphuric acid loves water,* Susan thought. *And we're all 70% water. The acid unites with water molecules in organic substances and decomposes them completely.* She knew that the effect of this liquid on the human body is burning heat and destruction of any tissues it encounters. Susan smiled.

Susan automatically repositioned the syringe horizontally across her palm with the needle toward her little finger, and closed her hand. With this grip she could strike a downward blow to the neck or shoulders, or a more subtle jab to the arm or torso. Her thumb rested on the plunger. The needle was sturdy, made of surgical grade stainless steel and was unlikely to break from the vial. She gripped it tightly.

Zeke was talking on his cell phone as Susan stepped forward as if to pass him and swung her arm easily to make contact. The blow, aimed for the side of his neck, travelled about half way to its target and stopped.

Susan, who had looked away casually, thinking about her escape, was taken by surprise and quickly refocused her hand holding the syringe. Wrapped around her wrist with a painful grip were Kimmy's strong hands.

"What…" she stuttered, a question on her face, immediately feigning innocence. Kimmy twisted smartly and suddenly Susan's arm was locked behind her, high between her shoulder blades. The sudden pain caused her to drop the needle.

"No, stop," she said loudly as the needle fell to the ground. "I'm diabetic. That's my insulin. I need it."

When Zeke turned and joined Kimmy, Susan was flat on the ground, her wrists secured with steel handcuffs. Kimmy knelt with one knee on the woman's ear to keep her in place while they searched her pockets. Within a minute, a dozen Cambridge police officers surrounded the small group, their weapons drawn.

"Hands up," said the ranking officer. "Put your hands up."

Zeke and Kimmy remained kneeling, but lifted their hands to waist height.

"We're law enforcement," said Kimmy. "This woman is a

killer." She pointed to her Federal ID, now hanging from her breast pocket.

The officer in charge, still pointing his gun at them, signaled to another officer who stepped closer and eased the ID packet from her shirt pocket. He backed away and handed the ID to the ranking officer, who looked at it and said, "OK, at ease, men." Then to Zeke he said, "We've been standing by. O'Malley at BPD told us what to watch for."

"Thank you," said Kimmy.

Zeke slowly extracted his Federal ID and showed it to the cop, who nodded.

"We'll take care of this one. You two come with us," said the officer, and he nodded to two of his men who circled behind Zeke and Kimmy and took possession of the restrained woman.

CHAPTER 15

"What do you mean, she escaped?" asked Kimmy in a voice louder than was necessary. The female police officer who had delivered the news looked at her feet in sudden embarrassment, then rallied and returned her gaze to Zeke.

"You're kidding," said Zeke.

They had been in another area of the Cambridge PD building, being interviewed separately by two sets of detectives. Once their affiliation with Clive Greene and The Agency had been confirmed, the interviewers had visibly relaxed. Their statements were taken and they were ushered into a breakroom, waiting to be released.

Kimmy, sitting at a small table, a cup of black tea in front of her, stood abruptly and bumped the table, sloshing some of the tea over the rim of the cup. "How long ago?" she asked.

"It couldn't have been more than fifteen minutes," said the officer. Her nametag read "Branson."

"What happened?" asked Zeke, shaking his head.

"Her attorney showed up," said Officer Branson. "A

woman. She seemed to know that the perp was here and insisted on seeing her. I don't know if she'd ever made her phone call…"

"And?" asked Kimmy.

"And the officers let her talk with the attorney," started Branson.

"Why? What was the rush?" Kimmy asked, a bit more aggressively.

"I wasn't there, but the officers in charge thought it would be OK. They put them in an interview room." Then she added, "We don't get very many violent crimes in this station. This is Cambridge, not South Boston."

"How'd she escape?" asked Zeke.

"Switched clothes with the attorney," said Officer Branson. "She took the briefcase and just walked out of the precinct." Branson wasn't looking at either of them, now.

"That must have been planned," said Zeke. "It was too quick. What do you know about the attorney?"

"Blonde woman, about the same age and the same look as the perp. She took the perp's clothing and handcuffs and put them on and sat in the interview room quietly until one of our guys went in to get her. Then she said she'd been threatened, that the perp told her she'd have her family killed if she didn't help her escape."

"You still have the attorney in custody?" asked Zeke.

"Yep."

"You've arrested her for aiding and abetting?" asked Zeke.

"Yep. And as an accessory after the fact."

"Has anyone gone after the killer?" asked Kimmy, getting loud again.

"Yes, right away, we've got guys all over the streets looking for her," said Branson.

* * *

"Yes?" asked the deep voice on the other end of the phone call.

"Benny, this is your Boston connection," said Susan. "This is a burner phone but we're not secure."

"Then why did you call?" he asked simply.

"I need your help," she admitted. "I'm on the street."

"You're out. Good. I will call you back in a minute." He hung up.

He's switching to a burner, too, thought Susan. She waited thirty seconds, and then her phone rang.

"Yes?" she asked.

"This is about as good as we can do," said Benito Diaz. "Don't use names."

"OK. You are aware of where I was?"

"Yes, of course. We sent our friend to see you," said Diaz.

"Thank you," said Susan.

"Did she equip you?" he asked.

"Yes, money, credit card and I.D. I bought this phone."

Benito Diaz waited.

"Can you call and get me a ride?" Susan asked.

"I'll call an Uber for you," he said. "Be looking for him downtown. He'll call you directly to arrange the pickup."

Susan knew that the Uber Benito Diaz was referring to would be someone in Freddy Hanson's organization. "Very good, thank you," she said.

* * *

"Thank you for coming to get me," said Susan politely. "I would like a ride to Providence."

The man behind the wheel nodded sharply and said, "About an hour and a half. Do you need to stop, first?" He looked at her in the mirror.

Susan shook her head slightly. She had bought and changed into some light jogging gear and had her blonde hair pulled into a ponytail, held back with a rubber band. Her fluorescent green running shoes set off her black and green top and black tights, and she was wearing no makeup. She carried a small backpack, almost purse size, with nylon strings for her arms.

"Where do you want me to drop you?" asked the driver.

She hesitated, used to sharing as little information as possible. But this was different. "The airport," she replied.

"Which airline?"

"No, General Aviation," she said. "It's a private plane."

The driver shrugged and turned his attention to the road. He was a large, swarthy looking man, dressed in dark colors and wearing his shirt out, over his belt. He wore dark sunglasses and a Red Sox baseball cap. Susan had never seen him before.

Twenty minutes into the drive, the driver said, "So you're the killer, huh?"

She looked at him, thinking, *What a breech of protocol!* But she said nothing, as if she hadn't heard the question.

He looked back at her, in the rear view mirror, but she was looking out the side window.

"How'd you get a job like that?" He pushed the subject.

Susan rolled her eyes to herself, but said nothing. She had, in fact, achieved the position inadvertently, almost by accident.

When she didn't answer he looked away and said, "Bitch," under his breath.

Susan wasn't overly attracted to men. She had married young, and she had chosen poorly. Her husband, Manny, came from humble beginnings. His father was a petty thief in Cuba until 1980, when Castro emptied the prisons and sent the Mariel boat lift north to Florida. His mother had worked in a cigar factory, packaging Cuban Cigars for export.

They had all escaped the island with about 135,000 other Marielitos and at first had assimilated into Miami's Cuban community along with Santeria followers, criminals, and the mentally ill, mixed in with honest citizens. Manny's mother was killed when the boat she was crossing on capsized, only a few miles from the Florida Keys.

Manny's father, Javier, had been on a different boat with the boy. Once ashore, he quickly found his way to the Cuban community in Miami and was hired as an enforcer and collector by some of his former Cuban prison acquaintances. But mostly he drank rum and played dominoes in the park.

A few years later, Manny's father moved himself and his boy to join the Cuban community in Chicago. There had been a position that opened up with the Chicago mob, and it was offered to Javier.

The position was actually with a relative of the gangster Paul Ricca, a first cousin twice removed to the mobster. Ricca had been fond of Cuba in his time, escaping from Naples, Italy in 1920 and arriving in New York by way of Cuba. He had a history of running Cuban whiskey to Chicago during prohibition, and Ricca went on to be an important Capo in the U.S. Mafia.

Ricca had died ten years earlier, but the first cousin had taken over after the old man's funeral, and had established himself. After the boatlift, he'd sent for Javier and given him responsibilities in Chicago and the Midwest. The position was short-lived, however, and Javier's propensity for alcohol and women ended his life. He died of a gunshot wound, drunk and in bed with his employer's mistress.

Surprisingly, there was an inheritance and an insurance policy, which was enough to keep the son, Manny, now alone and unemployed, in alcohol and pills to the point that his sense of reality twisted in circles like a cyclone.

After her mother became sick, Susan, also in Chicago, was never enrolled in school. She was left to manage herself most all day, every day, while her father gambled and waited for another assignment from his bosses. She quickly found trouble, from petty theft to selling drugs, and she became an accomplished con woman as a teen. She bounced around from thing to thing for years, aimless, until she met Manny.

Manny was five years her senior, and seemed worldly and

wise. To a sixteen-year-old girl, his charm and dark Latino looks were alluring, and when at a neighborhood party he focused them on her, she was captivated. Over the ensuing months they became inseparable. Smitten, Susan would do whatever he asked of her.

Manny, numbed by the drugs, had developed a sense of self that included casual cruelty and an extreme level of self-importance, which later morphed into a self-indulgence that bordered on the narcissistic. Initially, Susan was enamored by the handsome young man with the deep brown eyes, the inexhaustible wealth, and the untamed sex drive. He seemed to command the respect of everyone around him, which was an aphrodisiac to the young girl.

"Here, take this," he'd said to her when they first started dating.

"What is it?" She looked at the small capsules with uncertainty.

"No, it's fine. I want you to take them so we can enjoy the party. I took some already," he said.

"Upper or downer?" asked Susan.

"It's a benny. Amphetamine," he said.

The result was that Susan stayed up for the next twenty hours, high on speed and partying. She was on the edge, and life was crisp and colorful and would go on forever. With Manny, she felt like she was a part of something important, something wonderful.

At seventeen, Susan left her father and moved into Manny's apartment. She was mature for her age, a result of her hard life and her confidence from the streets. And she looked older than most girls her age.

Manny bought her jewelry and drugs and clothes that he wanted her to wear, and he wore her on his arm like a Barbie doll. Susan was in love with Manny, and he could do no wrong.

"Let's get married," Susan said one day.

"You're seventeen," said Manny, as if that explained everything.

Susan looked at him. "I have a fake drivers license that says I'm eighteen," she said.

"OK," said Manny. A month later, they were married in a small ceremony by the local parish priest.

The friction started a couple weeks later.

"Where have you been?" Susan asked him one night, when he arrived at the apartment drunk and late.

"I was out," he shouted. This wasn't their first fight. "And it's none of your business what I do."

"You were with someone." Susan sized him up, looking at him, then smelling his shirt. "I told you, I won't put up with that."

Manny turned away and said, "Too bad."

"You're just stupid," said Susan in anger.

He turned back toward her and stared at her for a minute. Then he said, "You're gonna respect me," and he punched her in the stomach, hard.

* * *

"Chica, I have to tell you something," Manny started. His drug use had increased in recent months, and he'd started doing odd jobs for his supplier, in order to stay closer to the source.

Now what? thought Susan. She'd been watching his decline, his slow spiral downward.

"I'm doing some work for Rolando."

Rolando Ortega was Manny's supplier, and he was responsible for about half of the drug distribution in Chicago's Cuban neighborhoods. He was also ruthless and unforgiving.

"What kind of work?" asked Susan. "What are you doing, Manny?"

"Nothing to worry about. You know that Rolando and I go back, right?"

She was silent. She could tell that he was high on something. Probably bennies again.

"What are you getting into?" she asked.

"That's what I'm trying to tell you. I'm doing it for us. Rolando needs some help with his operation. This is a chance to show him what I can do. I can be a part of his organization. I just want what's best for us, Chica," he continued, nuzzling her neck with his face. His beard scratched her skin, but she didn't pull away.

"Manny, you smell like you've been with another woman," Susan said suddenly. She sniffed again.

Manny stepped back, out of range. "No, no," he said. "I was just over at Rolando's apartment. There was a party there."

Rolando lived on the seventeenth floor of one of Chicago's newest high-rise condominiums, with a spectacular view overlooking Lake Michigan. It was one of six residences that he kept, all in other people's names.

"So what are you going to do?" she asked.

"I can really make a name for myself," he said. "Rolando will respect me. I've got it figured out."

* * *

"He wants you to what?" asked Susan, more surprised than disturbed.

"To kill someone," said Manny. They were spread out on their living room couch, lines of coke in orderly rows visible on the glass coffee table.

Manny had done some rough things for Rolando, but as far as Susan knew, he hadn't killed anyone yet.

"Who?" she asked.

"A nobody, no one important," said Manny with a flip of his hand, discounting the potential victim. "Someone who stole from him."

More and more, Manny would stay out late and come home wasted, when he came home at all. He'd become more and more abusive as Susan objected to his lifestyle. They would scream at each other, her angry about the drugs and women in his life, him resisting her interference. Frequently the arguments would turn physical.

"Don't hit me again," she said one day.

Manny looked at her with glassy eyes and screamed, "Puta!" Then he slapped her across the face.

She looked at him, unblinking.

Do I even have a soul? she wondered. Then she shot him.

* * *

"Daddy, I need your help." Susan had called her father immediately, instinctively knowing that she was way over her head.

"Susan?" her father asked. He had lost his wife earlier in the year, and she knew he was alone for the first time in many years. She knew he missed her, as well.

"Daddy, I just shot Manny. He was abusive and he threatened me and he, he slapped me…"

"Is he dead?" asked Frank Del Gato.

"Yes. You taught me how to shoot. He's dead."

"Did anyone hear it?"

"I don't think so. It was a .22. I shot him in the eye."

"OK," said Frank Del Gato. "I'm coming over now. I'm gonna pick up Jimmy and we'll be there in twenty minutes to clean up. You, you're at your apartment? What room is he in?"

"He's in the living room, on the carpet by the fireplace."

"OK, you stay there, but in the bedroom until I get there. Pack a suitcase," he said.

* * *

After that, Susan moved in with her father. And Frank Del Gato seemed to realize that he'd been given a second chance. He made an effort to drink less, and he tried to be home as often as he could. The loss of his wife of almost twenty years seemed to have sobered the man and given him a sense of his own mortality.

The matter with Manny was investigated and Susan, coached by her father, claimed self-defense. Eventually, the Chicago police, unable to gather evidence that could lead to charges against the girl, let the case drop.

Over the next few years, Frank taught Susan everything he knew about killing. And when he retired, she stepped in and took his place.

* * *

General aviation at the Providence, Rhode Island airport was a modern brown building sandwiched between the Fedex terminal and an open hanger. Susan's mob-connected Uber driver pulled into the parking lot. Susan said "Thanks," got out of the car with her backpack and purse, and walked into the building. Inside, there was no one at the reception counter, so she set her bag on a nearby couch and walked to the back of the building. There were a dozen planes on the tarmac and a couple more near the fueling station.

"Can I help?" a woman asked from behind her.

Susan turned and walked back to the counter. "I'm being picked up by someone with Monarch Air," she said. "Private charter."

"What time are you scheduled?" asked the woman, looking at a clipboard.

"Four-thirty," said Susan. "My name is Gloria DuPont."

"OK, I see you on the list, Ms. DuPont. Providence to Pittsburgh International." She looked at her watch. "They should be here to pick you up within a half-hour. Make yourself comfortable. There's coffee and soft drinks in the lounge over there."

* * *

The flight back was uneventful. Susan was using a driver's license she'd bought several years earlier, with matching credit cards and a government I.D. The co-pilot had looked at her driver's license quickly, compared it with the reservation slip stuffed in his flight notebook, and nodded and said, "Welcome aboard, Ms. DuPont."

There were no TSA agents and virtually no security in General Aviation, which made for a quick and comfortable return flight.

CHAPTER 16

"Let's get a change of perspective and talk this through," said Clive Greene. It was late afternoon, and he and Zeke had been reviewing the fallout that resulted from Susan Del Gato's escape from the Cambridge police. "I'm looking at possible relationships, you know."

"Sure. It seems like there are a lot of possible connections, just under the surface," Zeke added.

"First, we know that Jorge Ramirez knew Raul Diaz from when he was in prison," said Clive.

"Ramirez was a prison guard, and Raul was doing time."

"Quite so," said Clive. He was quiet for a minute.

Zeke said, "OK, second. Unrelated, as far as we know, Freddy Hanson is somehow connected to Jobare Worthington and/or Paul Richardson."

"Because of the attempt to, ah, dissuade you in Cambridge? Roy and Louie?"

"Right," said Zeke. "It was cause and effect. I audited, and someone called Hanson to stop me."

"At that point, though, it was probably just threats," said Clive. "That was early on."

"Or threats and a beating. I agree," said Zeke.

"Could have been someone from one of the other schools you visited," said Clive.

Zeke shook his head. "I don't think there was time. I spent time at Raleigh University first. By the time I got around to visiting the other schools, Ray and Louie were already dispatched. I'm sure it took a day or two to contact Freddy Hanson and activate them."

"So most likely, Hanson and, who, Jobare?"

"Or Hanson and both men," said Zeke. "OK, what else?"

"Three attempts on my life," said Zeke, dryly.

"What's the motivation? The source of that?" asked Clive.

"Lots of possibilities, but the chain of events started when I first went to help Ramirez and ICE with the Benito Diaz takedown. Feel like I've had a target on my back since then, with the Mara's, then Luis Cruz. And then there's the woman assassin," said Zeke.

"Yes, the woman who tried to kill you. Where does she fit in? Where did she come from?" asked Clive.

"It's likely that those three attempts originated from the same source," said Zeke. "Think about it… The Mara's were there to stop me, almost as soon as I got there. Almost as soon as they failed, this Luis Cruz character shows up to finish the job."

"But with a different M.O." said Clive.

"Right, but maybe for the same reason. To take pressure off of Diaz and his operation."

"OK," said Clive.

"The woman seems to be a continuation of the same effort," said Zeke. "But very clever."

"Indeed," said Clive.

"I'm going to say that the three assassination attempts were arranged by Benito Diaz. Which means that the killers- and Diaz- are all connected in some way," said Zeke.

"I can see that," said Clive.

"Two more possible connections that I can think of," said Zeke.

"OK," said Clive. Zeke could hear him making notes over the phone line.

"With the Student Loan scam, we've identified some of those involved, but there's got to be more to it. Something at a higher level than we've seen so far," said Zeke. "Some sort of controlling entity that is independent of the schools."

"A brain trust of sorts? A group, perhaps, that put the scam together and has managed to keep it going, and keep it hidden, for years?"

"Yes. Some politically and financially connected entity that's running the scam."

"Could be," said Clive. "They may have something to do with the most recent attempt on your life…"

"That's possible, too," said Zeke. "And here's my last connection, and this one's a stretch, I admit."

"Let's hear it," said Clive with a smile in his voice.

"Based on what's happened so far, you wouldn't need to take it too much further to assume that Benito Diaz and Freddy

Hanson are connected somehow."

"Hanson is a local bloke, though, right? Boston?" asked Clive. "Runs the mob there?"

"I believe so," said Zeke.

"So, he's into prostitution?" asked Clive.

"Most likely that, and drugs. And bookies and protection. The usual," said Zeke.

"Are you thinking what I'm thinking?" asked Clive.

"Probably. Hanson may well get his prostitutes from Diaz."

"Human trafficking. We know Diaz is in that knee deep," said Clive.

"It's a safe bet Hanson does business with Diaz," said Zeke.

"I could see that. So, what's next?"

"Don't know for sure. I think I'll rattle Hanson's cage a bit," said Zeke.

* * *

"Hey, Roy, Roy Calhoun," Zeke called across the crowded bar. "I thought you might be here."

Holding his pool cue, Calhoun looked around for the voice, then stood still looking confused. A moment later, a light of recognition crossed his face. His eyes narrowed. "You," he said. Kimmy jumped up on an empty bar stool.

Zeke, who had edged closer to the thug said, "It is."

The bar was a south side working class joint that had been retrofitted with enough inexpensive television sets to earn the designation of "sports bar." Five of the TV sets were replaying a variety of football games. The sixth was showing the Red Sox hosting someone at Fenway Park. Roy had been playing eight ball with another man.

Zeke and Kimmy had found the place after asking Deputy Chief O'Malley where Freddy Hanson typically held court. The police chief said, "Let me call the Organized Crime guys and I'll call you right back."

"His nickname is 'Handsome Hanson,'" said O'Malley, when he called Zeke back. "But nobody calls him that to his face. OC says Hanson can be found at a place called "Murphy's Law" in South Boston off Dorchester Avenue."

"Then we'll be heading south, paying him a visit," said Zeke.

"I'd be careful with those boyo's," O'Malley had said. "Like I said, they'd just as soon kill you as shake your hand."

Now Roy looked rigid, and several of those watching the pool game around him noticed and followed his gaze. He was staring at Zeke, the pool cue in his right hand. The room had become very quiet.

"So what is it you want?" Calhoun asked.

"Not trouble, Roy. I stopped by to talk with Freddy Hanson."

"About what?" the thin man snarled, becoming more aggressive on his home turf.

"About the attempt to kill me yesterday," said Zeke. Kimmy was sitting on the tall stool and watching the room from behind Zeke.

Roy looked at Zeke for a long moment, and then at his friends. Then he said, "No one's tried to kill you. You'd be dead if they had." This brought a few chuckles from the men around the room.

Zeke smiled. "Well, I still want to talk with Freddy Hanson. Is he back there?" Zeke asked, pointing to the hallway that led to the restrooms and then the back of the bar. He took two steps toward the hallway.

"You don't need to go back there," growled the bartender from behind the bar. He was a large man with long black hair and a matching, messy beard.

Zeke ignored him and continued across the room toward the hallway. Kimmy stepped down from her seat and followed him. The men in the room looked uncertain for a minute, and then they glanced at one another and then at Roy Calhoun. Roy stood his ground, tall and thin and menacing. As Zeke approached, Roy stepped into his path.

"I'm not backing down, this time," said Roy, moving his feet further apart, stabilizing himself.

"Suit yourself," said Zeke.

"I'll wrap this cue around your head," Roy continued, showing off for his audience.

"No, you won't," said Zeke. He was no more than three feet in front of the thin man, now, facing him. "You've got to take a backswing."

"What?" Roy said as he started to swing the cue back in his right hand.

Zeke stepped in close and quickly planted his left foot between Roy's feet. He moved, hooking Roy's ankle with his free foot and pushing, driving the man to the floor, following him down. He felt the wind expelled from Roy's lungs in a burst as he hit the ground with Zeke on top of him.

Ouchi Gari, thought Zeke. *The Great Inner Reap.* "You lose, Roy," said Zeke as he punched the thin man twice in the solar plexus.

Zeke stood and easily took the pool cue from Roy. He looked around the room at the seated men. No one moved. Kimmy was on the other side of the pool table, her Jerico 941 casually in hand, but pointed at the floor.

Zeke nodded to himself, and stepped over Roy Calhoun, toward the hallway. Kimmy followed, watching the room as they left. Past the restrooms, the hallway ran the length of the building, and ended at a solid exterior door. The door was closed and barred shut. *Probably doesn't meet fire code,* thought Zeke.

Between the restrooms and the back door, on the left side of the hallway, Zeke found a closed door that apparently led to the area behind the bar. He knocked on the door and waited a moment, a bit off to the side and out of the path of bullets, should they fly through the door.

"Hear anything?" asked Kimmy.

"No," said Zeke. "But we know Hanson's in there. Otherwise Calhoun and company wouldn't have tried to stop us."

Zeke knocked again, and the door swung open about halfway. Louie Brennan stood in the doorway, looking down at them.

"He takes up the entire doorway," said Kimmy. Then, "Did I say that out loud?"

Zeke looked Louie in the eye and said, "We're here to see Freddy Hanson."

Louie hesitated a moment, and a voice from inside the room said, "It's OK, Louie, let 'em in."

Louie hesitated a beat longer, then stepped back and stood against the wall while Zeke and Kimmy entered the small room. It was an office with paneled walls and two four-drawer file cabinets. The desk was an old, metal thing that looked like it came from Army surplus, and the floor was covered in vinyl tile. There were no windows in the room.

"You looking for me?" asked Freddy Hanson.

"We are," said Zeke.

"Who are you?" he asked, disinterested.

"I'm Zeke Traynor."

Hanson stopped and looked at Zeke with a surprised expression.

Freddy Hanson was young and pudgy. He had a meaty neck that lapped over the collar of his dress shirt, and his hands and fingers looked like plump sausages. His face was fleshy and his nose and jowls were pronounced. His only hair was on his eyebrows. Sitting behind the desk, he looked like a fat Pillsbury doughboy. Or an obese version of the Michelin Man.

"Well, what can I do for you?" Hanson asked Zeke, regaining his composure. His inflection was sarcastic while his voice was high and whiney. He sounded like a twelve-year-old Valley Girl.

"I'm here because someone tried to kill me. And you're culpable," said Zeke.

"Good word," said Kimmy, smiling.

"I didn't try to kill you," said Hanson.

"He's obviously a millennial," said Zeke, mostly to Kimmy.

"How do you know?" she said.

"He thinks he's entitled. Not responsible. And apparently self-indulgent."

"Hey," said Hanson. "What're you talking about? I'm right here."

"Yeah, I see that," said Kimmy with a smile.

Hanson looked at Louie Brennan and said, "Just get 'em out of here."

Louie looked at Zeke, obviously remembering their confrontation in Cambridge.

Then Louie wrapped his arm around his big body, reaching for his gun.

"I wouldn't," said Kimmy, leveling the Jerico at the big man. "Just sit still."

Louie looked at Hanson and shook his head slightly.

"So, OK, someone tries to kill you, and you think it's me?" said Hanson. "That's a stretch. People die everyday in Boston. But I'm not responsible for them."

"You're responsible, or you know who is," said Zeke. "That's the way things work."

* * *

There was an urgent knock on the door.

Hanson said, "Yeah?"

The door opened and Roy Calhoun stepped inside. "You OK, boss?" he asked, eyeing Zeke.

"Yeah, fine," said Hanson. "Sit." He pointed to a chair near the door, and Calhoun sat. He was wheezing hard, still trying to catch his breath.

Hanson looked at Kimmy and then at Zeke again. "So... what?"

"You can start by calling off whoever's trying to kill me," said Zeke.

Hanson spread his fat hands and adopted an expression of innocence. "I don't know what you're talking about," he said, shaking his head.

"There was an attempt on my life yesterday," said Zeke again. "In Cambridge. And I can't imagine that anything like that goes on in this town without your permission."

Hanson thought for a minute. "My guys had nothing to do with it," he said, and looked away.

"Right, this was a pro," said Zeke. "Nothing like these amateurs," he said, looking at Roy and Louie.

"Don't know what you're talking about," said Hanson with a grin. He rubbed his neck.

"Thing is, I don't think it was you," said Zeke. "I think someone ordered the hit with your permission. You're a businessman, right, Freddy? That's what Chief O'Malley told me. He said you're a business man, now."

Hanson was silent. Then he said, "Does O'Malley know you're here?"

Zeke nodded.

He could see Hanson weighing the options, his eyes intense.

"You received a call from someone. He asked you for permission to kill me on your turf. They tried yesterday," said Zeke in small sentences. "This was too big for you to handle, Freddy," said Zeke.

Hanson riled again and stood up. "You have no idea who I am," said the fat man. "I'm in control here. People come to me when they want something done. I say 'Yes' or 'No,' you know. Nobody but me."

"Uh-huh," said Zeke, skeptically.

"Even big drug lords respect me. Even the MS-13's respect me. They stay out of my way." Hanson was almost screaming, now, demanding respect and recognition.

"Sure," said Zeke.

"When the guys from out west come to Boston, I'm the first one they talk to," he continued. "Doesn't matter what they want, they show me respect," he continued.

"We're wasting our time here," said Zeke to Kimmy. "Let's go."

Roy looked at Hanson, who screamed at Zeke, "Good riddance, and don't come back! If you come back, I'll kill you!"

* * *

"That was interesting," said Kimmy when they'd exited the building and were driving away in their rental car. He can't help but talk about himself."

Zeke nodded. "He was lying about not knowing," he said.

"What did you see?" asked Kimmy.

"Couple of things," Zeke said. "Did you notice how willing he was to change the subject? He never answered my question about giving permission, and when I gave him an out, mentioned Chief O'Malley, he took that and ran with it. Trying to distract us from the issue."

"Hmm," Kimmy said. "Anything else?"

"Just a couple of common things. Liars often touch their face or neck when they're lying. Hanson did."

"Right, I remember," said Kimmy.

"And he looked away when he said he had nothing to do with the attempt on my life."

"He did," said Kimmy.

"Add it up and you've spotted a liar. But that was really to be expected," said Zeke. "Hanson had no reason to share anything with us."

Kimmy nodded, bouncing in her seat happily as they drove back toward Cambridge. It looked to Zeke like she had a song playing in her head while they talked.

"I don't think Hanson's the guy in charge," said Zeke. "Even if he inherited the business."

Kimmy nodded again, in time to her silent music.

"He clearly knew about the attempt to kill me," Zeke continued. "He was surprised to see me alive."

Kimmy thought about it.

"And think about the minds behind the student loan scam. That's someone with a long reach, and a lot of power. You'd need to keep a lot of people in line and scared to death to make that work," he said.

Kimmy was still nodding.

"So who has that kind of power?" he continued.

"Mob bosses?" she asked.

"Could be. Who else?"

"Politicians? Congressmen?" she asked.

"Perhaps. And more probably the Senators, right?"

"Sure."

"And money men. Hedge fund guys and mortgage bankers, like that."

"So how do we narrow it down?" Kimmy asked.

"It's time to follow the money," said Zeke.

* * *

Sarah Helms took a chair near the window in Clive Greene's office, sitting quickly and setting her briefcase on the adjoining end table. She straightened herself and sat erect, waiting.

"Sarah, we need your help with some of this," said Clive. "Need to shortcut the investigative process some."

"Sure," said Sarah. "I'll help if I can."

Kimmy sat next to Clive, and Zeke was standing, across the room from the window.

"It's the money," Zeke said. "We've talked with people involved in the scam. Students, Administrators, kids who are soliciting other kids to fill out fake applications…almost everyone in the food chain."

Sarah nodded slowly.

"But there's too much money involved. The people at the

top have to be connected, powerful and, well, bulletproof," he continued.

"We sort of thought the mob was running it," said Sarah.

Zeke was shaking his head. "I think it's beyond the mob's comfort level," he said. "This is being coordinated by some people who understand the law, the way the program was set up, the way the money moves, and they are essentially untouchable. It's an organized operation, and there are a lot of people involved."

"Like Washington insiders?" asked Sarah Helms.

"Or Manhattan. Or Chicago, or even L.A. But definitely financial and political guys with a lot of clout. And a lot of knowledge about how both money and government work."

"And how they work together," said Clive Greene. "Pretty extensive, specialized knowledge, I'd say."

"To find the soft spots in the system and exploit them, I'd agree," said Zeke.

Sarah was wearing a casual green sweater over brown corduroy pants and brown closed toed shoes. She had a minimum amount of makeup on today. It was Saturday.

She thought for a moment and then said, "If it's Washington, we can find out who it is." She paused. "Or at least isolate the possibilities."

She spoke in the same short, terse sentences as when they had met in Assistant Deputy Director Stiles offices.

"What would you need from us?" asked Zeke.

"Is there anyone you can push from the other end?" she asked.

"We followed the trail to two academics," said Zeke. "One

is already in custody for the Student Loan violations. He gave us the other one's name, and we spoke with him. He's supposedly the one with the connections."

"You think he may be a starting point?" asked Sarah.

"I do," said Zeke. "We'll give him another push and see what happens."

"OK, I'll work from the other end. Look for the leadership," said Sarah.

"We'll get it set up. Should have something more for you in a couple of days. Let's stay in touch," said Clive Greene.

* * *

"I'm glad you're here, gentlemen," he said smoothly, as if either of them had had a choice in the matter.

Stuart Williams III sat at the end of the small mahogany table in his Wall Street office, chatting with his two companions. His father had been a banker, and his father's father had founded the First Bank and Trust of New Jersey, over a hundred years ago. That bank had evolved from a small lending institution in the late eighteen hundreds to become a megabank after World War I, based primarily upon first railroad lending, and later war industry lending. The conservative bank prospered during the great depression and World War II. And then, during the bank failures of the early 1990s, First Bank and Trust had worked closely with the Resolution Trust Corporation to gobble up a number of weaker, failing institutions and expand its scope nationally.

After the latest recession, the hungry bank had allied itself with the FDIC and expanded even further, nationally and internationally, taking over failing banks during the crisis. Presently, Stuart Williams III's family bank influenced elections and dictated policy to governments.

The men sitting with Stuart Williams III were seasoned veterans of the finance world, and neither would show any weakness. In their world, as in the jungle, weakness meant death.

"No worries, Stuart," said the closest man. "I trust there's no problem with our arrangement." He was a tall, white haired man with skin like parchment paper. He looked to be eighty years old, but he could have been older. Baron Holmes knew where all of the bodies were buried. Some, he had buried himself.

He reached and poured a glass of scotch from the decanter on the table. Stuart watched to see whether Holmes' hand shook as he poured. It did not.

Holmes looked at the third man. "Milo, will you indulge? And you, Stuart?"

Milo Christianson was of a lineage that traced itself back to the Mayflower, and before that to the royalty of Britain. His relatives were known to have been Dukes and Earls, a fact that his wife, a Christianson by marriage, talked about endlessly. He said to Holmes, simply, "Of course."

Stuart Williams nodded absently.

As he poured the drinks, Baron Holmes said, "So, Stuart, what has brought us together this time?"

The other two men held prominent positions in Wall Street firms and were no strangers to wealth. Old fashioned wealth.

"Well, Baron," Stuart began, "it's this Student Loan thing." He paused, not quite certain where to start, or so it appeared.

"Yes?" asked Holmes.

"It may be in jeopardy," continued Williams.

Both men stopped fiddling with their drinks and gave Williams their full attention.

Williams said nothing for a moment, and then Baron Holmes said, "How so, Stuart?"

Milo Christianson watched Williams carefully. His gaze never wavered as he set his glass of scotch on the table.

"It appears that someone, and by that I mean some organization, government or otherwise, is investigating the high number of student loans in default," he continued.

"They've done that before," said Holmes.

"Yes, but my sources say that we should be worried. They're apparently looking for some correlation between defaults, lax admission standards, students withdrawing from the schools, and other such factors."

"That hits close to home," said Holmes. "Who's this, 'looking for a correlation'?"

"It seems to be coming from the ED," said Williams. "Highest levels." Both men recognized the abbreviation for the Department of Education.

"Do our contacts within the department know about this?" asked Holmes. Milo Christianson was silent, listening attentively.

"They say it came from the Director's office," said Williams, simply. "From the top."

"He's a politician," said Holmes. "He can't afford to take it too far. He'll make too many enemies."

"Just so," said Williams. "But the reports I've received are disturbing, nonetheless."

"What's the extent of the damage?" asked Milo Christianson.

"We're not sure, Milo," said Williams. "But I suggest we take it seriously until we hear differently."

"Yes, of course," said Christianson, looking away.

"What are you suggesting?" asked Holmes, quietly, sitting very still.

"Well, that's the thing. I'm not sure. The attempt to, ah, neutralize the auditors on our behalf failed," said Williams. "We can't let this get out of control."

"Will they try again?" asked Baron Holmes.

"We want them to. We've communicated that to our Boston contact, Hanson," said Williams. "Through Worthington, of course. And Hanson said he shared it with his friend, Benito Diaz."

"Can any of this lead back to us?" asked Christianson.

"Not directly, no," said Williams. "There are layers. But the fact that someone's looking into the situation is disconcerting. There are too many people involved. I wouldn't doubt that someone would cooperate with the authorities in lieu of a prison term."

The three men sat silently for a moment. Then Holmes said, "Yes. Well, what do you propose we do?"

CHAPTER 17

"I'll heading out to Phoenix; we've got to wrap up this Ramirez thing," said Zeke. "It's a big loose end." He was talking with Clive Greene in Clive's offices in D.C.

"Now that you've pointed it out, it seems like Ramirez may have been involved from the start. Mostly blocking the ICE progress into some of the key investigations," said Clive.

"Yep. And mostly by omission, by not doing anything when he could be taking action. Kind of a passive-aggressive approach to law enforcement," said Zeke.

"So you think he's helping out his old friend, Benito Diaz," said Clive. "Wouldn't have seen that without digging deep into his past."

"And even with the connection, it's still all circumstantial," said Zeke. "I want to prove it."

"What do you suggest?" asked Clive.

"We need to set a trap and monitor Ramirez's reaction and response," said Zeke.

"We're not law enforcement," said Clive. "We don't really

have jurisdiction here."

"I know. We'll need to be very careful," said Zeke. "Let's talk with Clark Hall and get his support."

"Good. OK, I'll set it up. Plan to meet with him before your trip to Phoenix."

"Will do," said Zeke.

* * *

"How would this work?" asked Deputy Director Clark Hall. Zeke and Clive were in the Department of Homeland Security offices in Washington, D.C., discussing Special Agent in Charge Jorge Ramirez. In addition to the three of them, a young man of about twenty-five sat at the table, writing furiously on a legal pad.

"Clark," said Clive, "I'd rather we didn't, eh, air the dirty linen, if you know what I mean."

"You want to speak privately?" Hall asked. "Sure." He turned to the young man and said, "Robert, please excuse us."

Robert paused and looked around the room. Then he slipped his pen in his shirt pocket and took his pad and left the room. In a moment, only the three men remained in Clark Hall's office.

Hall looked at Clive and then at Zeke. "My question stands."

"Is your office swept for listening devices regularly?" asked Zeke.

"It is," said Hall. "It was checked again last night."

"Outstanding," said Clive. "We need to draw Ramirez into

a situation that will force his hand. Something that will cause him to feel an urgency to contact Benito Diaz and communicate with him, tip him off." Clive paused. "And we'll need to monitor that communication."

"I'll authorize it, if you have a method for monitoring," said Clark.

Clive nodded. "Our people can set that up."

Zeke said, "Here's the play. We'll let Ramirez know that you asked us to look into the assassination attempt, to interview the Mara killers."

Clark Hall nodded.

"The last time I tried to do that, Ramirez told me there was no use trying, nothing to be gained. He said they'd tried and couldn't get the MS-13's to say anything," said Zeke. "He was pushing hard, and so I gave in, told him I agreed. And when I did, a small smile crossed his face. Very quickly. That happens when a liar thinks his lies have been accepted as truth. Happens more often than you'd think, sort of a sigh of relief."

Clark Hall nodded again.

"So when we reopen the matter, Ramirez will not only lose face with Diaz for not controlling the situation, but he'll also feel the threat of our interviews with the Mara's actually resulting in some useful data. It should push him around a bit," said Zeke.

"His first play will probably be to contact you, Clark, and tell you we don't need to do this, that he has it all under control," said Clive. "But you keep the pressure on. And call him away from the Phoenix office. Maybe a meeting in D.C."

"Then we'll conduct the interviews with the Mara's without

Ramirez in the room, so he'll be wondering what we've uncovered. He'll have to talk with Diaz, to let him know about these changes," said Zeke.

"And when he does, we'll have him," said Clark Hall. "When do you want to start?"

* * *

"I can't leave right now, boss," said Jorge Ramirez. "We've got too much going on."

Clark Hall, on the other end of the phone line, said, "It's not optional, Jorge."

"But a training seminar? Where does that fall in the levels of priority? I've got a team to run."

"Sorry, Jorge, this is mandatory for all personnel. Plan on coming to D.C. tomorrow. The seminar will be in our offices in two days," said Clark Hall. "It's important."

Ramirez tried to wiggle. "We're very close to cracking the human trafficking thing here, boss," he said. "Can I take a raincheck?"

"Just plan to be here, Jorge. I'll see you when you get in."

"OK," said Jorge.

"Incidentally, I've asked Zeke Traynor to interview some of the prisoners in Phoenix. The guys that took a shot at him in your parking lot," said Clark Hall.

"Boss, no, there's nothing we'll get from them. I've had my best people on it, and the Mara's won't talk. They just look at us from across the table."

Clark Hall said, "Zeke's a trained interrogator, and he's not employed by us. He may be able to push some buttons that you can't."

Ramirez was quiet for a moment.

"So, set it up, and head this way. I'll put you on my schedule here tomorrow afternoon, we can talk more then."

* * *

The ICE agent shook his head.

"No, man, I don't see any clearance for you to interview the prisoners."

He was a tall, broad shouldered man in his early thirties with hair graying around his ears. He wore it in an FBI-style haircut, held in place with too much gel. His gaze was steady and unblinking.

"We've gotten approval from your Director," said Zeke in a conversational tone. "Clark Hall."

* * *

Zeke looked through the plexiglass at the short, brown man. He was dressed in a gray shirt somewhat reminiscent of medical scrubs with his white t-shirt visible at the collar. He was sitting at the small desk space in the visitors section of the FCI, the Federal Correctional Institution in Phoenix. Behind the man was a guard dressed in a green uniform and sitting in a plastic chair against a concrete block wall.

"Hola," said Zeke in Spanish. "I'm here to ask you some questions."

The man frowned and sat, silent.

"My name's Zeke. Zeke Traynor," he said with a smile. "You're Rolando Acosta."

The man looked at Zeke, then turned and looked at the guard. He turned back to Zeke and shrugged.

He was in his late twenties, with short black hair and a blocky, almost square head. He was clean-shaven except for a small patch of beard beneath his wide lower lip. The right side of his face, curling up from the back of his neck, was a canvas upon which a series of complex and colorful drawings had been tattooed. There was a prominent M and an S, one on each cheek, in Old English style lettering. Beside the S were the numbers 1 and 3, but smaller and arranged vertically. His neck and upper chest, where visible, were covered in inked designs. The skin around his eyes was tattooed black, giving him an almost zombie look.

Tats are so hard on your liver, thought Zeke. He waited.

"You tried to kill me and my partner," Zeke said.

Rolando Acosta looked indifferent.

"You underestimated us," said Zeke. "Subestimado."

The man said nothing.

"Who sent you to kill us?" asked Zeke.

"No, man, we weren't there to kill you. If we were, you'd be dead."

"Then what?" asked Zeke.

"We were there to kidnap you. You and the girl," he said.

"By whom?" asked Zeke.

"I don't know," said Rolando. "The guy who was in charge is dead now."

"The guy carrying one of the rifles?" asked Zeke. "He was the boss?"

Rolando nodded.

"You know that you can make it easier on yourself, right?" asked Zeke.

The man looked away.

"Right now, you're looking at maybe twenty years in prison," said Zeke. "Twenty years away from your family."

"My family is MS-13. My family is everywhere. Including in prison."

* * *

The man sat in the chair that Rolando Acosta had vacated moments before. The guard, on the other side of the plexiglass from Zeke, signaled with a nod and returned to his chair against the back wall. He looked bored.

"Ernesto Reyes," said Zeke in Spanish. "It looks like they did a good job reattaching your nose."

Reyes, wearing the same gray prison clothing as Rolando Acosta looked at Zeke with cold eyes.

"It's all fair," said Zeke. "You tried to kill me. I just tore your nose."

The man shook his head. "No, not to kill you."

"Then what?" asked Zeke.

"We were told to take you, to bring you to a warehouse by Phoenix."

He's telling the truth, Zeke thought. "Whose orders?" he asked.

The man shook his head.

"Think about it, Ernesto. We have four of you here. Somebody is going to tell the story in return for a reduced sentence, right?"

Ernesto sat silent.

"How well do you know the other MS-13 guys? You trust them with your life? With the rest of your life?" asked Zeke. "Or are they pretty much focused on themselves?"

* * *

"Any luck?" asked Clive Greene. Zeke had called him from Phoenix to report the results of his interviews with the Mara's.

"I think we planted some seeds," said Zeke. "It may take a little time for them to germinate."

Clive said nothing.

"I did discover something curious though," said Zeke.

"Which is…" asked Clive.

"The attempt on us in the ICE parking lot here in Phoenix, a couple of the Mara's told me their intention was to kidnap us and take us to a warehouse here. Not to kill us."

"Any idea why?" asked Clive.

"I don't," said Zeke. "And I don't think they know, either. But they were telling the truth about that."

"Hmm," said Clive. "Alright, what's your next move?"

"I'll interview the other two here. Then I think it's time to give Jobare Worthington a little push. Before the FBI gets around to him."

"Very well. Enjoy Boston," said Clive.

CHAPTER 18

"Now, what's this about?" asked Jobare Worthington. He was sitting behind his desk, a large wooden table topped with a rich, dark stain. His chair was a brown leather Paris club chair.

That's not standard furniture for a college office, thought Zeke. He said, simply, "Someone's stealing your students' loan money."

Jobare Worthington's theatrical face tried several expressions before he landed on amusement.

He said, "And this is interesting to me because…?"

He was a tall, thin man with a gray ponytail that contrasted poorly with his large nose. His overall look was that of a circus clown, lacking only the white face paint.

Zeke looked across the desk at him and said, "I think you're involved."

Jobare Worthington waited for a moment, then he said, "Surely you don't think that I would be involved in something like that!"

He's going for outrage, now, thought Zeke. He waited.

"I'm going to have to ask you to leave," he continued, working himself up toward anger. "This is, well, outrageous."

"I'm deadly serious about this, Jobare," said Zeke, using his first name to further upset the academic. "There's a lot of money missing."

"What does that have to do with me?" asked Worthington, whining. "Why are you asking me about this?"

"Your fingerprints are all over it, Jobare," said Zeke, not giving an inch. "We've studied the files. Sarah Helms, ADD Styles' staffer and I have gone over it all."

"I don't know what you're talking about," said the academic. "And I won't sit here and listen to this any longer."

"The FBI has Paul Richardson in custody," said Zeke. "He's named you as complicit."

"I highly doubt that," said Worthington in his high, almost feminine voice. He choked on what was probably intended as a small, sarcastic laugh.

He's uncertain, thought Zeke.

Jobare rose and walked to the door. "You can show yourself out," he said, and he left the room.

* * *

Outside on the campus green, Jobare Worthington was less confident than he looked. He was thinking about the Boston mob and how unhappy they would be with him and with Paul Richardson, now that the student loan scam was starting to unravel.

266

Damn Freddy Hanson, anyway, he thought. If he'd had the auditor taken care of in the beginning, when Jobare had first told him about it, none of this would be happening. But now, with Paul in jail, things had taken a turn for the worse. A bad turn for Jobare Worthington.

Worthington knew Paul and knew that he had a weak constitution. He rattled easily and would roll over on Jobare several times before he would go to prison for the scam. *Hell, he's probably cutting a deal with the prosecutor right now,* he thought.

He dialed his cell phone.

"Yes?" said the voice.

"I need to talk with your boss," said Jobare, simply. "No names."

"Hold on, then," said Roy Calhoun. He turned to Freddy Hanson, who was counting a stack of money and handed him the phone.

Hanson said, "Who's this?"

"The professor," said Calhoun. "You can tell by his voice."

Hanson nodded, made a note, and said into the phone, "Yeah?"

"We've gotta do something more," said Jobare. "That auditor was just in my office."

"What did you tell him?" asked Hanson.

"Nothing. But it seems that Paul Richardson may have. He knows a lot about the loan thing."

"Will he talk?" asked Freddy Hanson.

"No. I don't know," said Jobare Worthington. "I can't say. He has a lot to lose." His voice whined a bit.

The leaves of the Cambridge maple trees were mostly brown and red now, and the air felt as crisp as Freddy Hanson's voice.

"Is he fishing? The auditor?" asked Hanson.

"No, he seems to know some of it."

"Then we can't risk it," said Hanson. "Richardson was a fool to get caught. We'll take care of this."

Jobare Worthington stared at a maple tree and said, "What do you mean?"

Hanson said, "Don't worry about it. Just do your job."

"OK," said Jobare. "And the girl in D.C., the one running the investigation from the ED office."

"Yes?"

"She needs to go, too. Sarah Helms."

"I think that's being taken care of," said Freddy Hanson. "But I'll check."

"OK, but hurry," said Jobare.

The phone went dead.

* * *

Clive Greene said, "The FBI said Richardson is, ah, sharing a lot with them."

Zeke smiled. He's pretty much a weak link," he said.

"How did you know? His ego?" asked Clive.

Zeke nodded. "Plus, the situation he's in now is way outside of his comfort zone. Way outside of anything he's experienced before."

Clive nodded. "He's given up Jobare Worthington about a

dozen times, so far," said Clive. "He's naming Worthington as the ring leader for the Student Loan scam."

"No," said Zeke, shaking his head. "Worthington doesn't have enough scope, enough power and resources to pull this off. He's somewhere in the middle, I'd guess. Moving the money around for the brain trust. Maybe recruiting students or monitoring the process."

Clive thought for a moment. "OK," he said.

"There's one thing I am worried about," said Zeke.

"What's that?"

"I'm worried about Sarah Helms' safety. If they tried to take me out in Cambridge because of my audit, it wouldn't be a big leap to think they might do the same with the lead investigator. The one who initiated all of this."

"How would they know about her?" asked Clive.

"Not hard to figure," said Zeke. "An operation that sophisticated must have huge resources. And the leadership—not Worthington but the leadership up the line—must have contacts with the ED. Or possibly spies within the department."

"I can see that," said Clive. "For the leadership, getting her out of the way would defuse the investigation, I suppose."

"It could," said Zeke. "I think I'll visit with her and her team in D.C."

* * *

"Has there been any, ah, relief? Changes for the better, I'm hoping," Holmes asked.

The three men were sitting comfortably in Baron Holmes private club on antique Louis XV gilt fauteuil chairs, their frames colored in a gaudy gold leaf with vines and roses stitched busily into the fabric. Baron's bodyguard, a tall man in a black suit, stood a discrete distance from the men.

"No, not to speak of," said Stuart Williams III. "Things haven't really changed since we last met."

Baron Holmes nodded sagely.

The room was a dark library with small, quiet alcoves and sitting nooks that assured privacy for the most sensitive discussions. Men dressed in tuxedos stood discreetly by to accommodate any request from the club members.

"There will be another effort, I assume," said Milo Christianson.

"That's what I've been told," said Williams. "They've done some research into the auditors," he continued. "Seems the request originated from the Director's office."

"You mean," said Christianson, "the Department of Education? Cabinet level?"

"It seems so," Williams repeated.

"Is your source credible?" asked Holmes.

Williams nodded. "They've invited an outside firm to do the audit," he said. "But not accountants. They've hired Clive Greene's group, 'The Agency.' They're troubleshooters."

"I've heard of them," said Holmes. "They seem to be a formidable group."

"Yes. Well, the effort in Cambridge was directed against one of their operatives, not a Department employee."

"Yes?" asked Christianson.

"We'll still need to deal with the threat, then," said Holmes. "We need to. There's too much in play right now."

He was speaking of both the money, millions of dollars in student loans in various stages of the scam, as well as the sheer volume of public loan documents already processed and vulnerable to scrutiny by government review.

"We'll continue on this path," said Williams. "And now we'll also need to deal with the threat from the Director's office."

* * *

Benito Diaz looked across the table at the woman. She was strikingly beautiful, and he knew that she was as deadly as a snake.

"How did this happen?" he asked.

Susan had flown from Providence to Pittsburgh via rented private plane, called a real Uber driver for transport from General Aviation to the Pittsburgh International Airport's Main Terminal, and then she'd caught a commercial flight from Pittsburgh to Phoenix using a false identity. Once there, she'd rented a car and drove to Scottsdale to visit Benito Diaz.

"It was unusual," said Susan. "I was set up."

"You failed. That's very unusual for you."

"Yes," she said. "Thank you for sending the attorney."

"That was in place in case something happened to you. You were fortunate," said Diaz. He looked into her eyes from across the table, studying her expressions.

Susan nodded. "Yes, thank you."

"You can thank me by finishing the job, Susana." He used the Spanish form of her name.

"Yes, I know," she said, simply. "It will be a little bit trickier, but I'll do it."

"This Traynor has caused us a lot of trouble. First with the Mara's, then with Luis, and now in Boston at the schools. That's why you were hired in the first place. I contacted you and Luis to provide the best solution for the problem," he said.

"Yes," she said. "I'll head back east as soon as things calm down some."

"I've been told that he's living on Cape Cod," said Diaz. "You can take care of the problem there."

"OK."

"And there's another part of the assignment," he continued. "Actually, two."

She waited quietly.

"There's pressure from Washington, from the Department of Education. We were asked to deal with that, also."

"A group, or an individual?" asked Susan.

"An individual. A woman asking the wrong questions. Sarah Helms. We think she's heading the Department's investigation into our friend Freddy Hanson's activities. He called me for help with that situation. The thought is that she should also go away. And it will slow things down a bit in Washington. They become distracted easily."

Susan smiled. "Can you get me the details?" she asked simply.

"We will,," said Diaz.

"And the second part of the assignment?" asked Susan.

"There's a student involved in the Student Loan, ah, project. Her boyfriend seems to be telling everyone about the thefts, talking way too much about something he knows nothing about."

"And…" asked Susan.

"And our friends in Boston are nervous. Extra nervous. They've asked for our help in putting that situation to bed," said Diaz.

"A student's boyfriend? That seems innocuous, Benito."

He hesitated for a moment. Then he said, "Yes, but nevertheless… Consider it a favor for our East Coast partner. They are good buyers for our product."

Susan knew that he was referring to the human trafficking. A good number of the victims ended up in the northeastern United States.

"Very well. Can you send me the details for that one, also?"

"Yes, we will," he said.

"And Susana?"

"Yes?" she answered.

"Take care of the Washington problem first."

CHAPTER 19

Sarah Helms barely noticed the sprinkling raindrops as she walked down C Street to her office in the Lyndon Baines Johnson Building. She was caught up in thought about the progress they were making, working to isolate and identify the likely leaders of what her team had christened "The Student Loan Scam." As usual, cars were parked on both sides of C Street with every available space taken and several vehicles circling, waiting for a parking spot.

Sarah entered the building with the 'come to work crowd' and waited in line to pass through the metal detector. Once through, she caught an elevator to her floor and walked briskly to her office. Five of her team were already there, ready for their nine o'clock briefing. Sarah entered her office and stepped behind her desk. She said, "OK, what do we have?"

The team was made up of three younger staff members and two agents, on loan from the FBI at the request of ADD Cy Styles. The FBI agents were from the White Collar Crimes unit and were experienced in following the money.

"We've been running down the Raleigh University situation, like you asked," said Tessa Walton, an ED staff member. "The guys at The Agency are pushing, and we're pulling."

"What are you finding?" asked Sarah.

"We're watching Jobare Worthington. Richardson gave him up, and we're gathering evidence to support that." This from Sammy Lee, another staffer. "He's got an academic's income… which means not much at all…but he's living way above his means." He looked at one of the FBI agents, who nodded in agreement.

"What about his wife. Does she have her own money?" asked Sarah.

"Not this guy. He's as gay as they come. Flamboyant," he said. "And no steady partner."

"So he has control of the distribution of the funds…"

"For Raleigh University, yes," said Sammy. "And we've been monitoring his communications."

"If he only has access and control at Raleigh University, it's not likely that he's at the top of the food chain," Sarah added. "Right?"

A thirty-something man in a blue suit and a blond crewcut, Agent Slater of the FBI, said, "Best we can tell, there's a central infrastructure at the top that supports this type of activity in a number of schools. It's been going on for years. Long enough for them to get their people in place in a number of colleges."

Sarah said, "Really? They've filled some personnel slots with their own people? In college administration?"

"We're talking years, Sarah. And lots of money. This has

been a very well planned operation," added Agent Slater. "And every time the rules for student loans have changed, they've found a way to modify their business plan to take advantage of it."

* * *

Outside of her office at the Department of Education, Sarah Helms was well respected. Her education, a Ph.D. from Harvard, was impressive, even though the degree had been in Modern History and Government. It had clearly positioned her for this job.

She was smart and well connected and she came from a family with strong political ties. Her father had been a congressman and now worked as a lobbyist inside the beltway. Her mother's family had been involved in politics since the DAR was formed.

But now, Sarah was intent. As she walked down the cold Washington street she could almost smell the end of their investigation. Based on this morning's briefing, they were close to having the testimony they needed to arrest the people behind the Student Loan Scam. The power brokers.

She knew they had to be there, lurking in the shadows and hiding, while they pocketed the majority of the money and kept everything quiet through the fear and greed of others. She was so sure they were there, she could just about see them. And it would be just a matter of time until someone gave them up.

Sarah stepped into a coffee shop and stood in the late

morning line behind congressional aids and interns who were picking up the standing orders for their offices. The song playing in the background was "How You Got That Girl" by Ex Hex. Sarah was busy, thinking through the scenarios again, looking toward the end game and her team's victory. To herself, she already called it a "win."

"What can I get you?" asked the girl behind the cash register.

Sarah said, "May I have a light roast? Medium."

The girl said, "Sure, what's your name?" and she wrote it on the cup.

Sarah stepped to the side to wait for her beverage. Behind her, a well-dressed blonde woman ordered a black coffee.

"Room for cream?" asked the server.

The woman rolled her eyes. "I said 'black' didn't I?"

"Sorry," said the server.

The woman said to Sarah, "Can't get good help anymore. You know, most people today don't even know how to count change."

Sarah nodded politely and waited for her coffee. When the barista called her name, "Sarah," she stepped forward and took the cup. She stepped to the service bar and poured some cream into her coffee.

The woman retrieved her cup from the barista and stepped to the service bar beside Sarah. She poured some half and half into her cup and added a sweetener. Then she said to Sarah, "Here, I took an extra one," and she handed her a yellow packet of sweetener.

Sarah said, "Thanks," politely and poured about half the contents of the packet into her coffee. She grabbed a stir stick and stirred.

* * *

Sarah tried to sip some coffee on the way back to her office, but it was too hot. She put her mouth over the opening in the cup cap and immediately knew she would burn herself if she tasted it. She blew on the opening, and then decided to wait until she got to her office.

As she walked, she rehearsed her presentation to the Deputy Director. When this was over, she would be in the spotlight, having taken down what she was sure were some of the power elite in this country.

Back at her desk, Sarah was surprised to see Zeke Traynor sitting across from her.

"Hi, Zeke," she said. "You back in D.C.? Done in Cambridge?"

She set the coffee on the desk corner and took the lid off of it in order to let it cool.

"I am," said Zeke. "I wanted to bring you up to speed and also to warn you, Sarah."

"Warn me?" she asked, a shocked expression on her face. "About what?"

"Clive and I were backtracking, and it occurred to us that you may be a target, too."

Sarah looked at Zeke blankly.

"Think about it, Sarah," Zeke continued. "You're driving an investigation into a multimillion dollar scam with some very powerful people at the helm. It just seems logical that they'll take a run at you sometime soon."

"I suppose…" she said.

"Have you noticed anything different? Has anyone approached you, or contacted you that made you feel strange, weird? Instincts are important," said Zeke. "Have you noticed anyone following you?"

"Not really," she said. Sarah picked up her cup and looked at her coffee. "There was a woman who shared a sweetener with me at the coffee shop just now," she said. "It seemed kind of awkward or something, you know?"

Zeke nodded encouragingly.

"And, come to think of it, how did she know that I use sweetener?"

Zeke said, "Set the cup down, Sarah. Very carefully."

* * *

"She was clever," said the lab technician. "She didn't leave anything that would have a fingerprint or could lead back to her. She essentially handed Sarah the poison in a packet and watched while she administered it to herself, via the coffee. It was cyanide."

With Clive's help, Zeke had arranged for the coffee to go to the FBI lab at Langley. The technician had called him as soon as the results were in.

"Cyanide, sure," said Zeke, thinking aloud. "Small dose, fast acting. Smells like bitter almonds, but mixed in acidic coffee, it could be virtually undetectable."

"We don't see a lot of cyanide deaths, though," said the technician, who's name was Carol Goodman.

"Where would the killer get it?" asked Zeke.

"Well, from apple seeds," said Goodman. "But more conventionally, you can buy it on the web."

"Jewelry makers use it for gilding. And small labs can get it, I expect," said Zeke.

"Right. Plus there's a black market for almost everything. Particularly if you're willing to go overseas."

* * *

"I'll arrange for someone to stay with you, Sarah," Zeke said. "Until we eliminate the threat against you. Looks like you got the attention of some bad people."

Sarah looked at him. "I can't believe they tried to kill me," she said, her green eyes beginning to water.

"Yes, they did," said Zeke. "Where do you live?"

Sarah took a deep breath. "I have a townhouse near Laurel, Maryland. It's a ways east of here, but it's affordable. And I take the MARC MTA from Union Station."

"We'll move you to another place, an anonymous one, and we'll provide transportation. Somewhere populated but away from Laurel. You'll only need to stay there a few days, I think. Until we catch the killer," said Zeke.

"OK," said Sarah, uncertain.

"Now, tell me about the woman in the coffee shop. Everything you remember."

* * *

"It's too dangerous," said Milo Christianson. He was sitting behind the wheel of his current year Mercedes Benz S-class. Baron Holmes was sitting next to him, and Stuart Williams III was in the rear seat.

"What happened with the girl?" asked Baron Holmes, ignoring the comment.

"We don't know. The packet was delivered to her. And she, our gal, saw it poured into her coffee," Stuart Williams said. "It's possible she spilled the coffee or tossed it for some reason. Or maybe she was distracted and left it sitting somewhere."

"Bottom line is that it didn't work, correct?" asked Holmes.

"Yes, that's the bottom line," said Christianson. "It was a dangerous risk, anyway. We could have been found out."

"But we'll still need to eliminate her," said Williams, "in order for the threat to go away."

"No doubt. But in a more subtle way," said Holmes.

"What do you mean?"

"Make it look like an accident," said Holmes. "They're too good with the DNA and such, nowadays."

"What about our gal? Did she get clear?" asked Holmes.

"Yep. She was gone before Ms. Helms got back to her office."

"Thank God," said Holmes. "No link to us, then."

"There were cut outs, anyway," said Williams. "You know that."

"So, what's the solution now?" asked Holmes, ignoring the comment.

"Leave it to me. I'll work something out," said Williams, cryptically. He was counting on the killer to finish the job.

"All right," said Baron Holmes. "But do it quickly."

* * *

Kimmy virtually danced into the office, her skirt billowing, trying to keep up with her.

"Sorry I'm late," she said.

"We just got here," said Zeke.

Clive said, "No problem."

Then he said, "You remember Sarah Helms from the Department of Education."

"Sure," said Kimmy.

Sarah was dressed in a gray woman's business suit and closed-toed shoes. Her blouse was light green, almost the shade of her eyes. Sarah said, "This has really got me freaked out. I mean, someone's trying to kill me."

"We won't let that happen," said Zeke. "We're going to eliminate the threat."

"How will you do that?" asked Sarah.

Zeke paused. Then he said, "We have a number of things we can do. Starting with assigning Kimmy to keep an eye on you."

"OK," said Sarah, looking at Kimmy. "But you're pretty small, Kimmy. Can you…?"

"I think so," said Kimmy.

Simultaneously, Zeke said, "Yes."

Clive, sitting at the table chuckled. "You're in good hands, Sarah," he said.

"Let's plan a couple things," continued Zeke. "First, we're moving you to an apartment outside of town. We'll want to change up your routine."

Sarah nodded. "Will it interfere with my job?" she asked.

"ADD Stiles has blessed the effort," said Clive. "I just spoke with him on the phone. He wants you alive and well, as we all do. You can work from the apartment, and make appearances in the office at random times. You'll be going for unpredictable."

Sarah nodded.

"What about your family? Friends? Anyone local?" asked Zeke.

"No, I'm an only child. My folks both died a few years ago. Mostly, I work. And not many acquaintances, outside the ED. I know, it sounds like a sad life."

"Or a typical type-A personality," said Clive.

"There's the issue of my work. Sensitivity and all. I tend to avoid relationships for security reasons."

Zeke nodded. "You burrow down in the apartment for a while, OK?"

"And in the meantime, we'll be looking for the killer or killers," said Clive.

"This attempt with the poison, it had to be a hired killer," said Zeke. "Too well planned, too professional."

"They must really want me out of the way," said Sarah.

* * *

Sarah Helms sat in the afternoon light on the balcony of her temporary apartment that overlooked a lovely inner courtyard. She was sipping tea and reading the results of her team's most recent investigation into the Student Loan Scam on her laptop.

Kimmy was sitting across the room at the kitchen table, reading a cozy mystery. Occasionally, she'd look over at Sarah.

Both women wore blue jeans. Sarah wore a beige cable sweater a size too big, baggy on her thin torso, and Kimmy wore a loose peasant shirt with embroidered cuffs and collar. They had been in the apartment for seven days, and nothing significant had happened.

Sarah said, "Are you hungry? Do you want to go out for a bite?"

Kimmy thought for a moment and said, "Sure. What do you have in mind?"

The apartment was located in a suburban neighborhood in Tysons Corner, a six-story elevator building with an interior lobby and good security. Kimmy had installed her own cameras in several key locations and she could access them from her phone or iPad. The building, which looked a lot like many others in the neighborhood, was two long blocks from the Galleria Mall.

Sarah stood and came into the living room.

"Let's go to the mall and grab something," said Sarah. "There's a good seafood place there called 'Coastal Flats'. You'll enjoy it. I've eaten there when I was out this way on business."

"Sounds good," said Kimmy. She stood and pulled on a light jacket that covered her Jerico 941, holstered at the small of her back. "Do you have your body armor on?"

They had decided that Sarah should wear a light Kevlar vest under her sweater as additional protection whenever she was out of the apartment proper, including when she was on the balcony.

"Yep, I do," said Sarah with a laugh, pulling up her sweater and flashing Kimmy. *She's nervous. That was out of character,* thought Kimmy.

Kimmy smiled. "Let's take my car," she said.

They took the elevator down to the parking garage and found Kimmy's car parked near the elevator. After a quick once-over, Kimmy nodded and the women got into the front seat.

"You want to navigate?" she asked Sarah.

"Oh, sure, nothing to it." Sarah looked at her phone. "We could have walked," she said. "Just turn right here, then onto International Drive, and to the mall. It's like three blocks."

Kimmy dialed a number and spoke quietly for a moment, then looked at Sarah and said, "OK, here we go."

CHAPTER 20

"Hey, Zeke, it's all quiet here," said Kimmy, reporting in by phone. "Nothing happening."

"Any chance the killer knows where you are?" asked Zeke.

"We've been pretty careful, but I don't know. She found Sarah at the coffee shop," said Kimmy.

"Yep. But that was an easy guess, based on where Sarah works and all. The new location would be harder."

"But like you say, people always leave footprints," said Kimmy. "Cell phones, cars, clues in her patterns…"

"Which is why you're with her," said Zeke. "Keeping her safe."

* * *

In fact, Susan had staked out the ED building, watching for Sarah's unscheduled visits.

It's a tedious chore, she thought, *but necessary. I can't have her mucking up the money and causing trouble for my clients.*

Dressed in uniform as a private security guard—there were many of them in D.C.—Susan stayed in an area close to the entrance to the LBJ Building and monitored the people who came and went. Apparently, Sarah had abandoned her townhouse and, based on Susan's earlier inspection, she'd taken her car and disappeared. No doubt with help from her friends at The Agency.

However, Susan Del Gato wasn't without resources. She'd touched all the bases, checking Sarah's Social Media pages for comments or photos that might reveal her location, checking her mail for a forwarding address, monitoring her credit card charges and ATM withdrawals using passwords she'd taken from Sarah's townhouse. She also checked dealerships for Susan's car servicing, calling them with the VIN number and asking about recent appointments or visits.

She realized that there was a good chance Sarah was visiting the office occasionally. She arranged for the Security Guard uniform and took her post, watching the entrance to the LBJ.

* * *

"I found her," Susan reported. She'd called Benito Diaz on a burner phone a couple days later.

Benito said, "Excellent."

"She forwarded her mail. I sent her a letter, 'Address Correction Requested/Do Not Forward' and the post office did exactly as I asked."

Benito Diaz waited.

"I'm moving into phase two. I'll pick her up at her apartment in Tysons Corner, which is her new mailing address. It should be simple, now."

"Good. Can you finish the job, now?" he asked.

"Yes, I can," said Susan.

"Good. I'll tell the appropriate people," said Diaz.

* * *

Coastal Flats turned out to be a comfortable restaurant with a nautical theme. The walls were a bright yellow, inside and out, and the many windows were designed in a Cape Cod style and painted white. As they entered the building, the smell of roasting oysters and cooking fish greeted them.

"I didn't realize I was hungry until we got here," said Kimmy as they were seated. "Smells yummy."

"Let's get an appetizer to share," Sarah said. "I love their crab dip."

"OK, I'm good with that," said Kimmy, and they ordered it with glasses of water when the server arrived a moment later.

"Got it," said the server. "I'll be right back with your drinks." She walked off to fetch their beverages.

Sarah nodded. Then she said to Kimmy, "I still have trouble believing that someone wants to kill me."

"Don't worry, there's a big difference between 'wanting to' and actually doing it," said Kimmy with confidence. "It's not as easy as you'd think, to kill someone."

"You know this…how?" asked Sarah, suddenly cautious.

Kimmy ignored the question and said, "It's not like on TV."

Sarah just looked at her.

Kimmy shrugged and continued, "First of all, there aren't a lot of ways to make someone die. It's easier to hurt someone than to kill them, you know?"

"Like…" asked Sarah.

"Well, to be certain, you've got to be in close. And, think about it, getting close to a stranger isn't all that easy. Plus, once you've killed him, you want to be able to get away," said Kimmy. "That's a trick in itself."

"But if they have a gun…" said Sarah.

"Well, if it's a handgun, it's only accurate for about ten yards. Not at all what you see on television, really. It depends on the sight radius of the gun. From twenty yards, you may as well just throw it at your victim."

"What's a 'sight radius'?" asked Susan.

"The distance between the handgun's front sight and it's rear sight. The longer that distance, the more accurate the weapon," said Kimmy.

"Really?" asked Sarah.

"Sure," said Kimmy. "But most handguns are short barreled. Less accuracy. And in public there's seldom a clear ten-yard alley. There's furniture, people, walls, trees, cars… The effective range is limited by that, too."

"Yes," said Sarah. "But aren't there more accurate guns?"

"Sure. There are a lot of variables. Accuracy depends on the powder charge, the length of the barrel, the weight of the bullet, all variables. But most killers are carrying a handgun because they can conceal it, which implies a short-barrel and a relatively light gun. And with that, accuracy diminishes, almost logarithmically," she continued.

"I guess I hadn't thought…" Sarah started.

"Plus, if you're in a crowded place, you've got people in your line of fire," Kimmy continued. "You can't predict what people are going to do, either. They're very random."

The server arrived and set down their drinks, waters with lemon, along with the crab dip.

Sarah sipped her drink and then said, "Wouldn't they just start shooting?"

Kimmy was shaking her head. "No, for a number of reasons. First, if they kill two or more people, they're considered a 'mass murderer,' which results in all of the attention from the local and state police, as well as a likely FBI presence. That's like calling down the wrath of God on yourself…it just isn't worth the attention. It escalates everything quickly, and you're going to get caught."

"OK," said Sarah. "You've thought about this, haven't you?"

Kimmy smiled and said, "This crab dip is excellent!"

Sarah put some on a toast point and ate it thoughtfully.

"Also, they won't just start shooting. After all, they want to escape. The element of surprise is important, getting the shooting done and then getting out of the area before anyone realizes that the sound was a gun, not a backfire or an explosion."

"So the more bullets fired, and the longer it takes, the more likely people will start to realize that's it's not background noise…" said Sarah.

"Sure," said Kimmy. "So one thing we do is we take away the killer's ability to be alone with you. We avoid small, private spaces like elevators or bathrooms, any place that could give the killer an advantage."

"I see."

"And another consideration," said Kimmy. "The activity associated with drawing the gun, bringing it up, aiming it, and firing accurately is a difficult set of motions that have to take place very quickly. Unlike target shooting, there's a lot of room for error there, too, in those moments."

Sarah was nodding again, as their server arrived to take their lunch orders. She did so, then scuttled away.

* * *

At a nearby table, Susan sat with her back to the table Kimmy and Sarah shared and listened to their conversation. Her hair had been cut short and died red, and she wore several layers of clothing, shirts and sweaters and a light jacket that together made her look pudgy. Susan had also applied makeup heavily, accenting her eyes and her mouth, virtually transforming her appearance.

It's a matter of good planning, she thought to herself. *No,* she corrected herself, *excellent planning.*

* * *

Kimmy looked around the restaurant again, seemingly

fascinated with the nautical and seaside decor. There were crab traps and fishing nets cleverly placed on shelving throughout the building, and the interior walls looked like an ocean cottage, yellow with white trim painted over distressed shiplap.

Sarah sipped her water and said, "How long will this take?"

Kimmy said, "The whole thing? Keeping you safe? Just until we take the killer down."

Two tables away, Susan overheard and smiled to herself.

"It's already getting old," said Sarah, her green eyes welling up with frustration. "I can't get with my staff with any regularity. And I can't really plan, because of the uncertainty of it."

"I know," said Kimmy, "but we've gotta keep you alive. Or else you won't be going to any meetings anyway."

As they spoke, the red haired, pudgy woman paid her check and exited the restaurant, careful to avoid looking at Sarah and Kimmy's table. She walked to the front door, pulled it open and stepped out into the coolness of the Tysons Corner afternoon.

* * *

Earlier, in the parking garage of the apartment complex in Tysons Corner, Susan had no problem locating Sarah's Toyota Camry, parked beside a concrete pillar. She dialed her cell phone.

"We'll send someone out," said the dispatcher. Susan had called AAA.

"Oh, please hurry! I'm late and I'm stuck in this garage here at my apartment building," Susan said.

"You can wait inside, if you like. The locksmith will call when he gets close."

"I can't. I don't have my apartment key, either. How long do you think...?" she started.

"He should be there within twenty minutes, ma'am," said the bored dispatcher.

"OK, OK, I'll wait by the car," Susan said.

"Yes, ma'am. If you'll write down the car's VIN number, and the make and model and year of the car for the locksmith..."

"Certainly, sure, I can do that."

"And you have an I.D?"

"It's in my apartment. And the keys to my apartment were on the key ring I lost. I thought it was in my pocket, you know, but when I got here, it wasn't. In my pocket, I mean," Susan said.

"Yes, ma'am. He'll be along soon." The dispatcher hung up.

Seventeen minutes later, a white panel van with a lock-smith's sign on the side had pulled into the garage and stopped behind Sarah's car. Susan walked over to the driver's door hurriedly.

The driver shut the van off and stepped out. He was a thin man, average height, and had a thick, black beard. His skin was pale white and he had what looked like burn marks along both arms. He moved fragilely.

He's been in prison, thought Susan. She said, "Thank God you're here! Can you get me a replacement key? Here's the information."

She handed him a sheet of paper, which he looked at for a

moment and then said, "Sure."

The locksmith, who said his name was Steven, went to the back of his van and took out some equipment. Within four minutes of his arrival, the door to Sarah's 2012 Camry was standing open and Steven was programing a new key.

"I'm supposed to see your ID," he said to Susan.

"I know, but I think it's in my apartment. I lost my key ring between here and there. Or maybe I left my purse in the apartment. Anyhow, the apartment key is lost, too," Susan said. "I can't get in."

Steve looked at her for a minute, and then said. "What's your name?"

"Sarah Helms," she said without hesitation. "Here's my AAA card." She handed him the spare card she'd taken from the desk drawer in Sarah's townhouse.

"Well, that's what it says here in the system," Steven said, looking at his iPad. Then he looked at her. "You're not going to have a problem paying for this, are you?" Suspicious.

"Oh, no, no," she said. "I have some cash in my pocket, if that's OK?"

Steven licked his lips, just a flicker of tongue visible. "OK. It'll be $180, for the door and the spare key, Sarah."

Susan said, "That's a lot of money…"

"It is," said Steve, obviously used to that objection. "It's these new keys with the chips in them. Everything's electronic, now, so everything costs more. The key itself is ninety some dollars, and then I have to program it to work with your car. Plus the door opening, and travel to and from. One eighty." He handed her a detailed invoice.

Susan turned a bit and put her hand in her pocket and looked down at what she was holding. She sorted through some currency, obviously trying to keep Steven from seeing the full extent of her bankroll. In a moment, she turned back and handed him two hundred dollar bills and said, "I'm very grateful."

Steven reached into his pocket for change, and Susan said, "No, keep it. Thanks for helping me out here."

* * *

Susan drove from Coastal Flats directly to the parking garage and found an empty space.

She whistled quietly as she approached the car. Guilty people seldom whistle. Manny had taught her that.

It was light outside, but there were shadowy areas in the garage, particularly between cars. Susan stepped between Susan's car and another.

"Now we just need to get this in place," said Susan to herself. She opened the door with the spare key she'd acquired from AAA the day before.

The package she held was unobtrusive, a brown paper grocery bag, folded twice at the top. Susan retrieved it from under a car three down from Sarah's, where she'd left it earlier that morning. The bag wasn't particularly heavy. It contained three sticks of TNT and a magnet all taped together with duct tape, a blasting cap, some wire, a small battery and a tilt switch.

Susan was proficient with tilt switches, having used them to detonate bombs over the years. The switch, typically a small glass canister of mercury, was wired into the detonation circuit of the bomb. She then secured the canister behind the brake pedal, her favorite spot, and once armed, the bomb would detonate when the brake pedal was pushed and the canister tilted enough to make the connection.

The TNT was attached to the undercarriage of the Toyota, just under the driver's seat. The circuit wires were pulled through the floorboard near the brake linkage, and the small canister was secured behind the pedal. *Ingenious, and almost undetectable,* she thought. Susan hummed as she worked.

Susan then retrieved the GPS device she had attached to Sarah's car, put it with her gloves, car key and brown bag in her purse and walked out of the garage.

* * *

"I've got nothing to say to you, Zeke," said Luis Cruz. Dressed in an orange jumpsuit that was stenciled in black with a prison acronym across the back and down one leg, and his arms and legs secured with heavy silver manacles, Cruz nonetheless looked confident, even cocky. As if their roles were reversed.

"You enjoying solitary?" asked Zeke.

"It's fine. Just putting in time, anyway, watching the bulls wander around."

"I think the attempted murder charge will stick," said Zeke.

Cruz smiled a small smile and shook his head to himself.

"Hope the witnesses show up at the trial," he said, indifferently.

"You know, Luis," he said, then paused. "That's your name, right? Luis Cruz? You know, Luis, we've been looking into some other deaths. Deaths of Federal witnesses after they testified. We've found eight killings in six cities in the past three years, and I think we can pin them all on you."

Luis Cruz smiled a lazy smile.

"DNA, you know?" continued Zeke. "Now that we know what to look for, we can get the samples the ME's took from each victim's clothes and body, and match them to your DNA. You know you were in close on every one of those killings. A garrote, knives, poison. One was beaten to death."

Cruz shook his head.

"Four of those states have the death penalty. They're planning to hold the trial in Federal Court in Arizona for all eight murders and the attempt. On me. So you're basically screwed."

"You know who runs the prisons?" Cruz asked.

"You think Diaz is going to help you? I think he'll be cutting his losses as soon as he can get to you," Zeke said. "As soon as you're out of solitary, or in transport, or maybe in the prison infirmary. You've become a liability to him. And he doesn't want the trouble that will come if you give him up for ordering the hits. You can see that, right?"

The men were silent for a minute while Cruz thought it over.

"You could possibly avoid the needle, though," said Zeke.

"What's this, the stick and the carrot?" asked Cruz.

"Sure," said Zeke. "Why not?"

Cruz looked at him.

"You should also know that one of the Mara's who tried to kill me here in Phoenix is suddenly anxious to talk," said Zeke. "Just to throw some urgency in the mix."

* * *

"There's no way to track her," said Luis Cruz. He was sitting in an interview room at the Federal Correctional Institution in North Phoenix, surrounded by his attorney, a Federal Prosecutor, three prison guards and Zeke Traynor. A small camera on a tripod was standing discretely in the corner with its red light glowing.

"You mean Susan Del Gato?" asked Zeke.

"Sure. I'm not sure anyone knows where she is right now."

"But you know how to reach her," said Zeke.

"Well, I know how to get a message to her."

"We're listening," said Zeke.

"You'll take the death penalty off the table?" Cruz reiterated. "Leniency?" He looked around the table.

The Federal Prosecutor, a short man named Anthony DeForest, looked at Zeke, then at Cruz and nodded.

"Let's draw up the papers, then," said Cruz's attorney.

* * *

"It's an electronic dead drop," said Luis Cruz. "Simple, but effective."

Zeke said, "Where and how?"

"Like I said, it's simple, actually. It's a 'help chat room' on the web, with encrypted access to sign in. It's got a lot of old chatter about Windows 7 and hard drive formatting, that sort of thing, and it looks like an abandoned site. But it's not," said Cruz. "It's how we communicate when we're apart. We leave a general message there."

He's not lying, Zeke thought, watching Luis Cruz's movements. *He may not be telling the entire truth, though.*

"Does she check it often?" asked DeForest.

"Maybe every couple days," said Cruz. "It depends. She hasn't heard from me for a while, though, so she probably thinks I'm dead or in prison."

"I imagine she checks it from a public computer," said Zeke, thinking out loud.

"Yes, usually," said Cruz. "Maybe an Internet café where she can rent time on a computer. Make us invisible. Something like that."

"If you suddenly post to the chat room, it might make her suspicious," said Zeke.

"It might," said Cruz. "Or she might believe that I got out of here. She'd probably be careful, though."

"OK," said Zeke. "Tell me about your codes."

Luis Cruz looked confused for a moment. "What?"

"If you're communicating like that, you've got to have code words for emergencies. Like 'stop' or 'run' or even a word to confirm that it's you sending the message," said Zeke.

"There aren't any codes," said Cruz, suddenly blinking and looking away.

He's lying, thought Zeke. "Sure there are. If you went to

this much trouble, you'd have an 'abort' code. Either a word or phrase…or possibly the absence of a word or phrase."

Cruz looked around the table.

"You realize it's you or her, now," said Zeke.

DeForest nodded. "This agreement isn't any good unless you cooperate fully, Luis," Deforest said. "If not, I'll just tear it up. If you lie, and she escapes, the deal is off the table."

For the first time, Cruz looked shaken. His attorney leaned over and whispered something in Luis Cruz's ear.

"IOS," said Cruz. "The abort code is IOS. Anywhere in the communication."

* * *

"I'd suggest something plausible and simple," said Zeke. He was talking with DeForest, the Federal prosecutor.

"That's your expertise," DeForest said. "You should get the Feds involved at this point."

"It was a US Marshals bust. We have a call into their offices," said Zeke. "And we'll need to go forward carefully."

In the end, Zeke got Marshal Brown on the phone, and they talked through the jurisdictional issues.

When they were done, Zeke said, "OK. Let's set something up."

* * *

The message was terse. "I need help with a Windows problem.

Anyone available?" And it was signed, 'Bear44.' The message became a part of a thread of online chats about operating system diagnostics and repairs, many of which were ancient in terms of today's technology.

The message sat alone and unanswered for two days, monitored by members of the US Marshal service's cyber team. Then there was a terse response: "I can help. What version are you using?"

* * *

"That's a standard response," said Luis Cruz. "Acknowledgement, and she's asking what I need. She'll check in a couple times a day, now."

"That'll speed things up a bit," said Marshal Brown. "OK, let's set up a meet."

"The message would be, 'Windows 7. Having trouble accessing the UI code. Thanks for offering."

"And it translates to…?" asked Brown.

"I want to set a meeting with her this week," said Cruz. "And asking where she is."

"OK, we'll send it."

"If she's nervous, she might disappear. We want to tell her that I'm OK, safe. So say, "Been working on this myself for a week, but I'm stuck."

"I'll have it sent."

* * *

"She came back with this message," said Brown. "Root is C++. Are you fluent? I have another project that's taking longer than expected, but I'll try to help. Traveling this week, though."

"She's finishing up a job. Luis Cruz says it's most likely a hit," said Brown when he'd reached Zeke. "Says she's telling him she's not around here, and she's on a job. He'll have to wait to get together with her."

Zeke thought for a minute. "OK, if she's not in Phoenix, then she's either in Boston or D.C. coming after me again, I suspect…"

* * *

"Sarah's OK?" asked Zeke as he stepped through the threshold. He'd arrived at Sarah's temporary apartment and Kimmy opened the door to his knock, Jerico in her right hand, pointed at the floor.

"She is," said Kimmy. "We've been playing it cautious, ever since you called with the information about Susan from Luis Cruz."

"We haven't found her yet," said Zeke, by way of update. "They're still monitoring the chat room."

"We've been playing cards and working on this jigsaw puzzle," Kimmy continued. Sarah was sitting on the couch while looking at her laptop when Zeke and Kimmy walked into the spacious living room.

"Anything odd going on? Any reason to worry?" asked Zeke.

"Not really," said Kimmy. "It's been pretty quiet."

"You're not visiting the office again until we catch Susan Del Gato, right?"

"That's the plan," said Sarah.

"According to Luis Cruz, that may be difficult. We have a message out to her from him, and she's responded. But it could take a while. She said she's not in Phoenix. Luis said he thinks she's traveling, on a job somewhere."

"A job to kill someone?" asked Sarah. "That could be me…"

"Or me," said Zeke. He paused a moment, thinking.

"Do you two have any intuitions about this?" Zeke asked. "Anything happen recently?"

"There was one thing," said Sarah, remembering. "It didn't make any sense."

"What was that?" asked Zeke.

"Well, I got a call from AAA about my car. They wanted me to take a survey about the service call."

"Service call?" Zeke asked.

"The woman who called said something about a lock-out, and she wanted to ask me about the service I received. A survey. It must have been a mistake," said Sarah.

"When was this?" asked Zeke.

"Yesterday," said Sarah.

Zeke and Kimmy exchanged a look.

"They had your name and number?" asked Zeke.

Sarah nodded. "From my account information, I guess," she said.

"Have you had any trouble with your car?" he asked.

"No," said Sarah. "I haven't driven it in the past week. Kimmy's been driving when we go out."

"OK, do you know if the AAA operator had your correct member number?" he asked.

"Actually, yes, I got my card out of my wallet to confirm it with her," said Sarah. She looked confused.

Kimmy said, "So, someone called AAA using your membership ID, and asked them to unlock your vehicle. Has the car been moved?"

Sarah said, "No, I saw it yesterday when we went to lunch at the mall. It was in my parking space."

Sarah was wearing a crimson sweatshirt with 'Harvard' written across the front, a matching pair of sweatpants and white sneakers. She had little makeup on and her hair was tied in a ponytail.

"Someone wanted access to your car, Sarah. Either to search it, or to steal it, or maybe something worse," said Zeke.

Sarah thought for a minute, then shook her head. "I've been a fool," she said. "I should have seen it right away."

"This killer's a pro," said Kimmy. "We were just lucky that triple-A called you on your registered phone number. If they'd called back on Susan's phone, we'd never have known."

"It could have been an accident," said Sarah. "Or a mistake."

Zeke shook his head. "Susan sent Cruz a message that she's not in Phoenix, and she's on the East Coast finishing up a job. I thought she might be after me, but now I'm thinking it's you, Sarah. She may be here in D.C. tracking you."

"So, what do we do?" asked Sarah.

"Let me have the keys. I'll head downstairs and take a look at the car. You two should go for a ride, take Kimmy's car and get out of the area," said Zeke.

* * *

As soon as Kimmy and Sarah had exited the building, Zeke approached the Camry and looked in the windows. He didn't touch anything. If it were an explosive device or some kind of booby trap, it could possibly be set off by motion, or by unlocking the car door. *Can't be too careful,* he thought.

There was nothing visible through the car windows. Zeke checked all the way around the vehicle. Everything appeared normal.

But a check under the car revealed what looked like three sticks of dynamite with a small battery taped to them, strapped to the undercarriage under the driver's seat.

Car bomb, he thought. Simple, effective and deadly. Zeke knew that such devices caused an explosion that would ignite the fuel tank, magnifying the explosion and destroying any evidence.

Slowly, he eased away from the car, stood up and called Kimmy. Then he called a contact in the D.C. FBI office and reported the bomb.

CHAPTER 21

"Look, sometimes I drink too much and my mouth gets me in trouble," said Hank.

The woman said nothing.

Hank was sitting in a metal chair in the apartment of the dining room he shared with Judith Henderson. His wrists and ankles were taped to the chair with duct tape and there was a brown leather belt wrapped around his neck.

"Look, I didn't do anything on purpose. I just got mad and started venting. At the bar, you know?"

He was terrified and almost incoherent, Susan noticed.

"What did you tell them?" she asked him.

Hank had seen an angle, and approached Eddie George asking for money. Blackmail, actually, threatening to tell the authorities about the student loan money, and Eddie's part in arranging the scam. Eddie George had told Jobare Worthington, who told Freddy Hanson. Freddy shared this information with Benito Diaz.

"I won't say anything else. I was just drunk and mad. It was stupid," he continued.

Yes, it was, thought Susan Del Gato, *threatening to expose them.* She said, "It's OK, Hank." And she stepped behind him.

Franticly he twisted, looking over one shoulder, then the other, trying to keep her in view. His secured wrists and ankles kept him in check.

Susan took the end of the belt and tightened it. She wrapped it around her hand, made a fist, and pulled harder.

Hank, still frantic, started to yell. Susan hit him on the top of his head with the cast iron frying pan, hard, and then she took her time.

* * *

"It seems like it's been months since I was here," said Tracy Johnson. She and Zeke were sitting on the deck of his Cape Cod rental, watching the waves break gently against the shore. It was early evening, and the weather was cooling off. The full moon was already visible in the southern sky.

Zeke sipped a glass of red wine and said, "I know. But it's only been a couple of weeks."

Tracy said, "I hoarded my vacation days to make this trip. I even borrowed a few from next year."

"They let you do that at the Secret Service?" Zeke asked. "They're flexible."

Tracy smiled. "I know people," she said cryptically.

They were silent for a minute. Then Tracy said, "You're like a cat."

"The nine lives?" Zeke laughed.

She nodded. "First the eight Mara's in the Phoenix parking lot, then the assassin in Cambridge. And that was all within the same month, wasn't it?"

Zeke nodded, looking at the sea. "Nothing too much to worry about," he said.

"Do you think they'll try again? Whoever's behind the attempts?"

"Don't know. But we're being careful," Zeke added.

Tracy set her drink down and sat back in her chair. The light breeze from the south washed across their faces and brought with it the smell of salt and ocean. The sounds of the waves lapping were relaxing. The tension melted away.

"I'm so glad I'm here," said Tracy. "This is so nice."

"Don't get too comfortable," said Zeke, wryly.

Tracy's eyes were closed. "Mmm," she said.

"We've got work to do," he continued.

Tracy said nothing. Then she opened her eyes and stood up. She walked to Zeke and leaned over his chair until their noses touched.

She smiled a wide smile. "Not tonight," she said. "Tonight is a special night. I have plans for you."

Zeke smiled and kissed her upper lip. He pulled on it gently with his lips and then kissed her again.

"Be careful what you ask for," Tracy whispered.

He nodded slightly, slowly. "We should go inside," he said.

"What's inside?" she asked, teasing.

"You'll see," he said.

* * *

Susan Del Gato sat in her car and watched. It was difficult here, because the streets were narrow and private, and there was no good place to park and watch the house. She couldn't quite see the front door from this angle, and she felt vulnerable in this spot.

She watched for a moment, calculating, and then decided that the exposure wasn't a good risk in this small, wealthy Cape Cod neighborhood. Carefully, she started the rental car, a green Range Rover, and eased away from the curb back toward Barnstable.

She parked on Main Street in front of Tim's Books and, window shopping, wandered down the street. She knew there were cameras, but her floppy hat and dark sunglasses obstructed her face enough to make her feel anonymous.

The trick was to find a way to watch this Zeke Traynor without giving herself away. She'd thought she had him once, in Cambridge, but they had anticipated her presence. That didn't happen very often. Now, a quick strike while they expected her to be in hiding could make up for it. She found a coffee shop, ordered a cup and started planning.

* * *

"I'm from the security company," the man said. He was a tall, black man, neatly dressed in workman's clothes wearing a shirt with "Cape Cod Security" stenciled over his pocket. "I'm Byron," he continued.

"How can I help, Byron?" Tracy asked.

The man looked at his clipboard, and then at the house number next to the door. "I have a work order for this address, for a Zeke Traynor," he said.

"Can I see your ID?" she asked.

Byron slipped the laminated ID card from his pocket. Tracy checked it carefully. Then she nodded. "Zeke's not here right now. We're renting," she said. "So the owners may have placed the order."

Byron said, "This is for a system check and a software upgrade. We sent out an e-mail about the software upgrade, offered it for free. The owner probably authorized it."

Tracy said, "Do you know where the system is?"

Byron looked at his paper again. "It's in the kitchen," he said.

"Come on in," said Tracy.

They walked across the cottage to the kitchen. Appropriately, Aerosmith's "Looks Like A Lady," from the album *Permanent Vacation* was playing in the background. Tracy opened a couple cabinets, then found the equipment.

"Is this it?" she asked.

"That's it," said Byron. "This won't take long. Your Internet will be down for, oh, five minutes, tops."

Tracy's laptop was open on the kitchen table where she'd been sitting. "OK, time for a break, I guess."

While Byron upgraded the equipment, Tracy took a cup

of hot tea out onto the deck and watched the ocean roll in and back out. *I'd never get tired of this,* she thought. *Or of Zeke.*

A few minutes later, Byron stuck his head out the sliding glass door and said, "All done."

Tracy nodded and turned back toward the house.

"Could you sign here, please? Just saying that I was here, and the work was done," he said, handing his clipboard to her.

She signed where he indicated, handed it back and said, "Thanks."

He walked to the door.

"Sure. Have a nice day," he said, and he let himself out.

* * *

"You were successful?" asked Susan.

"Yep, planted an infrared video camera and an audio device that will monitor the entire cottage. Military grade, wide angle lens, body heat activated, all that. The best money can buy," said Byron.

"Did you have any trouble?"

"No, he wasn't there, like you said. It was just the girl," he said. "Guess where it is?" he asked, meaning the camera.

She waited.

"It's a book, with the camera in the spine and the audio device inside. Small microphone in the spine, too. I mean small, as in pin-prick small," he said.

"Do you have the receiving equipment? Can we test it?" asked Susan.

"Yeah, sure, I've got my monitor." Byron pulled a small video monitor from his case. "It should be working now, if she's still in the cottage."

They watched as the small monitor came to life showing the inside of the cottage from a spot apparently high on a bookshelf. They could hear Aerosmith still playing in the background.

"That's it. I've got it wired into the Internet, so you can monitor it from any computer or your phone with this URL and password." He handed her a slip of paper. "The alarm code is on there, too."

"Pleasure doing business with you, Byron," said Susan. She handed him a small stack of currency. "Five thousand, correct? Parts and labor." She knew it was.

He nodded, put the money and the monitor in his case, stood and walked away.

* * *

Susan started the video over again for the third time. In it, she had watched Zeke Traynor and Tracy Johnson in their small cottage, cooking breakfast, eating, and reading a newspaper, sharing sections. They were in the open living area, Zeke sitting on the couch with his paper spread out on the coffee table, while Tracy sat cross-legged on the floor. Her part of the paper was on the ground in front of her.

At one point, Tracy looked over at Zeke and said, "We should just stay here forever."

Zeke smiled at her and said, "The highs are in the thirty degree range in January."

The video monitor was very good quality, and the small HD camera fed it excellent images even in low light. Today, however, the sunshine reflecting on the ocean lit up the space.

Zeke got up and poured himself and Tracy more coffee, handed the cup back to her and took his seat on the couch.

"What would you like to do this afternoon?" he asked.

"We should go to town, shop a little bit and then drink some wine," she said.

"Sounds good to me," said Zeke. They read some more.

Tracy said, "I'm going to change."

"Why?" asked Zeke.

"I can't shop in my pajamas, silly," she said, laughing.

"OK, I'll help you," said Zeke, and he followed her into the bedroom.

Susan sighed. It seemed that at least twice a day the two of them found a reason to go to the bedroom, and each time they stayed there for at least twenty minutes, sometimes much longer. She flipped off the monitor, knowing that the camera would start again when it sensed their body heat.

I'm surprised it can't feel the heat from the bedroom, she thought with a smile.

Over the past two days, Susan had gathered all of the information she needed to complete her assignment. There wasn't much she didn't know about Zeke Traynor's routine, his relationship or his reactions.

Now, all I need is the right opportunity, she thought.

* * *

They were sitting outdoors at a small sidewalk table in front of an Italian restaurant on Main Street in Hyannis. The wind was light and still warm, as they ate. Tracy was picking at the remains of a Caprese Salad, and Zeke had finished his Tuscan Chicken Sandwich. They were sipping an Italian Pinot Grigio.

"Good food," said Tracy. "Good company and a great location."

"I know. I'm always sorry when you leave," said Zeke.

"Soon," she said.

"It's probably better. We need to take care of the business here, and I'll feel better knowing you're safe."

Tracy nodded. "Do you think we're convincing them?"

"I do. The killer's almost certainly watching and listening to everything we're doing," said Zeke. "Looking for the right opportunity to eliminate me. Since she missed in Cambridge, I mean."

"She's resourceful and she's resilient," said Tracy, looking around on the street. "Maybe I should stay and protect you. I'm Secret Service after all…"

Zeke smiled. "Maybe."

"It is kind of creepy that someone's watching us in the cottage."

"It is. But they can't see in the bedroom," he added.

"Good thing," said Tracy. "I'm hardly ever wearing anything substantial in there."

Then she thought and said, "You're sure? They can't see in the bedroom?"

Zeke smiled and nodded. "Well, you said the security system guy was in the kitchen and living area..."

Tracy nodded. "So how do you think it'll go down?" she asked.

"I'm counting on a planned attack in the cottage. That's what I'd do," he said. "Breech the back doors, and wait until we return. There's not a lot of space, but at night, there are several places she could hide, conceal herself until we return."

"Then pop up with a gun and take you out?" asked Tracy, sweetly.

"Or a knife. Or more battery acid."

"Yeah, that was pretty creepy," said Tracy. "So, do you have a plan?"

* * *

It was after dusk when they made their way back to the cottage. They'd spent the late afternoon wandering in and out of Main Street shops on the Cape, and eventually returned to their car and pointed it south toward the ocean.

"This really is a romantic spot," she said. "The moonlight is just right."

Zeke smiled.

In a couple of minutes, they pulled into the cottage driveway and Zeke hopped out and opened the passenger door.

"Thank you, sir," she said, and gave him a small kiss on the cheek.

Together, they walked the short distance to the front door, shopping bags in hand. Zeke pulled out the keys and unlocked the entrance and opened the door. They stepped inside and Zeke set down his bag and said, "I'll be right back; I need to use the restroom."

As he walked across the small living room a shadow shifted by the window behind him. A woman's silhouette was visible in the moonlight that splashed into the room from the porch. She was quick and silent and all business. Her shadow was sleek and efficient in the small space. She leveled her handgun at Zeke's retreating figure.

Suddenly, without warning, the handgun flew into the air, immediately followed by a loud explosion. The woman grabbed her right hand and cradled it in her left, bent over at the waist in pain.

Kimmy hurtled the small couch and knocked Susan Del Gato to the ground, cuffing her hands behind her despite the blood and the visible muscles and bones in her right hand. "I should let her bleed out," she said to no one in particular.

* * *

Kimmy had brought a small team of specialists with her from The Agency in D.C., and they were able to clean up the mess quickly. Susan was bandaged and secured and loaded into a black SUV that immediately headed south toward Washington, an eight and a half hour journey, mostly on Interstate 95. The FBI in Washington was awaiting her delivery.

"That went well," Kimmy said.

Zeke nodded. "I thought substituting you for Tracy might be the right move," he said. "You're deadly from that distance, and deadlier any closer."

Kimmy smiled and wandered around the room. "Nice place, Zeke. I see why you hang out up here." She turned on the CD player and a Jason Mraz song started playing.

"Thanks," said Zeke. "What it lacks in size, it makes up for in views."

"Sure does," said Kimmy, looking out the windows at the churning ocean, visible in the cottage's outside lighting.

A technician from The Agency knocked on the front door and opened it. He stuck his head into the room and said, "I'm Allen, and I'm here to get the bugs out."

* * *

"I'll be heading down to Washington tomorrow," Zeke said. He was talking to Clive Greene on the phone in his Cape Cod cottage. Agency people had come and gone all evening, but the place was thinning out.

"Very well," said Clive. "Let's plan to meet over lunch."

"Somewhere with British food?" asked Zeke, innocently.

Clive ignored the comment. "We may have a lead on the human trafficking organization," he said. "We're getting close."

"Good," said Zeke. "I put Tracy on an airplane yesterday. She's back in Atlanta. I'll fly down to see you tomorrow morning."

"We'll be here," said Clive.

* * *

The restaurant was small and local, and Clive was immediately recognized and treated as family when they entered. Zeke looked around the room and picked a table that allowed unobstructed views of the front and back of the house. A long bar ran half the length of the restaurant and the ceiling was painted a bright red.

The young waitress followed Zeke and Clive, and as they were sitting, she said, "Welcome to the Irish Channel. Can I get you something to drink?"

"An Irish pub in Chinatown," said Zeke, shaking his head. "Go figure."

"How about the red ale," said Clive. "A Smithwicks."

"Very good, sir."

Zeke said, "I'll have a Harp, please."

When the server had left, Zeke said, "What do you have on the human trafficking?"

"Yes, well, now that Ramirez isn't running interference for Diaz, Clark Hall has asked us to continue our original investigation," said Clive.

"You mentioned a lead?" asked Zeke.

"Yes, well, it appears that one of the killers, one of the Mara's that tried to kill you—sorry, kidnap you—in Phoenix, changed his mind and is suddenly talking to save his skin," said Clive. "It could be an opportunity to derail Diaz's operation."

"What made him change his mind?" Zeke asked about the Mara.

"Apparently, it was something that you said when you talked with them in Phoenix," said Clive. "Did you find some leverage?"

"Maybe. Which one?" said Zeke.

"Ernesto Reyes."

"Sure," said Zeke. "He seemed the weakest. I thought he might give it up when they charged him with attempted murder. The Mara's in the ICE parking lot were apparently there to abduct us, not kill us. I'll bet the escalated charges by the Federal Prosecutor scared him enough to get him to talk. I just loosened him up some. The charges opened him up."

"Maybe so," said Clive.

"Regardless, that's good news," said Zeke. "Has he given us anything specific? Anything useful?"

"It seems that he wants to cut a deal for himself," said Clive. "He says he's willing to tell it all."

CHAPTER 22

"We need to chop off the head of this Lernaean hydra," said Clive.

"That would be lovely," said Kimmy. "I'm ready." She was standing next to Clive, looking out the window of his library-like office, bouncing slightly on the balls of her feet.

"Which head, though?" asked Zeke, sitting in a comfortable chair across the table.

"Don't know. Maybe all of them," said Clive. "We'll keep going until it dies, I suppose."

Sally, Clive's researcher and assistant, was looking at her laptop.

"I know where we can start," said Zeke. "Benito Diaz was connected to Ramirez, and also to Susan Del Gato, the killer. We know he's heavy into human trafficking, as well as prostitution and drugs."

"Yes, and somehow he's connected with the attempt on Zeke in Cambridge," said Kimmy. "His hitman, well, hit-persons, were responsible for the WITSEC murders as well as two attempts on Zeke's life. West Coast and East Coast."

"I thought these were separate investigations, the human trafficking and the student loan scam," said Clive.

"We did, too, initially," said Zeke. "But it's curious. We're coming across some of the same players in both investigations."

"Right," said Kimmy. "Freddy Hanson. Susan Del Gato, who worked with Luis Cruz. Maybe Benito Diaz…"

"It's a loose connection. Hanson has some business dealings with Benito Diaz," said Zeke. "Luis Cruz confirmed that. He said that someone involved with the Student Loan scam wanted me out of there, and Hanson called Diaz for help. There aren't that many killers available…"

Zeke looked at Clive. "Raul Diaz connected with Jorge Ramirez while he was in prison. Jorge was a guard there, right?"

Clive nodded.

"I wonder what Raul Diaz's current status is, then. He's either a felon who served his time, or he may have gotten out early…" said Zeke.

"Which would possibly put him on parole," said Clive. "When was he released from prison?"

Sally typed for a moment and said, "He was released in 2015. Part of the Federal Inmate Release program."

"What's that?" asked Kimmy.

Sally said, "There was a change in the sentencing laws for drug offenders. They reduced the sentencing guidelines for drug traffickers, basically instituted shorter sentences, and they applied the changes retroactively."

Clive shook his head.

"So Raul Cruz was in prison for drug trafficking, and when

this program went into effect, he was released on parole?" asked Kimmy.

"Well, drug trafficking and child porn," said Zeke.

"Yep. And according to this," said Sally, tapping her computer, "he's still on parole."

"I think we need to chat with Clark Hall," said Zeke.

* * *

"Look, I'm not going back to prison," said Raul Diaz. "I don't care what it takes."

"Why don't you tell us about your brother's businesses?" asked Clark Hall. He was one of about a dozen law enforcement people crammed into the small room with Raul Diaz. Officially, Acting Special Agent in Charge Jose Fernandez was hosting the meeting, but Clark Hall outranked him.

In addition to the half dozen ICE personnel, Raul Diaz's United States Probation/Parole officer and his attorney were in the room. Zeke and Kimmy were connected by phone to the speakerphone in the small conference room in ICE headquarters. Raul looked around the room nervously.

"No, my brother's a businessman," he started. "He's in transportation and logistics."

"Really," said Clark Hall.

"Mr. Hall," said the attorney, "My client hasn't done anything illegal, here. He's reported on time and has kept his nose clean. He's not involved with anything sordid or illegal. That would violate the terms of his parole."

Clark Hall looked at the attorney. "Actually, we have extensive and rather arbitrary powers over ex-cons," he said. "We can put Mr. Diaz here back in jail any time we choose to do so. He lost his rights when he was convicted of a felony."

Raul Diaz seemed to shrink in his chair.

Zeke said, "Raul, perhaps there's some other information you'd like to share with us. Something about the Boston connection?"

"I don't know anything about that," said Diaz, looking around nervously. "I can't help you with any of that…"

His attorney said, "Don't say anything else, Raul."

Raul's blink rate had increased and he had shrunk in on himself physically, often clear signs of lying.

Zeke said, "We don't care much about you, Raul. I don't care whether you go back to prison or stay on the outside. But we need to know what's going on in Boston."

"Why would I know about that?" he asked.

"Maybe you overheard something. Maybe your brother said something to you," Zeke continued.

"I heard some things," said Raul. "Some things that may help you find what you're looking for."

"What did you hear?" asked Clark Hall.

"One of the guys I know, a driver, he works for my brother. He makes runs to Boston. Told me that Freddy Hanson is the guy in charge. He's supposedly involved in stealing money from some student loans or something."

"How did your guy know about it?" asked Zeke.

"He was making a delivery and he said he overheard this

Hanson talking on the phone. Telling someone that he'd take care of the problem, that their arrangement was still good."

"How do you know it was about the student loans?" asked Zeke.

"When he hung up, he said, 'These academics make me sick,' and he told the driver 'that with all the money they're stealing, they should clean up their own messes.' It was like a rant, our guy said."

* * *

Freddy Hanson stood in the street, handcuffed, with three large Boston Police officers surrounding him.

"You're looking pretty pathetic, Freddy," Deputy Chief O'Malley said. Standing next to him, Zeke smiled.

Roy Calhoun and Louie Brennan, also handcuffed, were both sitting on a curb, feet in the street and with blue and red lights washing over them in the darkness.

"I'll be outta there in five minutes," said Hanson with what Zeke interpreted as a lot of false bravado.

"Sure, Freddy," said O'Malley. "This time, though, I think we've got you dead to rights."

Freddy Hanson looked confused. "What?" he said. "What makes you so sure?"

"It's the source of our intel," said O'Malley.

"What's that?"

"Have you ever heard of Diaz? Out of Phoenix?"

Hanson paled for a moment. Then he said, "No way! No

way Benito Diaz had anything to do with this. You guys are lying to me."

"No, not Benito Diaz," said O'Malley with a grin. "It's his brother, Raul Diaz. Sang like a bird after the US Marshals arrested him. He had a lot to say, Freddy, trying to save his own skin. Said he didn't want to go back to prison."

Freddy Hanson opened his mouth, and then closed it again. Then he said, "Federal? You're not Federal."

"No, we're not. We're just helping out, detaining you until they get here. They sent the arrest warrant ahead this time. They should be here in a couple of hours."

Louie Brennan, listening, said "Federal? What?" and started to stand up.

"Sit down, Louie. I don't want to have to tell you again."

"I'm not going down on a Federal charge," said Brennan. "We're local. You got all this wrong." He kept getting up, and even with his arms handcuffed behind him, he looked formidable.

"I'm not, I'm not," said Brennan, agitated. He started jumping around in small circles, on one foot, then the other, with what looked like crazy ballet moves. Then he ran directly at Deputy Chief O'Malley.

As the big man passed him, Zeke lashed out with a knee kick aimed at the inside of Brennan's far knee. It was a small, quick move, and suddenly the big man was lying in the road, screaming in pain.

* * *

"I'm not taking the fall for this," said Freddy Hanson, again. "No way. I didn't do anything."

"Diaz says you were a part of the human trafficking coming in from Central America, Freddy. Said you bought boys and girls from him," said O'Malley. "Bet you preferred the boys."

"No, that wasn't me," said Freddy.

They were in an interrogation room in the Boston PD's downtown precinct, O'Malley and Zeke talking with the mob boss, along with a Boston FBI agent.

"And there's the drugs. And prostitution. And…"

"Look, I don't know why you guys decided to do this," said Hanson, taking another tack. "We pay a lot for your protection." He looked at O'Malley.

"I don't know about that," said O'Malley, "but I do know that this is Federal."

"OK, look, get a Federal Prosecutor in here. We can cut a deal," said Hanson.

* * *

After the introductions, the Federal Prosecutor, a woman named Gail Regent, said, "What do you have for me, Mr. Hanson?"

She was a veteran prosecutor, a lifer, about forty-five years old with graying hair. She wore a brown business suit and no wedding ring. Her eyes looked tired.

"Look," started Freddy Hanson, "You guys are trying to jam me up with some bogus charges…"

"Freddy, let me talk," said his attorney, a slick looking man with white hair, a rep tie and what looked to Zeke like a Brooks Brothers suit. "OK?"

"Yeah, sure," said Hanson. They had conferred earlier, while awaiting Gail Regent.

"I believe you'll have trouble proving these charges," said the attorney, whose name was Gerald Howell. "This case seems to be built on a lot of hearsay and information that's suspect at best."

Gail listened.

"But hypothetically, my client may be privy to information that could help you with a much bigger crime."

"It's his duty to report that, if it's even true," said Gail Regent.

"Of course," said the attorney, and looked across the table at her.

"Let's hear what you've got," she said to Freddy, "and if it's as good as Mr. Howell has implied, we're willing to reduce the charges."

"Dismiss," said Howell, not giving an inch.

"It had better be good to merit that," she said under her breath.

"We'll probably need to put my client in Witness Protection after this," said Howell. "It's that big. Hypothetically speaking."

The attorneys talked for a moment and then reached agreement.

Gail said, "OK, go ahead, spill it…"

Hanson looked at his attorney, who nodded, and Hanson

said, "OK, I'm not involved with this. I just know about it…"

Gail Regent, taking notes, nodded.

Freddy Hanson said, "Have you ever heard of Jobare Worthington?"

* * *

"This is almost too easy," Zeke said.

"But we'll need to move fast, while we still have momentum," said Kimmy.

They were eating lunch at a small Irish restaurant on Harvard Square, sandwiched between a textbook store and a bicycle shop. Kimmy was working on a roasted beet salad, while Zeke devoured an excellent cheeseburger topped with aged Irish cheddar and garlic aioli.

"This is great," he said about the food.

"Do you think the white-collar guys from the FBI will get up to speed in time to arrest Jobare?" asked Kimmy.

"They didn't have enough to hold him with Richardson's testimony. Said it was too little to get a conviction. But they're pretty sharp," said Zeke. "I think, with Freddy Hanson's testimony, they'll be able to put Dr. Worthington away for a while.

After the interview with Freddy Hanson, the Federal Prosecutor had called the FBI and asked them to look into the falsified Student Loans. The FBI, already involved because of Dr. Richardson's arrest, responded quickly and sent a team out of their Boston offices, to be assisted by members of the white-collar crimes division in D.C. Zeke had turned over the details of his audit and pointed the agents in the right direction, to give them a running start.

"So what's next?" asked Kimmy.

"We'll see when they pick up Dr. Worthington. It shouldn't take too long, now."

* * *

"I don't know what you mean," said Jobare Worthington, sounding sullen in a pitchy voice.

"Do you know a Freddy Hanson?" asked the FBI interviewer. He was a tall man in a white shirt and tie who took his time and talked slowly. His name was Colbert and he seemed patient and competent.

"Freddy Hanson? Is that one of my students?" asked Worthington. "Because I don't know all the students' names…"

"He identified you as the ringleader for the student loan thefts. Freddy Hanson?"

"He did?" Jobare looked blank.

"When we arrested you, we also had a warrant that allowed us to search you, your phone and your computer. Can you guess what we found in your phone?"

"What?" asked Worthington.

"Calls to Freddy Hanson, as recently as yesterday. And e-mails you sent from your office last week," said Agent Colbert.

Worthington was quiet for a moment. Then he said, "We're small cogs in this wheel. We're not calling the shots."

"Fair enough," said Colbert. "Who is?"

CHAPTER 23

"This is crazy," said Zeke. "The amount of money we're talking about is huge."

"It is," said Sarah Helms. "Like I said, we tend to get used to the big dollar amounts. But yes, it's huge."

Sarah had joined Zeke and Kimmy in Cambridge with ADD Styles' permission. They felt that she may have some insight into the details of the Student Loan Scam. Jobare had named his contact, Milo Christianson, in his statement to the FBI.

Christianson was from old money, according to Jobare. They had first met years ago at a Raleigh University fundraiser; Christianson was a Raleigh alumnus. After several donor meetings, Christianson felt out Worthington and found him to be receptive to discussing the student loan process. Over old scotch and with a touch of shared larceny, the men began to speculate on the soft spots in the system, and how they might be exploited.

"So, where do we find Christianson?" asked Kimmy.

"FBI says he's a prominent Wall Street banker. A principal

with Harrison, Hart and Christianson. One of his ancestors founded the company," said Zeke.

"So, New York?"

"Sure. But the FBI got a whiff of this and they've pretty much taken over. They're organizing a small task force to coordinate and take down Christianson," said Zeke.

"Do you think he has partners? Or is he in it alone?" asked Kimmy.

"Jobare said he's certain that there are more people involved at that level. He just claims that he doesn't have their names," said Zeke.

"The FBI guys will get that information, I'm sure," said Sarah Helms. "What do they want from us?"

"The Boston FBI is sending some people to meet with us and discuss the Student Loan scam. They'll want all the details that we can share."

* * *

"I believe that Milo will be talking about us," said Baron Holmes.

Stuart Williams III nodded in agreement.

They were eating a power breakfast in Williams' offices, served by a waiter and his cook, who was Cordon Bleu trained. The food had been prepared in the industrial kitchen adjoining his office.

"He's been detained by the Feds," said Stuart Williams. "That's not a good sign."

"They're getting close, circling the wagons, it seems."

Williams nodded. "And our killer is out of commission," he added.

"Yes. She was taken down on Cape Cod." Baron Holmes took his cell phone from his interior pocket, looked at the screen and put it back. "She wasn't as good as Benito Diaz had led us to believe."

"No, disappointing," said Williams. "I thought she was the answer to our auditor problem."

Holmes said, "Yes, me too. It's after ten, so I'll need to be going."

Stuart Williams said, "What's our plan from here?"

"Well, Milo will most likely give us up," said Holmes. "Yes, let's count on that. So, it'll have to be his word against ours."

"Can they prove that we were involved?" asked Williams.

"No, I don't think so. The money's well hidden and there's no direct paper trail to us. We were too clever for that," said Holmes.

"It was smart, getting all the money overseas quickly," said Williams. "Who would have thought of diplomatic courier bags? And your family connections in Scotland?"

It was a rhetorical question, and Holmes didn't answer.

"The less said, the better, of course," said Williams.

"Yes," said Holmes. "Just so."

* * *

"You've got them," said Zeke.

Agent Randolph nodded and said, "I agree."

Special Agent in Charge, George Talbert said, "Me, too."

The FBI technicians had remotely activated the microphone in Baron Holmes cell phone and were listening to and recording the breakfast conversation of the two men. It was as if the agents were sitting at the table with Baron Holmes and Stuart Williams III.

They both looked at the FBI attorney who was there to assure the operation was legal, and that the wiretapping was within Federal guidelines. She was also to be responsible for the chain of evidence considerations, once the recording was completed.

She nodded.

The three of them were sitting at FBI Headquarters in New York, monitoring the cell phone transmission over the 4G wireless network. Milo Christianson had quickly coughed up the names of the other two men.

"It just gets easier and easier," said Agent Randolph. "We didn't even have to leave the office."

Zeke said, "I guess you've got enough to pick them up."

"Yes, and thanks for the information about the Student Loan scam," said the agent. "It pointed us in the right direction."

"Don't forget the attempted murder," said Zeke. "I'm thinking that, between the two of them and Susan Del Gato, you'll be able to turn someone."

"It's what we do," said SAC Talbert. "I'm dispatching men to pick them both up right now."

* * *

The tall man in the black suit glanced east and then west on the sidewalk, and then he stepped to the curb and opened the door of the limousine.

Baron Holmes stepped out and blinked in the sunlight. He stepped up onto the curb. Baron Holmes waited a moment, as was his habit, until his bodyguard had closed the car door and joined him for the walk to his offices.

The building was a sixty-two story glass and steel creation of Renzo Piano, whom Baron Holmes considered to be one of the greatest living architects. Holmes' penthouse offices were spectacular, boasting twenty-foot ceilings, floor to ceiling windows and views of the East River and Governors Island in the distance. Looking east, one could see the Brooklyn Bridge.

"And if you like that, I have a bridge I can sell you," said Baron Holmes, mostly to himself. It was his daily mantra, a routine.

The man in the black suit appeared on Baron Holmes left side, and they walked together. A doorman opened the front door and bowed slightly at the sight of New York royalty. Inside the building, the man in the black suit nodded a greeting to the security guard behind the desk and, without breaking stride, the two men approached an elevator. Baron Holmes' private elevator.

Just then, as they waited for access, a voice called out from behind them.

"Hello, Baron," said Zeke Traynor. "I understand that you're trying to kill me."

The bodyguard stepped between Holmes and Zeke, and a handgun appeared in his right hand. He was totally focused on Zeke as he separated the two men with his body movements.

"You won't shoot in here," said Zeke, holding his right hand palm up and indicating the surrounding lobby area, presently filled with people. "You might injure your boss with the ricochet."

The man hesitated a moment, judging the angles and distances. That small doubt was all Zeke needed. He quickly stepped toward the man, his hand still extended and grabbed the gun barrel and rotated it forward, as if shifting into first gear. The gun came free in Zeke's hand.

The elevator dinged, the door opened and Baron Holmes stepped briskly toward it.

Kimmy said, "Not so fast," and stepped between the octogenarian and the open elevator, cutting off his advance.

He tried to push past her, but Kimmy executed a quick move that left Baron Holmes sitting on his dignified ass.

Four men in white shirts and windbreakers with 'FBI' printed in capital letters on the back stepped into the lobby. Three surrounded Baron Holmes while the fourth man stood next to the bodyguard, blocking his access to the action.

"Baron Holmes, you're under arrest," said the oldest FBI agent. "You'll be coming with us, now."

* * *

"Talk about being highly connected," said Clive. "This guy is like a spider in his web."

Zeke and Kimmy had joined Clive in his office. It was Saturday, and they had driven the four plus hours back to D.C. after the FBI had taken Baron Holmes into custody. Three black FBI SUV's had squealed to the curb as the four agents walked Holmes and his bodyguard out the front door of his building in handcuffs. Holmes was composed until three local press photographers appeared and started snapping pictures as quickly as the motor drives of their cameras could go. Then he'd lost it, yelling and trying to cover his face with his hands while being pushed toward the vehicles.

"No doubt," said Zeke. "From what I know, he's a part of the power elite. A former congressman, he's connected to judges and Senators and bankers, just about everyone with money and power. He's a presidential advisor."

"Those connections are everywhere," said Clive. "I spoke with my contact in the New York FBI office. It seems that Baron Holmes is active in D.C. and Boston and Palm Beach, as well as New York. He knows just about everyone."

"Bet he's got a great attorney," said Kimmy, looking out the window, relaxed, but missing nothing.

"Did the FBI share any details?" asked Zeke.

Clive said, "They've detained Holmes as a person of interest right now, while they're digging through the paperwork and following the money trail. But they're very confident that they can find the connection. Between Holmes and the Student Loan thefts, that is."

"And Stuart Williams?" asked Zeke.

"He's also been detained," said Clive. "The New York FBI has had a busy day."

"What about the bodyguard?" asked Zeke.

"For hire," said Clive. "Not really involved in the rest of it."

"Who else was in it with him?" asked Kimmy.

"Well, Milo Christianson, we know that," said Clive. "And Stuart Williams III. We recorded their conversation when we remotely activated the speaker on his cell phone. And possibly others, we expect. But that will all come out in the investigation, won't it?"

CHAPTER 24

The sky shone in bright reds and oranges, cast by the setting sun. The mountains reflected the colors and created deep shadows between the crags and valleys. Arizona's landscape is particularly conducive to colorful sunsets.

Zeke Traynor pulled up to the curb and parked his rental car in front of the small bodega. The store was located in a popular commercial strip in Scottsdale, between a dry cleaner and a wine store. He stepped out of the car, locked it, and walked to the corner.

Benito Diaz's compound is just up the street, here, thought Zeke. He waited at the corner until a black Lincoln SUV turned and stopped for him. Zeke hopped into the passenger's side, and the car moved toward the compound at a reasonable speed.

"Just take me past the house," said Zeke.

"OK. Then I'll roll around to the back of the compound," said Kimmy.

"As planned. Good," said Zeke, looking hard at the Diaz house.

After Raul Diaz talked to Clark Hall and the ICE agents, he had been detained in their Phoenix facility on a charge of possible parole violation. That prevented him from alerting his brother, Benito, to ICE's scrutiny.

In the meantime, based on the cell phone wiretap of Holmes and Williams' conversation over breakfast and their later testimony, ICE had issued a Federal warrant for the arrest of Benito Diaz. Fearing that there might be additional leaks in the Phoenix ICE office, Clark Hall quietly deputized Zeke and Kimmy and agreed to let them arrest Diaz.

The compound looked quiet in the twilight as Zeke approached, the outside lights illuminating the yard and the front of the house. Several palm trees occupied the front yard and the iron gates across the driveway were closed. There was an Audi RS3 in the driveway.

Zeke crouched near the driveway and watched through the iron gates. A few moments later, a large man strolled across the front yard.

A guard, thought Zeke. He spotted the man's handgun tucked into his belt and covered by his shirt.

The guard stopped near the car and lit a cigarette, the match flashing in the low light. He shook out the match and continued on his patrol.

As soon as the guard turned the corner, Zeke vaulted over the fence and made his way up on the front veranda. The space on the wide veranda was packed with chairs and chaise lounges, outdoor furniture that could easily be moved into the yard. It made for convenient cover as Zeke edged to the windows and snuck a look at the interior of the house.

Inside, the house had an expansive, open floor plan with a living area toward the front of the house, followed by a dining area and a kitchen. The back wall was primarily made of glass, and the outdoor living space was visible just past the kitchen. There were four people in the dining room, three sitting at the table. From his photograph, Zeke recognized Benito Diaz as one of them.

The others at the table were men, with the exception of the woman who was circling the table and serving them food. It looked to Zeke like she was serving enchiladas.

Mentally timing the guard's probable route around the house, Zeke moved to the front door and waited. A moment later, through the glass he saw the guard circling through the back yard. When he was no longer visible, Zeke pulled his gun and waited just a moment longer.

Seconds later, a bright flash came from the back yard, followed by two loud explosions that originated at the far corner of the yard near the privacy wall. The men at the table all turned toward the noise and two of them stood, guns drawn, and ran to the sliding glass door, quickly exiting the house into the outdoor space. Benito Diaz sat at the table, watching them as they joined the outdoor guard and surrounded the still burning fire. They pointed their guns at the device and squinted in the darkness to see if anyone was lurking there.

* * *

Zeke opened the front door quietly and slipped inside.

I've got about twenty seconds, thought Zeke. He walked directly to the dining room table, touched the muzzle of his Walther PPK to Benito Diaz's temple and said, "No te muevas. Don't move."

Diaz paled, but he was very still. Slowly, he moved his head toward Zeke and said, with no expression, "You're a dead man."

"Eventually," said Zeke, "but not today." He was watching the action in the back yard.

The woman who had been serving enchiladas looked at Zeke, then at the gun, and sat down at the table. She put her hands flat on its surface.

The men outside seemed confused. The fire was going out, and nothing had happened for almost a minute. One of the men looked back into the house and saw Zeke standing over Benito Diaz. He spoke a flurry of words in Spanish, and the others looked back into the house through the glass walls.

Suddenly a small ghost-like figure rose from the grass and in a single movement leveled an Uzi Pro at the three men.

"Ponte de rodillas," said Kimmy. "Get on your knees." She let off a three-round burst pointed at the fire.

The three men looked at Kimmy's automatic weapon, a sinister and efficient looking tool, and they thought about their odds for a moment. Then each man lowered his handgun and they slowly dropped to their knees in unison.

* * *

"I can make you very rich," said Benito Diaz, simply. "Or I can have you killed." Having executed the warrant, Zeke and Kimmy were awaiting the ICE agents to take the arrested man to prison.

"You've been trying," said Zeke. "To kill me, I mean. How's that going for you?"

Benito Diaz looked at Zeke, his eyes not blinking. "Yes," he said. "But you should be very careful." He looked around. "Coming into my home, this was a big mistake."

The three men were still outside, kneeling in the yard and outgunned by Kimmy and her Uzi. Zeke had secured Diaz's hands behind him in the chair with a pair of handcuffs. The woman, across the table from him, was secured in the same fashion.

Zeke said, absently, "I make my fair share of mistakes." He was clearly thinking about something else. Then he said, "Your two killers are in custody. Without them, I don't think I have much to fear, Benito."

* * *

"I'm wrapping things up here, closing up the cottage and I'll be back in D.C. next week," said Zeke.

"Righto," said Clive. "I know that ADD Stiles is interested in talking with us."

"Another debriefing?" asked Zeke.

"Of sorts. But he wants a private audience. The man seems almost paranoid, afraid that all of this will reflect poorly on the President."

"Strange priority system for anyone who lives outside the Beltway," said Zeke under his breath. "OK. I'm out for the weekend, then I'll come back down here to see you."

* * *

This was short notice," said Tracy, tongue-in-cheek. "I'm lucky I was able to get away again."

"No, I'm the lucky one," said Zeke.

They were sitting on the floor of the cottage in front of a lively fire, the constant sound of the ocean complimenting the low sounds of the Oscar Peterson jazz trio playing in the background.

Tracy had a plaid blanket wrapped around her, bare shoulders showing. She was curled up, eyes closed, snuggling close to Zeke.

"Too bad you need to give this up," said Tracy, eyes still closed.

"It'll be cold before you know it," said Zeke. "Time to move on."

"Where to next?" asked Tracy, lazily. She opened her eyes and picked her wine glass off the floor beside her and sipped some more merlot.

"You have a suggestion?" asked Zeke.

Tracy smiled. "Atlanta's nice this time of year."

Zeke looked as though he was seriously considering that, but then said, "No, I don't want to be anywhere where I'll need to plan my day around the traffic. Besides, Atlanta's land locked…"

"Hmm," said Tracy. "True."

"I was thinking about Marathon, in the Keys," said Zeke. "It's isolated, but not horribly far from the Miami International Airport."

"For when you're working?" she asked.

"Sure. And Naval Air Station Key West isn't far, in case they need me in D.C. quickly," Zeke said. "It's down on Boca Chica."

"That might be nice," she said. She tasted the words, "The Florida Keys."

"I grew up there," said Zeke, casually.

"On the sailboat. Yes, I remember," said Tracy. "I'll bet it'd be nice to go back."

Zeke thought for a minute. The jazz floated over them gently.

"I'm enjoying this," said Tracy.

"I'm glad," said Zeke. Barefoot, he was wearing cargo shorts and an open denim shirt. The fire warmed them both.

"The video bug sort of cramped our style," Tracy continued, gesturing toward the cottage's kitchen. "It's creepy to know that a killer is watching what you're doing."

"It is. But it worked out," said Zeke.

"It did," she said. "But I was getting tired of going to the bedroom every time we…"

"I know," said Zeke. "The camera's gone now, though."

"It is," she said, and she snuggled closer to him. "It's warm in here. You should lose that shirt…"

Other Zeke Traynor Mysteries available at
http://amzn.to/2DL2jyF

If you enjoyed Zeke's latest adventure, consider leaving a
review on Amazon.com.

And visit the author's website at www.JeffSiebold.net

About the Author

Jeff Siebold loves a good mystery. A life long reader, he has embarked on a personal journey in creativity designed to contribute to the delight of mystery readers everywhere.

Jeff and his wife Karin live on a barrier island in North Carolina, not far from the Cape Fear River (made famous by one of his favorite authors, John D. MacDonald). They have three college-aged children and two unruly dogs.